THE EAGLE

Gerald Lowthin

MINERVA PRESS
LONDON
MONTREUX LOS ANGELES SYDNEY

THE EAGLE
Copyright © Gerald Lowthin 1997

ISBN 1 86106 504 3

First Published 1997 by
MINERVA PRESS
315–317 Regent Street
London W1R 7YB

Printed in Great Britain for Minerva Press

THE EAGLE

To Vera
with my love

Acknowledgement

The idea of writing this book was implanted in my mind during my services with the Royal Dragoons. Forty years later, in 1991 and with retirement not far ahead, I decided it was time to put the dormant idea into effect. I then realised that apart from the dispute as to who had captured the Eagle, I knew little else. I knew that an officer and a corporal were involved but I did not know their names. As a result I contacted the Regimental Museum of the Blues and Royals at Windsor and its Curator, Major A.W. Kersting. I am extremely grateful to him for his help and also for selling me a copy of the History of the Royal Dragoons, 1661-1933, which enabled me to plot the course of the Royals' participation in the Peninsula and the Waterloo campaigns.

I am also indebted to: Mrs J.M. Blacklaw of the Ministry of Defence, Whitehall Library; the staff of the Public Records Office, the National Army Museum, the Department of Manuscript Collections at the British Library, the Newspaper Library at Colindale, Woking Library and of the Military Attaché at the French Embassy.

Special thanks also to Bob and Shirley Edom for their interest, help and advice.

Contents

The Visitor 11

Ipswich 21

To Portugal 30

Lisbon 39

The Proving Ground 45

Fuentes d'Onoro 62

Diversions 68

Guerrillas 80

Maguilla 90

Return to Portugal 100

To France 106

The Great Bath Road 124

Northaw 133

Cornwall 146

Belgium 161

Waterloo – Sunday, 18th June 1815 178

Appendix 206

Conclusion 213

I send, with this despatch, two eagles, taken by the troops in this action, which Major Percy will have the honour of laying at the feet of His Royal Highness.

(Extract from the Despatch from the Duke of Wellington to Earl Bathurst, Waterloo, June 19, 1815)

Major the Honourable Henry Percy, riding in a carriage drawn by the best four horses that a Dover innkeeper could provide, was making fast progress towards London. In addition to Lord Wellington's despatch, written early on the 19th June 1815, he had two Eagles entrusted to him – the Standards of the 45th and 105th French Regiments of the Line. Because of their size, the Eagles, atop their Tricolours emblazoned with battle honours, hung out of the windows on each side of the coach. At each village and town the inhabitants turned out and cheered on Major Percy's progress. He considered himself as being most fortunate as he was the only unwounded officer among Wellington's ADCs and his role as "messenger" was one which he undertook with pride. In the case of one of the Eagles little did he know that the controversy as to its capture had already started and would remain an item of speculation in the future.

The story begins some years earlier in the early 1800s...

The Visitor

Not many people visited Northaw in Hertfordshire. This is not because it was an unattractive place. The village, although under a mile from the Great North Road, is approached by a winding, narrow lane, which, after running through dense woods, ends there. Such strangers who come are perhaps visitors to Nyn House, the home of the lord of the manor, or carters bringing in supplies, such as flour for the bakery. The former do not need to enter the village proper and the latter are mostly known by the inhabitants.

Yet Northaw is home for three hundred and fifty men, women and children. The main employment is in agriculture – growing crops of wheat, beans and roots. Large supplies of milk are sent daily to London. For the good of the villagers' souls there is the church of St Thomas of Canterbury, presided over by the vicar, the Reverend John Heathfield for these last thirty-five years. Other needs are met by two public houses – The Sun, and the Two Brewers. There are also a bakers and a blacksmith's forge.

It is outside this last mentioned building, early one afternoon in mid-May in the year 1804, that two men are engaged in their labours. The smith, one William Thomlinson, is busy shoeing a fine draught horse, while the other keeps a firm grip on the reins. It is a warm day for the time of year, but as yet the leaves on the oaks in the Great Wood have not shown themselves, so that there is no shelter from the sun's rays. Thomlinson pumps the bellows before pushing a shoe back into the fire. After a short while he holds it between a pair of tongs and skilfully beats it into shape on his anvil, before dousing it in water.

"Hold her head still, boy," he says to his companion. "Shouldn't be long now." He has gauged the fit perfectly and drives in the nails.

His companion, Francis Stiles, has brought the horse in for shoeing. Francis works on Nyn Manor Farm and at eighteen years of age stands tall at over six feet. He has worked on the land for almost as long as he can remember, is strong for his years, and admires the smith, not only for his skill and strength but mainly because of his obvious love of horses. Stiles hears the rasp of the blacksmith's file but also picks up another sound – the approach of a horse's hooves. He turns quickly. Riding towards them is a soldier.

Bill Thomlinson recognises the rider as a sergeant of Dragoons and says so. Stiles carefully takes note of the sergeant's dress – red tunic, white belt and breeches, long black thigh boots which gleam in the sunlight. His horse, also black, must stand sixteen hands high at least, if it is an inch. The sergeant approaches the forge and dismounts. He towers over Stiles. He addresses the smith.

"Hello, Bill! Don't you recognise me? I'm Joe Kyle."

"Damn my eyes!" replies Thomlinson. "What are you doing in these parts?"

The sergeant removes his hat and mops his brow. "Give me some water first," he says. He is handed a pitcher, from which he drinks long and noisily. "That's better. I'm off down to London. We're recruiting and I thought I'd look you up, you old bugger. I told the others I'd join them tomorrow. How long is it since we last met?"

Thomlinson scratches his head. "Must be all of eleven years since the campaign in Flanders. We were near Menin when I was wounded and sent home before they kicked me out. Luckily I had this to come back to. What about you? I see you have been made a sergeant."

Before Kyle could reply Thomlinson looked at Stiles, who was staring almost open mouthed at the soldier and said, "It's rude to stare, boy! Francis, meet a real man, Joe Kyle. We have been in some tight spots together when we served in the good old Royal Dragoons. He never let me down and it was Joe who came to look for me when I was wounded. If it were not for him, I wouldn't be here today. Joe, this is Francis Stiles, a good 'un with horses." They shook hands.

"Anyway, off you go, boy. I've finished the shoeing."

Stiles sprung easily onto the horse's bare back. The ease with which he made the movement and his self assurance drew a smile of approval from Kyle.

"You look a likely lad," he said. Ever thought of enlisting? You won't do better than the Royal Dragoons, the oldest regiment of horse."

Stiles' immediate reaction was to laugh off the invitation. "Why should I want to do such a thing? Goodbye, Mr Kyle." With that he dug in his heels and rode off.

The sergeant called after him, "If you change your mind, you'll find me at the George Inn at Southwark." Stiles raised his arm in acknowledgement.

"He could do a lot worse," said the smith. "Come on, Joe, get that saddle off and we'll go and slake our thirsts."

As he rode back to the farm, despite his comment, which was the only thing he could think to say at the time, Stiles thought that there were at least two good reasons why he should leave Northaw. There were six of them living in a small cottage. He was the second eldest of four children, and while his mother and father did their best, quite often there was scarcely enough to eat. It could get worse. The family had a small strip of land on the common on which they raised a small crop. They also grazed a pig there. If the enclosure of common land, which had already occurred in many places elsewhere, happened in Northaw Parish – and some said that it was only a matter of time – their strip would disappear and there would be nowhere for the pig. Times would then become very hard. Perhaps the sergeant's coming was an omen. Joining the army might not be such a bad idea after all. He would talk it over with his father.

William Stiles, the stockman at Nyn Manor Farm, saw his son returning. He certainly had something on his mind, as he was deep in thought.

"Francis, when you've stabled that horse, come and give me a hand bringing the cows in for milking." The opportunity for talk had happened more quickly than Francis had anticipated.

"Father, I want to ask you something."

"Can it wait until after milking?"

"I suppose so," replied his son.

"Well, what is it?" asked William. Milking was over and the beasts had been driven back to the field. The two men, father and son, sat in the shade cast by a hedge.

"Father, what would you say if I became a soldier?"

"I might say you were daft," replied William, "but I would want to know your reasons."

Francis told him of his meeting with the sergeant and his subsequent thoughts.

"Enclosure is the main worry," said William Stiles. "We both should be all right with our jobs, but the future could be uncertain. If you are really set on this, I'll have a talk with this Joe Kyle, if he is still about when we get back. Say nothing to your mother, meantime. Leave that to me!"

Francis anxiously awaited for his father to return from the Two Brewers. The public house lay opposite the cottage where the family lived. At last William emerged, accompanied by the sergeant.

"He wants to talk to you, boy," his father said. "From what he tells me it all seems fair enough. You could have a good future, and as far as I am concerned that's all right with me. Thanks, Joe," he said to the sergeant, adding, "I had better go and tell the wife."

The sergeant looked Francis straight in the eyes. "You'll need to come down to London," he said. "I can't enlist you here. You have a lot to learn and may change your mind yet. I expect to be in Southwark in two days time. Remember, I'll be at The George. Your dad says he can get you a ride down on one of the milk carts. So I'll see you in three days from now." With that he turned on his heels and re-entered the pub.

The atmosphere in the cottage had at first been tense. It wasn't that Mary Stiles disapproved of her son's action as such. If William said it was all right, then that was good enough for her. She doubted whether Francis would change his mind but could not help feeling worried for him. The lad hadn't been further than Barnet or Enfield and had never spent a night away from home. Now he was proposing to go to London. Neither she nor her husband had been there and the good Lord knew where that could lead to. It could well be the start of a journey to fight the French in foreign parts. She had no doubt that he was capable of looking after himself, but would she ever see him again? She silently cursed the money-grabbing owners and their enclosures.

Mary Stiles hugged her son. He stooped to kiss her on the cheek and said, "Don't worry, Mother, I'll be all right. Sergeant Kyle said that they won't take me straightaway so I'll probably be back in a day or two." For a moment they stood away and looked at each other until Stiles, unable to bear the signs of his mother's grief, got up beside the driver. The journey to London had begun.

By mid-morning the cart had reached Highgate. The driver, one Dan Smith, stopped to place a metal shoe under one of the wheels.

Stiles could well see why this was necessary. A steep hill led downwards and there in the distance, still some four miles away, was London spread out before him. A smoky haze hung over the city, and Dan pointed out the dome of St Paul's, which stood out well above the other buildings. Until now, the journey had been a routine of villagers about there business as they had passed through Barnet, Whetstone, and Finchley, where the cattle grazed on the common. There had been toll gates and at times they had been forced to pull into the side of the road, as a post horn announced the arrival of a mail coach. In truth what had seemed exciting to start with had become monotonous. That is until the moment the vista of London had opened up before him. They descended the hill safely, and now the road settled down to a gradual slope.

"No more hills now, lad," said Dan. "We'll be parting company soon. I'll point you in the right direction but it's easy to get lost. A word of advice. Keep your money in your pocket and don't get drawn away from what you intend to do. There's all sorts of strange folks about, as you'll soon discover. If you want a ride back, you'll usually find me at the Angel, where I'm dropping you off, at two o'clock or thereabouts in the afternoon. Do you understand?"

Stiles said that he did.

Some minutes later the cart stopped. Somehow it wasn't quite what he had expected. Ahead of them was a toll gate, but sheep and hens grazed and clucked. Nearby were two coaching inns, the Angel and the Peacock.

"It's in between times," said Dan. "I've been past here when you can't move for coaches." He stopped his horses at the pond and they noisily drank the water. "Follow that road down there," he said, pointing with his whip. "It'll take you down towards St Paul's, and when you get there you won't be far from the river. You need to get across. Ask someone for directions but remember, don't part with any money and don't get tempted by women or drink. Goodbye, lad." With that Dan and his cart vanished into the traffic. Stiles was alone, apart from the bustling crowd which swept round him.

He felt apprehensive as he walked along in the direction Dan had pointed. In one hand he held the small bundle which contained the few possessions he owned. His free hand, the right, was ready to fend off any potential attacker. It was a busy, straight thoroughfare, which on the face of it looked respectable enough, except that every now and again narrow, dark passageways ran off to the side. Judging by the appearance of the men and women who inhabited these entrance ways, the alleys must lead to some dubious places. Even looking at them would have been enough to have earned him a lecture from the vicar, had he been present, on the sins of the flesh. From what he had said to Stiles on being informed of his journey it was another Sodom and Gomorrah.

Above everything else was the noise – more of a continual roar made by the rattle and screech of iron-rimmed wheels on the stone sets and the smell. Street sellers paraded their wares. There were the shouts of the water carriers, costermongers, sandmen, and cherry girls. The songs of ballad singers and street fiddlers clashed against the ringing of bells by women selling gingerbread. There was the raucous demand of "Ring! Ring!" as space was demanded for the settlement of some quarrel by a fight. He didn't stop to watch. It was such a confusing place.

Wagon drivers and coachmen vied with each other for right of way, hurling insults and obscenities at each other and cracking their whips. Hordes of people jostled and pushed each other but in the main, seemed to know where they were going. All spoke at the tops of their voices in a variety of accents and tongues, but above all was the nasal whine of the cockney. Pungent smells greeted his nostrils, much worse than from any farmyard he had ever known. He clutched his bundle more tightly and did his best to ensure that as he was jostled, he did not fall prey to any pickpockets.

With much effort he reached St Paul's. The great church had not been visible as he walked, but at last he was almost beneath its great dome, which seemed to touch the sky. He paused to stare and was pushed into the path of a horse and cart. The driver cursed him as he jumped for safety. He observed a buttress to a building which offered protection from the crowd. He did not notice until she spoke the girl who had followed him for a good half mile:

"Where are you going, young sir?"

At first Stiles did not realise that she was addressing him. It was the first time in his life that anyone had spoken to him in that way.

"Er, are you talking to me?"

The girl's tone of voice changed as did her manner of speech. "Are you bleedin' deaf? I asked where you are going."

Stiles looked at her appraisingly. She was slim built with dark hair which needed a good combing. She didn't look particularly clean. Her dress was tattered and her feet bare.

"I'm going to Southwark, to enlist in the army," he replied at last.

"Have you come far?" she countered. "If you are feeling tired and need a rest, then I have a gaff up there." She pointed to the entrance of a narrow alley. "Won't cost you much."

This was too much for Stiles. He could almost see the Reverend Heathfield looking down on him and saying, "Beware of harlots". He declined the invitation, and now the girl asked him for money. He said he didn't have any.

"Sod you!" she said and flounced away. Stiles hurried off as quickly as he could.

At his third attempt to find the way to Southwark and the George, Stiles was successful in getting proper directions. He crossed a bridge – his informant told him it was London Bridge. The river below contained all sorts of filth and smelt awful. Once on the far bank, he had no difficulty in reaching his destination. The George was a large, three-sided building which was flanked by galleries on the first and upper floors. Stiles wandered around for a while before he discovered a soldier in the stables.

"Do you know where Sergeant Kyle is?" he enquired.

"He's in the taproom," the man said, pointing to a door across the yard.

Stiles entered the George and made his way across the smoke-filled room to where Kyle and a corporal sat on a bench. Both had tankards before them and they were smoking pipes. The sergeant didn't express surprise.

"You found us then. I knew you'd come. This is Corporal William Walker," he said, introducing his companion. "William, meet Francis Stiles, the lad I was telling you about." Both men were over six feet tall, and whereas the sergeant was about sixteen stone, the corporal, a very smartly turned out man, was of slight build.

"Fancy a drink?" said the corporal.

Stiles wasn't much of a drinking man. His mother didn't approve of him drinking but he did enjoy the occasional drop of ale. For some reason unknown to himself he replied, "I would like a glass of gin." Later he realised that he had said that to impress the two men.

The corporal went to get the drink, and Kyle said to Stiles, "Listen. This is the only time I will say this to you, but if you have any doubts at all about enlisting then go home. I say this because of my friendship with Bill Thomlinson, and having met your father I feel that I need to be straight with you. You'll find it a hard life in the army. A lot harder than you've been used to. The pay is not much good. The food is rotten, and once you're in they have got you for life.

"I'm telling you this now because once you have signed, that's it, and nobody can save you. You'll get no favours from me, but if you work hard and learn your trade, I think you will do well for yourself. As far as I am concerned, this conversation has not taken place, but once we've explained things to you, if you want to change your mind then go." The corporal returned.

Stiles was then given the official version of army life, details of the pay and the bounty he would receive.

"Do you still want to enlist?" asked Kyle.

"Yes," Stiles replied.

"In that case we'll take you upstairs to be measured," said the corporal. Kyle enlisted him into the Royal Dragoons and explained that his service would continue, "...until you are legally discharged. Sign this form and add the date. It's the 21st day of May 1804. There's one further thing," he went on, "I have to give you this." He held out a coin. "It's the enlisting shilling, but while I'm giving it to you now, the custom is that you use it to buy drinks."

On returning to the bar Stiles ordered another half pint of gin.

The events which followed seemed in retrospect to be somewhat hazy. He had a dim recollection of a woman, a lot older than the girl who had accosted him that morning. She was sitting on his lap, wriggling about and at the same time smothering his face in her ample bosom. She kept repeating, "What a shame it is to take this young boy away from his poor mother! Never mind, Nellie will look after you. Buy us another drink, love."

He didn't remember much after that but when he woke it was the next morning. He was lying on a bed, and the sergeant, who was sitting on a chair by the door, was grinning at him across the room. Stiles was at first filled with alarm, but as his head cleared he calmed down.

"You're awake then. We had a right job getting you up to bed last night; had to get that woman away from you. You were in no fit state and kept buying her drink. We didn't want you poxed up before you started. Hurry up now! We've to get you examined by the doctor and sworn in by a magistrate."

Stiles obeyed, got out of bed, and pulled on his trousers and boots. It was then that he noticed that the little money he'd had with him had gone. Later that day he received an advance of five shillings as part of his bounty.

"You can go home for a few days," said Kyle, "but be back here on the first day of June. If you're not back on time, we'll come looking for you, and Heaven help you! I know where you live and you'll wish that you had been press-ganged." Stiles, who had every intention of returning, hurried off to get to the Angel to meet Dan for a lift back to Northaw.

Stiles returned to his job on the farm without much enthusiasm. Now that he was going he was impatient to be away and almost resented the fact that Kyle had sent him home. He suspected that once the time came to take leave of his family, he would be filled with sadness. His grandfather had said, "Well, I don't suppose I'll see you again." It had been said in a matter-of-fact tone, but Stiles knew that in his heart the old man was worried.

He was returning home one evening two days before he was due to leave. So deep in thought was he that he didn't hear straightaway a cry of pain and a thin high voice demanding to be left alone. He turned off the track and approached a clump of ferns. This time he heard another, much older and deeper voice saying, "I told you what would happen if you didn't bring me money. Take that!" There was another cry of pain followed by a snivelling sob. A tremulous reply came. "My father keeps his money well locked up." Stiles recognised the voices – one belonged to Tom Bates, a bully if ever there was one, the other was that of Henry Jackson, the son of the local baker. Another voice joined in. This time it was a girl shouting, "Leave him alone, you big bully!"

Stiles came up behind the struggling group. Tom Bates had young Henry's arm locked up behind his back. The youngster was struggling, but as he did the pressure on his arm was increased, which caused him to cry out. Pulling at Bates from behind was a girl who he now saw was Margaret Hicks, the gamekeeper's daughter. The trio were so engrossed that they didn't know he was there until he spoke.

"What's all this then?" Stiles demanded. The result was instantaneous. Bates let go of the boy, who was now rubbing his arm, while the girl looked at him in anticipation. At first Stiles thought that Bates was going to make a run for it. His eyes darted from side to side.

"Just having a bit of sport," Bates at last replied.

"Not from what I heard," said Stiles. "What's this about money?"

"He wants me to steal from my father and give it to him," the boy blurted out. "I've told him I can't get any so he twisted my arm."

"Shut up, you little fool," Bates snarled. "I've a good mind to really hurt you." With that he raised his arm as though to strike the boy, but Stiles was too quick for him. He caught hold of the raised hand and quickly bent Bates' arm up his back.

"Now you know what it's like!" he said as he gave the arm a vicious twist. Bates sank to his knees as though this might bring some relief and could not avoid crying out as Stiles further increased the pressure. "Next time," said Stiles, "and there had better not be a next time, I'll break your arm off. Do you understand?" As though to emphasise the point, he applied further pressure. "You two. Go home now," he said to the youngsters. "Henry, tell your father I'll be round to see him later to tell him what happened." He pulled Bates to the ground and gave him a boot in the ribs. "I may be going away," he said, "but after I've been to see his dad and he's had a word with your father, I doubt that you will try it again." He gave him a final kick and walked away. He didn't see the two young ones who had hidden themselves to see what happened to Bates. The girl, ten-year-old Margaret Hicks, watched her hero depart with a look of adoration on her face.

Ipswich

At first they were only four. The new recruits waited outside the George, in the back of a cart which had been sent to collect them. They were soon joined by a fifth. Sergeant Kyle force marched a man across the yard and assisted him aboard the vehicle with such force that he tripped over Stiles' outstretched legs. The man fell with a thump. The chains on the cart rattled and the team of two horses backed up before being halted by the driver.

Kyle addressed all of them. "This one," he pointed with his finger to the new arrival. "This one wants watching. He's a thief. You might as well know it now and not come whining to me later that your stuff's been nicked." He looked at the subject of his short address. "You, Tom Banks, had better watch it. I warn all of you," – he let his eyes sweep the group – "if you attempt to run, it will be the worst thing you could ever do. If he," – and he prodded the still prone criminal with his crop – "leaves the cart without my say-so, I will hold you all responsible. Is that understood?" They all nodded dumbly.

Thus it was that Stiles' army service commenced on that day early in June 1804. To make matters worse, it was raining. The thin drizzle which had fallen since daybreak had developed into heavy rain. A crowd had gathered outside the George. Some mocked. Others wished them well. Stiles had met their greetings with good-humoured embarrassment.

"Where are you going?" shouted one. "You shouldn't have joined," cried another. A woman, heavily pregnant, forced her way through the throng. Stiles had seen her somewhere before... Of course! – she was the one who had accosted him when he was on his way to enlist. She wasn't pregnant when he'd last seen her. He knew that he was right as soon as she spoke.

"That's my husband," she shrieked, pointing at Banks. "What's to become of me and my children?" She turned to Kyle. "You have no right taking him. I'll tell you now, he'll be no use to you. He's trouble and always will be!" Kyle froze her with a glare. Since the woman had intervened, the crowd's mood had changed. There were angry murmurings.

Stiles was relieved when Corporal Williams got up beside the driver. "Move off, Corporal," Kyle ordered.

The cart rattled over London Bridge. So far no one had spoken.

Banks, whose composure had returned, pointed vaguely to his left. "I come from over there. Got caught doing a money-lender's place. There were some rich pickings, I can tell you. It was my own fault I was caught. I found a bottle of grog, drank the lot and fell asleep."

Stiles watched Banks as he talked. All the while, the man looked furtive. His eyes moved from side to side as if expecting something to happen. He spoke out of the corner of his mouth. It was his first meeting with a criminal and he took an instant dislike to the man. Quite involuntarily, he moved his bundle of belongings so that it was placed on the opposite side of his body, away from Banks. He would need to watch him carefully, he thought, but commented, "The army would be better than prison."

Banks mumbled something in reply. It sounded like "I hope I won't be in long enough to find out."

Waiting appeared to be one of the military's pastimes. This time they waited outside the guardroom of Ipswich Barracks. The cart had dropped them off at the gate and they were immediately greeted by the sight of a squat, ugly looking soldier, who stood on the veranda. He was, Stiles estimated, not much more than five feet six inches tall, but he had exceedingly broad shoulders. He carried a silver topped cane with which he continually beat the palm of his left hand. A leer crossed his face, revealing several missing teeth. Stiles was close enough to see the warts on his face and noticed that at some time he had sustained a broken nose.

The corporal stood at attention before him and handed over a sheet of paper. "The new recruits, Sergeant." The corporal came back down the steps and shouted, "Fall in in a single rank. Move yourselves. Attention!" They shuffled rather than moved smartly. It had been a long journey and they were cramped and stiffened.

The sergeant moved forward and looked at them. "My name's Else. Provost Sergeant Else to you. I've a feeling that I will be entertaining some of you coves in my palace." He jerked his thumb in the direction of the guardroom behind him. "If you are fortunate enough to enjoy my hospitality," – the tone of his voice, which until now had all the attraction of a rasp on metal, took on a note of venom and rose to a roar – "THEN HEAVEN HELP YOU."

"Answer your names. Banks."

"Yes."

"Yes what," snarled Else.

"Yes, I'm here," Banks replied.

Else leapt from the veranda and stood with his lips close to Banks' ear.

"When you address me, Private Banks, you call me sergeant!" The words were softly spoken. Then he bellowed so that Banks and the rest noticeably flinched. "Is that clear?"

"Yes, Sergeant," Banks replied.

The roll call over, Sergeant Else ordered Williams to march them away. Stiles noticed that the barrack buildings were arranged in a square, around an open space on which men were marching. Orders were being barked, and he became so engrossed that when Williams ordered the squad to halt, he didn't hear the command and marched into the man in front.

Williams, although he noticed the breach, chose to ignore it. "Private Stiles. You are in Captain Hulton's troop. Follow me." Stiles hurried after the corporal, who led the way along a stone flagged corridor, up a flight of stairs, down a passageway and into a room. His first impression was that there wasn't much daylight. Small windows were set high up in the walls, and the room was smoke filled to such an extent that he could barely see across it. A sea of faces greeted him as the men, seated at a long table, turned their heads in his direction.

"New recruit," said the corporal. "Who's looking after him then?"

"I am, Corporal." A man rose to his feet. He looked every part the soldier. He was much older than Stiles. He introduced himself. "I'm Benjamin Barrow. Call me Ben. What's your name?"

"I'm Francis Stiles."

"Well, I'm to instruct you in your soldierly duties," said Barrow. "You're in luck because it's dinner time. Shove along a bit," he said to one man at the end of the table. "Make way for young Francis here!"

Stiles sat down and had placed before him a plate of meat, a bowl of soup and a piece of bread. The food tasted better than it looked. His companions, once they had emptied their plates, took an interest in him and introduced themselves. Only one name apart from Barrow's stuck in his mind. A tall, fair-haired soldier introduced himself with a plain "Jim Burnside". For Stiles it was like looking into a mirror. They each had the same colour hair and eyes. In fact each very much resembled the other, although Burnside was the heavier of the two.

"There could be fun here," said Barrow, looking from one to the other. "Particularly when you've been kitted out. Come along, lad. I'll take you to the store to get your equipment."

Stiles was enraged. He'd been cheated. He lay on his palliasse, as did the other men in the cramped barrack room. It was hot, stuffy, and smelt of sweat. The others were asleep, judging by the snores and heavy breathing, which came from all sides. He turned on to his back and the fresh straw in the palliasse crackled. He could not get to sleep however hard he tried.

The source of his anger was the bounty. He had been due the remaining five pounds, but at the store he had been told that he would have to buy his necessaries.

"What are these necessaries?" he had asked.

"You won't get far without them," was the answer. The storekeeper had reeled off a list as long as his arm. There were flannel drawers, shirts, stockings, stable trousers, shoes, boots, gloves, comb, razor, cleaning utensils, items for the care of a horse, and a night cap. The cost totalled almost six pounds. The list, when he looked at it later, contained twenty-eight items. He was surprised at that rate that he didn't have to pay for his uniform. He had been looking forward to putting it on, but a further disappointment had followed when he was told that it would not be ready for at least two weeks.

Burnside had tried to cheer him up. "It was the same for all of us when we started. You'll soon get over the shock."

He'd had to borrow the rest of the money to pay for the items. He hadn't been in Ipswich for twenty-four hours and already he was in debt. To make matters worse, Barrow had told him. "You won't draw your full pay anyway. There are all sorts of deductions of the odd halfpenny or a penny."

In the days that followed, his resentment lessened. There was so much to do that there wasn't time for thought. One of the first lessons he learnt was that he wasn't supposed to think for himself. He was expected to obey orders without hesitation. At first it was a question of asking Barrow, "What do I do now?" but quickly he settled into a routine which was dominated by stable duties – feeding, watering, combing, brushing and mucking out, the big black horses of the troop. In between times came drill, first on foot under the watchful eye of Sergeant Battersby, who was hated by all. The drill sergeant was a fearsome man, who struck terror into the hearts of the recruits but gradually achieved his purpose. "Just wait 'til they get you on a horse," he threatened.

To Stiles and his newly-joined colleagues their former lives seemed nothing other than a far-off dream. Firing the carbine and practising using the sabre, a broad bladed weapon, thirty-five inches in length, involving the twenty or so positions, had to be mastered. Stiles soon came to realise that Captain Hulton's troop, to which he had been posted, comprising seventy or so men, was his family. As with most families the individual members were of different temperaments. He found the discipline to be harsh and was appalled when Barrow, with some relish, told him of the floggings he had witnessed. Burnside, who overheard the conversation, attempted to calm Stiles' fears.

"That's just one of his old soldier's tales. It doesn't happen that often and it has to be something really bad for that punishment to be awarded."

"Mount,", ordered the riding instructor. It was Stiles' first time at the riding school. He could ride, if riding a farm horse counted. Then it had been a question of grabbing its mane and pulling himself up onto its bare back. Now it was different. There were reins, stirrups and a saddle. He was wearing long leather thigh boots, with spurs, which hampered his movements. With an effort he got into the saddle. The horse, used to a series of beginners, stood placidly. The stirrups were long and he knew from what he had been told that he must keep a straight back. "Walk" was the next command. The horse, to Stiles' relief, responded to the pressure he exerted with the inside of his lower leg and moved round its familiar track in the riding school. "Keep your head up and straighten your back," came frequently. At last he heard the command to "Halt," followed by "Dismount.". He got down.

The corporal said, " You've got a lot to learn, but we'll make a horseman of you yet."

Stiles progressed and eventually reached the stage where he was riding confidently without stirrups and his arms folded across his chest. It was at one of these later sessions, that unbeknown to him, he was being watched by the riding master. Another onlooker was Joe Kyle who stood in the shadows.

"Let me see what this man is made of!" said the riding master to the corporal. The latter kept on telling him what a good prospect Stiles was.

"We've got some remounts being broken in. Get one of the rough riders to bring in that big black stallion." The corporal knew which animal was intended. They had nicknamed it 'Lucifer'. "He hasn't been properly broken in yet, sir, and is only just about used to the feel of a saddle," replied the corporal.

"Don't argue. Just do it!"

Stiles saw the corporal return followed by another man, who he recognised as a rough rider. They led a giant of a horse. The animal, by its demeanour, looked a handful. It pulled against its bridle, attempted to rear and crab sideways. It took the two men all their efforts to hold it. Stiles assumed that the rough rider was going to put the horse through its paces and was unconcerned when he was given the order to halt and dismount. As his feet touched the ground, the corporal turned to him and said, "Who's a lucky lad, then? The riding master wants you to show us how you manage with this one." He lowered his voice. "Try and stay on him for all our sakes. He has a tendency to bite." The corporal and the other man still kept a firm grip on the horse's head. As Stiles reached for the reins the stallion managed to turn its head slightly and Stiles saw a wild eye looking at him. Its jaws clamped shut with the force of a rat trap, narrowly missing his arm. Gingerly he got up into the saddle and the two attendants freed the horse's head.

"Walk."

He gave a slight tap with his legs. Nothing happened. The beast just stood there. Then Stiles felt a tremor run through the its body, before it raced towards the other side of the ring, slewed round and attempted to crush Stiles' leg between its side and a rail. Then it bucked back in the direction from which it had come in an endeavour, all the while, to throw its rider. Stiles remained seated and after the initial shock was beginning to relax. He soon realised his mistake. It was as though the animal had read his mind. It reared on its back legs, plunged forward and went round in circles. Stiles stayed with it until it came to a sudden halt and dropped its head. He was dislodged and hit the ground with such force that every bit of wind was knocked out of him. He lay one side of the ring. The horse glared at him from the other, pawing at the ground, Stiles noticed in a detached way, with its front near side hoof. He pulled himself to his feet. He was determined that this son of the devil would not get the better of him.

Kyle, by now impressed, was encouraged by Stiles' response.

It was after one of these sessions that Stiles had an argument with Barrow, who had asked for more money. He already paid him and was not ungrateful for his help in cleaning his equipment, particularly when he didn't return from riding school until dinner time at twelve o'clock and had to be ready for drill by two. Barrow's demands were increasing, and on this occasion Stiles told him to "bugger off". Barrow's attitude changed from wheedling to a threatening tone.

It was at this stage that Burnside intervened and said, "You have been told, now bloody well go away."

Barrow departed, still issuing threats. "The trouble with these old soldiers," said Burnside, "is that they don't know when to take no for an answer. How about coming into town this evening?"

Later they went to one of Burnside's favourite haunts in Ipswich, the Boar's Head. It was difficult to see across the room for tobacco smoke and the large numbers of soldiers and civilians present.

"I didn't expect that there would be so many here," said Stiles. He had noticed straightaway that a good-humoured atmosphere was evident and the townspeople and the soldiers mixed quite happily.

"I am surprised that the ordinary folk are here."

"That's because they know that they have nothing to fear if there is a press-gang about. The navy wouldn't dare show its face in here," replied Burnside.

Stiles looked round. "I don't see many of our lot."

"One of the reasons I come here," said Burnside, who appeared to be well known to the serving girls.

They had ordered two flagons of ale and were wedged into one of the corners at the side of the fireplace. The noise was tremendous. Soldiers were talking and laughing at the tops of their voices and a lone fiddler was attempting to scrape out a tune. They had to shout to speak to each other. It was then that Stiles noticed a door a little to their right. Burnside had followed his gaze. "That's to upstairs, but it's no use going up there alone, if you understand me." Stiles understood all right. He wondered what it would be like. He had never been with a woman. True he'd had a fumble or two with one of the village girls which had left him feeling frustrated. Back at barracks he joined in the conversation about such things, with an air of bravado. The truth was he had never had a woman.

Later, and it was much later, and feeling a little light-headed with drink he saw Burnside catch a serving girl's eye, point to the door and then to him.

Burnside said, "Go on, Francis boy, through the door and wait. She'll be with you soon. Her name's Lizzie. She'll take care of you."

Feeling nervous, he passed through the doorway and waited as instructed. It was pitch black. She didn't keep him waiting long, the door opened and there she was framed against the light from the bar. The hubbub subsided as she closed the door behind her.

"What's your name, me duck?" she enquired.

"Francis. Francis Stiles," he replied, in a tremulous voice.

"There's no need to be nervous," she said. She took him by the hand and led him up the stairs, by the light of the candle and into a room which had one of the largest beds he had ever seen. Quickly she took off her clothes, and Stiles was fascinated at the sight of her. He took her in slowly. She was probably a little older than him, with a pretty face. Her cap, which had been one of the first things to come off, had concealed long, dark brown hair, the unleashed ends of which had fallen over one of her large breasts. His eyes travelled downwards and she was aware that he was looking at her thighs.

"Well, don't stand there all night. Get undressed and let me see what I'm getting." With mounting excitement he obeyed her.

He woke and the girl was gone. Stiles stretched with contentment, reflecting that Burnside had been right about her. He'd better get moving, he thought, and he quickly hurried back into his uniform.

Stiles went down the stairs. The room was now much less full and he guessed that it was getting late. Burnside was sitting at a table with another of the wenches and he looked knowingly at Stiles and said, "You look as though you've enjoyed yourself. I've been well looked after too. Come on. We'd better go. We don't want Provost Sergeant Else looking for us!"

To Portugal

"Where have you been?" Stiles found it difficult to hide his annoyance. Burnside had just entered the barrack room having been missing for the better part of two hours. He didn't need to ask the question. It was obvious where Burnside had been. He wore a satisfied, smug grin and there were signs of his encounter in the form of pieces of straw on his trousers. If truth be told, Stiles was envious. It didn't matter where the regiment had been stationed in England, Scotland, and these last eighteen months in Ireland, Burnside always had the ability to coerce some woman or other into parting with her favours. They weren't usually the hard-faced type either. Somehow or the other, they would be young and pretty. Sometimes they were married. It was all the same to Burnside, who often explained to Stiles, "Once you get your hand on it, you're almost there."

Stiles knew what his approach was. "Take pity on a poor soldier who is on his way to fight the French. Who knows, it might be my last night amongst civilised folk." He would buy them a drink or two, and before you knew it, he and his woman would be off to the nearest barn or stable. Stiles had tried the method himself. It didn't always work for him, but Burnside never failed.

"Where have you been?" Stiles repeated. "Look at the state of you." Burnside mumbled something about a hayloft and started to remove pieces of straw from his clothing, which he dropped on the floor. "Not in here!" shouted Stiles, now quite beside himself. "We've been cleaning this place up for the last two hours, while you have been out whoring. It may have escaped your notice but we're away from here tomorrow."

Burnside replied, "She's not a whore but a respectable." He slurred his words, and it was obvious that he had had more than one or two. "She's a respectable young girl called Deirdra. You should have seen her tits!" With that he sat down on his palliasse and settled onto his back. In seconds he was snoring. Stiles took off his boots for him, and as he did so wished that he had a shilling for every woman Burnside had coupled with. He had no doubt that he would be a rich man.

"Deirdra Newell, will you come back into this house!" Her mother's voice echoed along the passageway, and Deirdra took one last look at the column of mounted men as they rode purposefully down towards the harbour. As yet she hadn't seen him and she waited a moment longer. At last there he was in the middle file, looking straight ahead. Her blood tingled as she thought longingly of the night before when he had possessed her in the stables. It had not been her first time but he had shown an unaccustomed tenderness towards her and she glowed at the memory. Her eyes followed him till he turned the corner and she waited until she could no longer hear the hooves. Where did he say he was going? Portugal! She had no idea where that was but hoped that he would return safely, despite all his blarney about "going to fight the French". She would have followed after him but obeyed her mother's renewed call:

"Deirdra, come back in here directly."

Robert Tatum, Master of the transport *Success*, stood on the deck of his ship moored alongside the quay of Cork Harbour. The port was a bustling place, which contrasted with the stillness aboard his and the other vessels. He awaited the arrival of a regiment of cavalry. The last few days had seen much activity. Ammunition, stores, provisions, including fodder and extra water for the horses, had been loaded. Tatum had needed to keep a close eye on the victualling agent. That breed needed watching at the best of times. Tatum pulled the watch from his waistcoat pocket, opened its case and looked at the dial. It was ten o'clock, almost time. His charter was for fifty horses and men, and apart from some regimental officers he was taking a major-general with aim. Tatum was quite used to carrying cavalry but this was the first time he would carry the Royal Dragoons.

In the distance Tatum heard the unmistakable sound of the clatter of many hooves on the cobbled roadway. Into view came the first files of the column, led by an officer. The soldiers, dressed in their bicorne hats, scarlet coats, white breeches and black leather thigh boots, rode their horses at a walk. Tatum noticed that they rode easily, with long stirrups, but there was no mistaking their disciplined approach.

"We will soon have them aboard," he said to the mate. The horses would, one at a time, be hoisted up and over the side and lowered down through the hatchway, to the deck below, where they would be stabled. Tatum turned to the mate and said, "If you please, Mr Keenlyside, get the crew on deck."

Five days later, on the 2nd of September 1809, the convoy weighed anchor and left harbour to rendezvous with its escort. The Royals were at last off to fight the French.

At the ship's rail on board the *Success*, Stiles and Burnside had watched the crew as they laboured to raise the anchor. The capstan bars had been pushed round, the pace being dictated by the men as they chanted a shanty. They weren't supposed to be on deck and had only brief snatches of fresh air these last five days. Their time was fully occupied. Apart from their own horses, there were the mounts of the officers to attend to. So far no one had objected to their presence on deck and they tried to remain as unobtrusive as circumstances permitted. They had fully expected the ship to have sailed long before now. The loading of the men and horses had been quickly undertaken, so that when the vessel had pulled away from the quayside and anchored offshore, they had felt disappointed. Now it was different, and they were experiencing a mixture of apprehension and excitement.

Stiles asked one of the crew, "How long will the voyage take?"

"Depends," was the reply. "Could be ten days with the wind in the right quarter. If we get contrary winds, could be a month."

Orders were shouted for "All hands aloft". Barefooted sailors swiftly climbed the rigging and spread themselves out along the yards. It seemed the wind had been waiting its opportunity to push against the newly spread canvas. The green hills surrounding the anchorage passed with increasing speed, and the ship, which now thrust itself forward as it responded to the stiff offshore breeze, began to pitch and roll.

Stiles was enjoying the sensation. "If it doesn't get any worse than this, it won't be too bad."

On the bridge Robert Tatum turned and said to the mate, "Won't be long now before some of our guests will be wishing that they were back on dry land."

Stiles had not enjoyed being in Ireland. For the most part the Irish people had been friendly but there had been an ever-present undercurrent of resentment, sometimes a downright hostility to their presence. The regiment had arrived from Scotland some eighteen months previously and that was the last time, until a fortnight ago, that they had all been together. Individual troops, sometimes half troops, had been quartered in various parts of the country and often at great distances from each other. Almost without exception they had been billeted on innkeepers, which suited Burnside more than him. They hadn't exercised together at squadron level in all that time.

Stiles thought how unfitted they were for the task which lay ahead. He turned to his companion. "I'm not sorry to be leaving this place."

Burnside, always on the lookout for fresh pastures, replied with a simple, "Me too, but I wouldn't have minded a little more time with that Deirdra." It always seemed to work in his case. All you had to do was to tell a woman you loved her and that you were off to face danger. They soon came round to your way of thinking.

Women didn't occupy his mind fully. Well, not all the time. If it hadn't been for the fact that they'd been anchored several hundreds of yards offshore and for the constant patrolling of the guard boats, he might have risked another visit to Deirdra. He would give a month's pay to hold that milky white body again.

By now the ship's motion had become more violent. They had crossed the harbour bar. Burnside turned his thoughts away from women and remembered the crossing to Ireland. That had been a rough one and judging by the way that the *Success* and the rest of the ships were leaping about, they would be better off below.

"Let's go. I feel like getting my head down," he said.

In a large day cabin in the stern, Major-General Jack Slade, who had joined the ship at the last possible moment, was holding court. Slade had commanded the Royals previously, and since his promotion a year ago had seen active service in the Peninsula. He was travelling out with his old regiment and feeling quite sentimental as the non-commissioned officers and men had presented him with a sword at the cost of one hundred guineas. For what seemed to be for the hundredth time to the onlookers, he pulled the blade from its scabbard and held it up against the light. The blade felt balanced in his hand.

"It was damned fine of them," he said yet again.

Seated round the table with him were Lieutenant-Colonel de Grey, Major Wyndham, and several other officers.

Slade put the sheathed sword down on the table and said, "A few months ago I would never have thought that we would return to the Peninsula. Things have changed now that we have got Wellington back in charge. I can tell you that when he was offered the Royals he accepted with enthusiasm. He's damn short of cavalry, you know!"

Privately, Slade was honest to admit to himself that he was fortunate to be returning. He hadn't exactly distinguished himself on the previous occasion and was regarded as being indecisive. Luckily for him, he had some influence at Horse Guards.

Lieutenant Alexander Kennedy Clark was sitting at the far end of the table. He took comfort from the fact that he was on the fringe of the conversation and, conscious of his junior rank, knew that apart from one or two hear hears, he wasn't expected to make a contribution. That would come from the colonel and the other senior officers. As the decanter was passed round, a little too often to his mind, he made the pretence of pouring more port into his already full glass.

Clark didn't mind being cast in the role of being a listener and he let his mind wander. He was a Scot by birth, the son of a landowner near Dumfries, and had joined the Royals from the 8th Hussars in 1805 when he purchased a lieutenancy for £650. Clark thought about those early days with the regiment at Piershill Barracks in Edinburgh, where an officer's duties had barely taken up two hours in any one day. The men had been thoroughly drilled by the non-commissioned officers, with a general tendency towards cleanliness of man, horse and equipment, rather than a knowledge and understanding of tactics and accomplishment in arms. He couldn't see how that would be of benefit where they were going. Well, we'll soon find out how good we are, he thought. A few of the men had experience of battle. Very few at that. No doubt he and they would learn as they went along. He hoped that it wouldn't be too hard a lesson. To any one of Clark's generation, England and France had always been at war. The Royals had been due to go to Portugal earlier in the year, but following the death of Sir John Moore at Corunna and the evacuation of the army from the Peninsula the order had been cancelled.

The sound of Slade's voice penetrated his daydream.

"Representatives of the Central Spanish Junta visited London recently to ask for our assistance. That's why we are going. I think most of us would agree that their regular army will not be of much help but their guerrilla forces will tie down a large number of French troops in Spain and reduce the numbers facing us. Britain, Spain, and Portugal are to undertake a combined effort, the ultimate aim being the invasion of France." Clark was often to remember these words over the coming years.

In the men's quarters were rows of swinging hammocks, which at first had been the cause of much good humour, although this had given way eventually to bad temper. The first night aboard, Stiles had been obliged to sleep on the deck as he could not master the art. The contraption had contrived to throw him out every time he relaxed. Eventually he got the hang of it and was glad that he had persevered. It would be at the least uncomfortable and at the most dangerous to be rolling about down there. Now the ship was alternately leaping, plunging and rolling. Unfortunately his stomach sensations were going in contrary directions to the ship's movements. To make matters worse, the normal onboard smells were accentuated by the odours from the horses, which were one deck below. Each of the beasts was in a separate stall with its heels towards the ship's side and a passageway between the two rows. They were fastened by double halters to strong mangers, so had no chance of laying down while they remained on board. The men had to attend to their normal stable duties, twice a day as usual. Watering, grooming, feeding and mucking out. Still, the horses seemed to have grown accustomed to their new surroundings.

Stiles found that closing his eyes didn't help. Opening them was as bad if not worse. The wooden walled enclosure was dimly lit by a lantern, which swung in sympathy with the ship's motions. It was hot and airless. He tried to concentrate his mind. Burnside, to his left, was already asleep and snoring. On his other side was Tom Banks. Stiles didn't trust him. Banks the convicted thief, who had chosen enlistment over imprisonment, on one occasion when he was the worse for drink, had confided to Stiles that he didn't intend to get shot by some bloody Crapaud. Stiles and his fellows didn't have much that was worth stealing. Their pay, as and when they got it, was a pittance, and most of the men spent the money immediately they received it. Stiles had managed to save a little of his, and because of Banks' presence slept with it between his legs. The added precaution was that, apart from any official punishment, Banks would be well aware of the rough justice which would be handed out by his fellows, if he so much as dared to touch their property.

Beyond Banks was Tinsley. Tinsley kept a journal and was forever writing in it. He'd told Stiles that he fully intended to keep it going throughout the campaign. He was not writing that night. Apart from the rough conditions, there was not enough light. Tinsley and Stiles were something of a rarity. Stiles had been fortunate in that Mrs Heathfield, the vicar's wife, had taken a liking to him and instructed him in his letters and numbers.

He must have fallen asleep. He became conscious that someone was shouting. His first thoughts were that the ship was sinking. With his feeling of nausea still persisting, he had reached the stage where he didn't care if it did.

"One of the horses has fallen. Come on, all of you," shouted Corporal Williams.

The men scrambled down the companionway to the deck below. Above the groans and creaks of the ship's timbers and the noise of the sea all around, Stiles could plainly hear the horses whinnying in alarm. They sounded like so many terrified children.

"Careful how you go," said the corporal. "You don't want to fall in among this lot and alarm them further. It's the mare at the far right-hand end." He had to shout to make himself heard. "Somehow she's got loose and has fallen."

It was too dark to see properly.

"We'll need some more light," said Burnside.

"Right, go back to your quarters and get the lanterns from there," replied Williams. "Stiles. Go and tell Mr Clark what's happened. He may feel that he should come down."

Stiles knocked at a door, hoping he'd got the correct cabin. There was no reply. This time he fairly hammered. The door opened. Clark stood there in his night attire.

"What is it?" he said testily.

"Begging your pardon, sir, but Corporal Williams sent me to tell you that one of the horses is down."

"I'll be along directly."

Clark sent his orderly to inform the officer of the watch. No doubt they would soon be seeing him. On arriving on the lower deck, Clark saw a knot of men. There were far too many to be useful. He made his way forward, clutching for support, and pushed his way through.

The fallen mare was plunging with her front hooves at the wooden deck, in an attempt to regain her footing, but to no avail. The other animals, in the immediate vicinity, were in a most agitated state. Clark looked back along the row. To his mind there was only one thing to do. They needed more room to work in. As luck would have it, at the far end there was an empty stall, where muck rakes, leather straps, and other equipment was stored.

"Corporal Williams, take all of the men, apart from Burnside and Stiles. Start by moving the farthest horse on this side into that empty stall and the remainder up one, so that we eventually have double space to work in here. Stiles, go and bring down the leather straps. In the meantime we'll do our best to calm the horses."

While Clark was talking, he hadn't noticed a sudden movement behind him. Whether it was the sudden lurching of the ship or a rush of blood to Bank's head, but Stiles saw Banks hurtling towards Clark. Stiles, who had hold of a post, reached out with his free arm and stopped Banks in full flight, and pulled him with force, running him head first into the post. He hissed, "Got you, you bugger!"

Stiles was never sure if it was a deliberate attempt to push Clark into the flailing hooves.

The first that Clark knew of the incident was when Burnside said, "Banks seems to have hurt himself."

Much to Clark's surprise it was not the Officer of the Watch who came down but Captain Tatum. Clark explained what he was trying to do.

"The wind has started to ease off," said Tatum, "but there is still a heavy swell running. I'll turn the ship's head into the wind to see if I can make things easier for you. Let me know if you need anymore help, but by the look of things you have enough help here already."

It was a matter of hours before they had created the space that was needed. They tried pulling and pushing, but to no avail. They ran a rope over a beam and attached it to the leather straps which had been placed under the mare's belly. The men heaved on the rope but their combined strength was not enough.

"It's no good," said Clark. "Let us see if we can get her to lie down. What is it, Stiles?"

Stiles had gasped in disbelief. The mare, now that she was lying down, disclosed the full extent of her injuries.

"Looks bad, sir," he said at last. "I'm afraid it doesn't look as though she'll last much longer." The thoroughly exhausted animal lay there. Now and again she attempted to raise her head.

"Corporal Williams, you may dismiss the men," Clark commanded. "Stiles, will you stay with her?"

"Yes, sir."

The end when it came was peaceful. They had sustained their first casualty.

Ten days later on the 13th September 1809, the *Success* tied up in Lisbon harbour. They disembarked the next day.

Lisbon

"Fall in," the troop sergeant-major ordered. Stiles, Burnside and the other members of the reunited troop had been lounging on the quay. It was good to be on dry land once more, although the sensation of being on a moving ship still lingered, to the extent that the ground 'rocked' beneath their feet.

Burnside, having sniffed the air, had declared, "It's like your English air, but it has a foreign smell to it."

Stiles' unspoken reaction was that you couldn't argue with such logic.

"Once the 'orses are off," the troop sergeant-major continued, "we will be going to the Queen's Stables at Belem Barracks. This, I am told, is not just any old place. The stables have marble mangers and there is enough space for a thousand 'orses."

"There'll be a bit of room left over then, sir," said Burnside, knowing that in all the regimental mounts totalled just under seven hundred.

The sergeant-major ignored the comment, but made a mental note that there would be plenty to do and Burnside could look forward to more than his fair share. "Now put your backs into it. The sooner we get away from here, the better."

The horses were being brought off in the same manner as they had been loaded, with slings beneath them, which in turn were attached to a large rope, run over a tackle on the main yard. Up and out they came. Through the padded hatchway and down onto the quayside. It looked undignified. Stiles, watching, was pleased that a group of sailors were doing the really hard work of taking the strain on the rope. At Cork it had been a body of convicts. The animals' coats were dull and once landed they moved stiffly. Each horse was walked up and down the dock for a few minutes before the troop moved off.

Belem exceeded their expectations. Fountains played majestically in the stables and to their surprise each man had a cot bed. This was in complete contrast to the cramped and indifferent accommodation that Stiles had endured since joining the army. The food was plentiful and much improved.

The days passed and they settled into their familiar routine. The horses got well-needed exercise and their black shiny coats was evidence of their improved condition. The men were constantly reminded that they must consider their mounts before themselves. They were, after all, the means of fighting the French, and on their state would depend the outcome. Then came the day when the regiment was inspected by Lord Wellington, the commander-in-chief, who expressed himself well satisfied. The main army and the war were still two hundred miles away. Rumour persisted that they might yet be withdrawn. In the meantime, there was Lisbon.

When they had first viewed Lisbon from the Tagus, the city had been an impressive sight, a place holding out much promise. There were clusters of white buildings, built on seven hills, and yet it wasn't as it appeared to be. Stiles and Burnside readily agreed on this point as they steadfastly plodded up a hill. They had gone into Lisbon with high hopes and on the lookout for drink and whatever else might take their fancy. Eventually they found what they were looking for but only after having to pick their way through the muck and filth which littered the streets and squares.

Stiles' first impression was that Lisbon was dirtier than London.

"When I walked through the city, on my way to enlist, I wondered what I had come to," he said, "but this beats all. Even Ipswich had street sweepers."

Burnside, who had already made his mind up that he didn't like foreigners or want to have much to do with them – although there might be one or two exceptions – replied, "Stands to reason that it's going to stink more than back home. Look at all the muck they eat."

The two Royals walked on, conscious of the stench and wondering if it was always like this. It didn't help matters to see people performing necessary functions in the street.

"Tinsley told me it was like this, but I didn't believe him," Burnside informed Stiles. "It seems as if they rely on the rain to clear most of it away."

"Doesn't look as though it has rained for some time," Stiles replied.

In stark contrast were the fine buildings and the elegant clothes of the rich. There were plump ladies, wearing white headscarves, being carried in painted litters or sedan chairs. The men were generally short, handsome, and wore tricorne hats. The peasants were dressed in long straw coats, white shirts and blue drawers. Pilchard dressers, lemonade sellers, beggars, friars, and ballad singers thumping their guitars crowded the streets, for this was one of the many feast days. Except for one aspect, Burnside was singularly unimpressed. He expressed the opinion that he wouldn't mind a few minutes with one of those fat parties. He'd give her what for!

A passing Portuguese man, who either understood English or, more likely, comprehended the accompanying gesture, muttered angrily to his companion, "These British soldiers are all alike. The sooner they get on with what they have come here to do and start fighting the French, the better."

They found a tavern. Wine was all they could get, and having some limited experience of its potency they had adopted a healthy respect for its effects. The place was in the poorer part of the city and they had progressed along a series of narrow alleyways, in which groups of people huddled in the shadows. The room in which they found themselves was full of redcoats, and on entering Stiles noticed Banks and his crony Willett. Both seemed to be well away and each had a woman with him.

Stiles and Burnside got their drinks and were standing near a party of men from the 95th, one of whom remarked to Burnside:

"I wouldn't get too settled, 'cos there might be trouble soon. Those two blokes of yours," he said, pointing towards Banks and his mate, "took those women away from two Portuguese. I'd keep my eye on them if I were you."

Burnside followed the man's pointing finger. Sure enough, in the background were two sullen-faced individuals, whose eyes never left their late companions. While he was still weighing up the situation there was a crash as tables and benches were suddenly up-ended. Stiles became aware of the pressure and hostility of the crowd. Their position had been halfway along the room, but gradually he and Burnside were moving ever so slowly towards the door. The momentum increased. They and the other occupants were swept, with a rib crushing force, through the door and into the outside. They still had their drinks in their hands. By chance, a corridor had formed, through which Banks passed, closely followed by Willett. They were going like greyhounds and being hotly pursued by the two women. Burnside saw some of the shadowy figures in the alleyway join in the pursuit.

The bar soon returned to normal and there was much discussion as to what had happened.

Stiles said, "I saw Banks wrench a bracelet off a woman's wrist."

"Wouldn't like to be in their shoes if the mob catches up with them," replied Burnside. "Do you think we ought to go after them?"

"From what I saw," said Stiles, "we would be well outnumbered. They brought it on their own heads. Let them get on with it."

In a merchant's house in a more affluent part of the city, Lieutenant Alexander Kennedy Clark and his brother officers of the Royals, Ralph Heathcote and Henry Carden, were being entertained to dinner. Clark had met their host, an exporter of wines, on a number of previous occasions and they were on the best of terms. The meal was first-class, and Clark, who was an excellent judge of wine, had been lavish in his praise. The hour was now late; the ladies had long since retired, and with their host the three officers sat in the salon, in deep comfortable chairs, drinking brandy and generally at peace with the world.

The merchant asked Clark, "How do you find life in Lisbon?"

"If I may say so, life has been easy since we arrived, or at least it has been for us." He waved his hand to include Heathcote and Carden. "I suppose the men are happy with their lot, provided their baser instincts are satisfied. The officers are never short of invitations, whether it be for a dinner or a ball. There are also the theatres and the coffee houses. If one wants to get away from the city," – Clark stopped just short of saying because of the oppressive smell – "the surrounding countryside is delightful. We are indeed fortunate to be based here. This may amuse you," he continued, "Lord Wellington has limited all leave in Lisbon, which doesn't apply to us as we are already here. His limit is twenty-four hours, which is justified on the grounds that no reasonable man needs longer than that in bed with one woman."

The host probed further. Sometimes he spoke in fluent English, but he occasionally lapsed into French, which was equally understood by all. "This must be completely different to Great Britain. Don't you miss home?"

"Home is in Dumfriesshire, where the family owns several farm properties. I went to university in Edinburgh with my two brothers, but on short acquaintance I prefer Lisbon. In all honesty, I haven't been home much these last five years. It has not been the same since my mother died. I was aged fifteen at the time. I must admit that I still miss her. Then, six years ago, my brother Walter was drowned when the *Hindoostan*, which belonged to the John Company, was lost at sea. My father is still alive, as are two sisters Jane and Christiana and my other brother John who is a surgeon." Clark became conscious that he had spoken of things in front of others which were matters he had kept locked away in his mind until now.

The host, noticing Clark's embarrassment, thought it as well to change the subject. "When is your regiment going to fight?"

Clark hoped he wasn't talking to a spy. "We await orders, sir," he replied. "The men, horses and equipment are in first-class condition – all we lack is practical experience. Lisbon – and I do not mean this in a disrespectful way – is our base, but for what it is worth my feeling is that Lord Wellington does not intend to evacuate the army. That would be unthinkable."

The merchant asked mischievously, "But are you going to win?"

"At the end of the day, most certainly," replied Clark. "His Lordship will continue to probe, and having chosen the ground he will fight battles on his own terms. As long as we, the Portuguese forces under Marshal Beresford, and the Spanish guerrillas all play our parts to the full, I am sure we will succeed." His delivery was accompanied by nods of agreement from the others. He concluded by saying, "The hour is now late and unfortunately we must take our leave." The party expressed their appreciation, bad farewell, and left by carriage for their quarters.

The British contingent left the bar as a body. There was no point in taking unnecessary risks. In ones and twos they might well provide an attractive target. On reaching the main thoroughfares they said their farewells and went their separate ways. As they walked along the now silent and almost deserted roads, Stiles and Burnside saw creaking muck carts collecting some of the dirt from the streets. As they passed one building, a shout came from above and Burnside quickly pulled Stiles to one side as the contents of a chamber pot narrowly missed him. They were now more than a little drunk, were tired and looking forward to bed. There was a figure in front of them. A soldier on his own, walking quickly. There was no mistaking the shambling gait.

"That's Banks," said Stiles. "I wonder what has happened to Willet?"

Next day Willett was reported missing at roll-call. Later his body was found. He had been stabbed to death.

The Proving Ground

The Royals' officers were awaiting the arrival of their commanding officer, Lieutenant-Colonel de Grey. He had called them together, and there was an animated buzz of conversation in the room as they waited. The regiment had taken twenty-one officers to the Peninsula. Most of them were present, including Majors Wyndham and Jervoise. Phillip Dorville, the senior captain, had joined as a cornet in 1795. None of them had previously served abroad.

It was the middle of December 1809 and the regiment was still in Lisbon.

"If we are to stay much longer, we will have a problem with discipline," said Clark to Lieutenant George Gunning, who had joined from the 9th Foot only the week before. "There is an increase in drunkenness, which I fear will only get worse unless we get proper work to do." His words were hardly out when the door to the room opened swiftly and with a clatter as the handle hit the wall.

The commanding officer, Lieutenant-Colonel the Honourable George de Grey, entered, accompanied by the adjutant. They all rose to their feet.

"Pray be seated, gentlemen," commanded de Grey. He paused while they did so. "I am pleased to tell you we have at last received our orders and will leave here on the 28th of this month. I am sure you will agree with me that we have had to wait far too long. Between now and the date of our departure ensure that all men, horses, arms, and equipment are ready. Overlook nothing. Take nothing for granted. Our initial march will be to Santarem, where we will receive further orders. We are to be brigaded with the 14th Light Dragoons under Major-General Sir Stapleton-Cotton, although at the moment he has handed over to Major-General Slade. Are there any questions?"

"Are the French advancing then, sir?" asked Clark.

"No," de Grey replied, "but we are at last to move in their direction. This initial move will provide further opportunities for acclimatisation. Inform the men, and remember, I rely on all of you to uphold the honour of the regiment!"

Stiles, Burnside, and the rest of the men were told at the afternoon parade. They were now eager to get on with it, even Banks, who had said nothing about being with Willett the night he was murdered. Stiles and his friend had decided to profess ignorance of the matter, on the basis that the less said the better. They weren't sure whether Banks had spotted them, but Stiles had his suspicions. He had observed Banks looking at them oddly.

"Better keep an eye on our backs, Jim, once we get to the fighting," he observed to Burnside. "We don't want to get caught from behind."

There was much to be done. The already well-cleaned arms and equipment were re-cleaned, time over, until they passed muster. Swords and bayonets were sharpened. Greater attention than ever was given to the horses, with new shoes fitted where necessary. The barracks and stables were possessed with a frantic sense of urgency. No one was allowed out. This was a precaution against possible desertions, but in any event every second counted. Burnside thought it as well they had been confined to barracks, as with all the cleaning and polishing he wouldn't have either the strength or inclination for his usual activities.

"Hope I get a bit before we come across the French," he said reflectively to Stiles.

On the day before they left Belem Barracks for the last time, there was a regimental inspection. The men stood by in their barrack rooms awaiting the arrival of the commanding officer. Stiles knew their turn could not be far off as he heard the sounds of command getting progressively nearer. There was the sound of marching footsteps, quickly followed by the order to come to attention. The colonel and his entourage, which included Captain Hulton, the troop leader, and Sergeant-Major Waddell, were suddenly in the room, which had been thoroughly cleaned and tidied. Every item of equipment, clothing and weapons in charge of each man was to be looked at. The colonel was not one to leave things to chance. Saddles were inspected to make sure that they were in good condition. Carbines, which were hung with their locks downwards; hats; cloaks, neatly folded; swords and bayonets, out of their scabbards; bits, boots as well as the men – all came under scrutiny. Stiles experienced, not for the first time, that heart-stopping moment when several pairs of eyes inspected him but the party passed on. Inevitably, and to no one's surprise, Banks was reprimanded for having dirty equipment.

When the inspecting party left the room, the troop sergeant-major rounded on Banks, threw his kit on the floor, and yelled, "Bloody well clean it again and bring it to me when you have done so!" While there was a feeling of resentment at Banks for having let them down, Stiles felt that the troop demonstrated its true spirit. The equipment was quickly shared among them and they all got to work to clean it. Banks did not, by word or gesture, show any appreciation.

They left Belem early on the morning of the 28th December, 1809 in high hopes that the coming year would bring a change in fortune. Their saddlebags were the last items to be packed with an assortment of articles and clothing. The packing was in a strictly prescribed manner. In all, the bags weighed about eighteen pounds, which meant that each horse was carrying, with its rider, approximately sixteen stones.

Burnside caught Stiles grinning at him and asked, "What's up?"

Stiles looked at Burnside, the sheer size of the man, standing with his saddlebags and said, "With all that weight your horse will be carrying, I wouldn't be surprised if it doesn't have a bowed back before we get to the Gate."

"Saucy sod!" was the reply.

They mounted and were on the march, formed in half squadrons, in column and six ranks abreast. At the rear came the forage carts, carrying such of the men's wives as had been selected to accompany their husbands from Ireland. These were followed by wagons for transporting the surgeon, veterinary officer, saddler, armourer, and the forge, all covered by the rearguard, which on this day included Stiles, Burnside, and Banks. Just as they passed through the barrack gate a Portuguese came out of the crowd and shouted something at Banks, at the same time running his right forefinger in a cutting motion across his throat. Banks paled visibly.

"Now we know why he hasn't been keen to leave the barracks," said Stiles.

"Quiet in the ranks!" shouted Corporal Lloyd.

The distance to Santarem was only thirty-six miles and was to be made in easy stages over four days. During a day's march, occasional halts were ordered so that girths might be adjusted and the horses watered. Strict discipline was enforced. The men rode in an upright manner, wrapped in their cloaks, and content in the knowledge that, for the time being, each day's march would end at noon, leaving sufficient time for foraging and unsaddling. They also travelled knowing that, although they were now dependent on the commissary for their supplies, the lines of supply were short.

"I don't know what we are doing here," said Burnside. "Christ! For all the good we are doing, we might as well have stayed at home!"

The troop was watering its horses at a stream outside a town near to the Spanish border. Stiles could only but agree. It was now April, four months after they had left Lisbon. Their initial destination, Santarem, had proved to be their base for a month, and when they had at last moved it had been to the east. Now they were on their way north, but as far as they knew the enemy were still a long way off. Their expectations were dulled.

"When we first went east to Niza," said Stiles, "there was some hope that the French would put in an attack, but we haven't seen hide or hair of them."

"You don't have to tell me," retorted Burnside. "What's this place called, again?"

"Portalegro."

"I don't know why I bothered to ask. They're all beginning to look alike. I see there is a patrol going out. Don't know why they bother!"

A little after dusk the patrol returned in some haste. Word soon spread round the camp that the French had been sighted.

"It wasn't that large a number of them," said Sergeant Lee. "Not more than fifty, I would say, but the light was failing and we didn't get a good sighting."

"How far off would that be?" asked Colonel Wyndham.

"About five miles, sir," Lee replied. "They looked as though they were setting up camp for the night."

Wyndham ordered Major Jervoise to put out a strong sergeant's picquet. "I cannot be certain whether it is merely a patrol or an

advance guard," he said. "We will have a look in the morning to see
what they are up to. It could be that it is only a reconnaissance. Send
Clark. He must take Lee with him, and I suggest you use half a
troop."

Stiles and Burnside were among those detailed for the patrol.

Stiles was excited. "Action at last!"

Burnside was more sceptical. "There'll be no action. I wouldn't
put it past them to have made up the whole idea. Sergeant Lee can't
be certain he saw the French. How would he know? None of us has
seen one yet!"

It was dark, an hour before dawn, when they mounted. Clark
pushed Lee on ahead with Stiles and they rode as point. Lee led the
way, slowly, along a track which was wooded on either side and rose
and fell intermittently.

Stiles strained his ears but could hear nothing above the horses'
tread. From time to time Lee stopped to get his bearings. Finally:
"Not far now. Just up there." He pointed into the gloom. "There is
an opening in the woods. That's where their encampment is."

Lee sniffed the air. "Can't smell any cooking."

"Maybe they are still asleep," ventured Stiles.

"Go back and tell the lieutenant that I have gone forward to see
what they are up to," said Lee. "If I am spotted, you will soon hear."

The patrol waited. There was not a sound. After what seemed an
eternity Lee returned. "Sorry to say, sir, but the beggars have gone.
There's no sign of them."

"We might as well go forward and take a look," said Clark in a
resigned tone.

"What did I tell you?" said Burnside triumphantly. "They've
buggered off!"

The promise of an early summer had given way to torrential rain.
The regiment was heading firmly northwards but its progress was
barred by the River Caterena, which was in full flood.

Wyndham called his three squadron leaders together. "As you
know, we have sent men up and down stream. There are no bridges
and apparently no other places more suitable for a crossing."

The rain continued to fall, and the puddles which had formed were
getting ever bigger. As he paused, Wyndham looked over what would
normally have been a gentle flowing stretch of water. Now it was
transformed into a thrashing, violent torrent, and was carrying whole

trees, branches, and all manner of debris. "We do not have any alternative but to cross here," continued Wyndham. "It could be days before the level drops, and I cannot afford to wait as long as that."

The noise made by the rushing water drowned normal conversation. Usually they would have crossed in groups but the conditions meant that there was only room for two horses abreast. Stiles gulped air and took a firm grip on his horse's mane. The river had spread beyond its banks and there was no knowing what lay beneath the surface. So far so good. His mount was now chest deep in the water and from his vantage point he kept a wary eye for larger items of debris. There didn't seem to be anything to worry about on that score at the moment, but the current was pulling so fiercely that it was impossible to keep in a straight line towards where the opposite bank should be. He was being forced diagonally downstream. He heard a cry from behind. On turning he saw George Acheson being swept away. His arms flailed above the water and were then lost to sight. Stiles noticed that Burnside, to his right, was having similar difficulties to himself, but at last they were nearing the opposite shore.

At last, he reached safety. He was soaked from head to foot and on dismounting took off his boots to empty them. The crossing, which had only taken a few minutes, seemed to have been one of the longest journeys of his life. Later, he was one of those detailed to look for George's body. It must have become trapped, for despite a thorough search it was not found.

"Keep a sharp look out!" ordered Sergeant Bell. Stiles, Burnside, Tinsley, and two other men were on outpost duty. The French were nearby but presented no immediate danger. It was a warm July night and a gentle breeze carried the voices of a body of Frenchmen, no doubt engaged on similar duties, towards their position. Bell's concern lay with the fact that Colonel Wyndham would be visiting the picquets, as field officer of the day.

Burnside at times could be annoying, otherwise he was a good soldier. "Colonel coming then, Sergeant?" he'd enquired earlier.

"Be quiet," Bell had replied.

That had been followed by "He's not here yet," and similar comments, until even Stiles had told him "Shut up!"

"I was only asking!"

In the distance they heard the sound of hooves, not, so far as they could tell, coming towards them but it was difficult to appreciate the true direction as they were on springy turf, so that the effect was more of a slight thump than a beat.

"That might be him," said Bell. "Stand to!"

The picquet had just got into line when on the breeze came a challenge. "*Qui va la?*" This was followed immediately by the sound of several weapons being cocked and then, disarmingly, by laughter.

"Stiles. Go and have a look and make sure you are not caught!"

He hugged the ground and carried his carbine at the trail. As he got nearer he could hear the far from silent and excited Frenchmen. Then a voice shouted, "Silence!" He was almost to the French position. They must be on the other side of that rise in the ground. Stiles got down on to his stomach and edged his way forward, cautiously, on his elbows and knees. He looked down on the French vedette and what he saw made him gasp so loudly that he thought that he must have been heard. There, in the light thrown by a lantern, looking equally disconsolate, were the unmistakable figures of the colonel and two privates. No wonder the French had laughed. The commanding officer had walked straight into their hands.

Stiles counted the enemy. In all they numbered twenty. Even if he went back and told Sergeant Bell, there was nothing they could do. A French officer walked forward and addressed Wyndham in heavily accented English.

"Colonel, I will have your sword, if you please. Will you please be good enough to ask your men to lay down their arms?"

The colonel nodded to his men, who put their weapons on the ground. At the same time he drew his own sword, which he handed over.

"Well, Colonel," said the Frenchman, Stiles was now concluding his report to Bell, "we must get you and your men safely to the rear."

"They grouped round Colonel Wyndham and the two men and rode off," Stiles concluded.

"Go back and tell Major Jervoise immediately," said Bell, "then come back here."

It was late August. Dorville's squadron, which included Clark's troop, was on picquet at Freixadas with a squadron of the 14th Light Dragoons. The bulk of the army had been withdrawn following the fateful explosion of the magazine at Almeida, which led to that town's surrender. The French, vastly superior in numbers, were seen approaching, and the two squadrons had, at Dorville's command, formed into line. The next order was, "Draw sabres!" There was a sighing sound as the swords were withdrawn from their metal scabbards, followed by, to Clark's surprise, a momentary stillness. No one spoke. The enemy was still some distance away, on the slightly descending plain. Eventually the only sound came from a horse which was snorting and pawing the ground.

The French drew nearer. Their cavalry was at the front, coming at a walk. The infantry followed, and their drums suddenly started to beat the *"Pas de Charge"*. Clark thought, 'Surely we are not going to receive them at the halt. We must advance!' It was as though Dorville had read his mind. He said in a loud voice, to no one in particular, "We'll let them get closer." The French marched on.

Dorville gave the order. The trumpet call signalling the advance rang out. They went forward at a walk, increased through a trot to a canter and then to a gallop as the trumpeter sounded the strident notes of the charge, which was answered by a yell from the men. Down came the sabres so that the points were towards the foe. Within fifty yards contact was made with the enemy, and while some stood their ground, the majority turned about and fled.

Clark engaged a French dragoon. Their weapons clashed. He managed to parry his adversary's sword, then put all his strength into a savage backhand cut. The blow caught the man on the shoulder but his epaulette turned the sword aside. The Frenchman had had enough. He turned and followed his retreating companions.

For days now they had covered the retreat. The Royals and other cavalry units were the rearguard. Still Wellington had found time, in late September, to give Massena a bloody nose at Busaco. The retreat had started the day after the battle and it was now into October. Stiles, Burnside, and their comrades wondered where it would all end. They were ordered to burn the corn, flour, and anything which might be of use to the enemy. They also found themselves in the thick of the action. Collectively they achieved the objective of buying precious time. Time to enable the army to retreat in good order. They soon became accustomed to the sound and effects of cannon and musket fire. They became used to the loss of life and the appalling wounds, both to man and beast. Stiles, on one occasion, cut a French soldier across the face with his sabre, laying him open from brow to chin. Later as he related the experience to Burnside, he'd said, "I could hear the drill sergeant's voice: 'When you make the cut, make sure that you don't cut your horse's ears off!'"

Now it all seemed to be a blur. Day followed day. A stand here, followed by a retirement and so on. A surprise attack on their camp, on a very rainy night, when they hadn't expected the French to come, had been a near thing. They had been lucky to get away and had lost some of their equipment and baggage in the process. One of the worst times was last week, when they had gone without hot food for days. Stiles chuckled to himself. They were skirmishing. Burnside had two live chickens tied to his saddle and a full haversack. They had all helped themselves to food which otherwise would have fallen into French hands. At the day's end a pleasant surprise awaited. They rode into a village to find Major-General Slade waiting for them. Much to the annoyance of the other regiments, he had requisitioned all the wine for the Royals. The last stages of the retreat brought constant heavy rain. The ground became churned up and the horses sank to their knees in the mud. There was a shortage of forage and the mounts were in a sorry state. They were all worn out. Horse casualties were over a hundred and many needed shoeing.

Clark, recently promoted to Captain, led a file of twenty men, who were to relieve a picquet on outpost duty. They rode uphill, slowly picking their way along a track which would bring them to their destination – a fortified farmhouse. Since early October there had been no action to speak of, other than the occasional exchange of small arms fire and it seemed that both sides were equally content to await developments. Marshal Andre Massena, Commander of the French Army in Portugal, had forced Wellington to retire and now had his headquarters in Santarem. It was said that the existence of the Lines of Torres Vedras, a well preserved secret, had come as a complete surprise to him. He was not the only one, mused Clark. As far as he was aware, apart from the duke, whose scheme it had been, and the engineers and labourers, who had been involved in their construction, the Army had been equally amazed. The regiment had arrived within the safety of the lines soon after the battle of Busaco. They had made life difficult for the French by their stubbornness. It had not been an easy pursuit for them. Busaco had cost Massena dearly, and his men, accustomed to living off the countryside, were short of provisions, due to Wellington's scorched earth policy. By contrast, the Allies were well supplied with food.

Following Wyndham's capture, Jervoise had taken over, quite successfully in Clark's opinion. Eventually an outside appointment had been made and he wondered how he would get on with the new man. Lieutenant-Colonel Benjamin Clifton from the 3rd Dragoon Guards was now their commanding officer. He had the reputation of being an authoritarian and had already been dubbed "Ben the Ruler".

Stiles and Burnside were among the party at the farmhouse, which had been turned into a fortified outpost. The building was placed high on a hill, which gave good all-round observation, and all possible cover had been removed, so that any would be attacker would be in for a difficult time. There was almost a sheer drop on three sides and there was only one main route in or out, except for a narrow winding path to the plain below.

"Put some more wood on the fire, Burnside!" ordered Corporal Rankin.

Burnside reluctantly got to his feet. He had only just sat down, having been on sentry duty. He picked up a billet of timber and threw it onto the blaze. The dry wood quickly caught alight and sent out a series of spitting sparks. He resumed his place on the flagged floor. 'One thing', he thought, 'there is no shortage of fuel.' He looked at Stiles, who had rested his back against the wall and had his legs stretched out in front of him. Stiles' eyes were closed and he appeared to be asleep. The wind, now blowing a gale, howled round the building as though seeking access to the room. Burnside pulled his cloak tightly around him and settled into a doze.

Stiles wasn't asleep but was deep in thought. If truth be told, Burnside hadn't stopped talking since he'd finished his guard duty and he wanted a rest from his voice. They hadn't argued or anything like that; it was just that the picquet had been cooped up for five days and he'd had enough of these confined quarters. Still, he was warm and ought to be grateful for that.

His thoughts were interrupted when he heard faint popping sounds. Immediately he was alert and he opened his eyes. Everyone else looked relaxed. He must have imagined it. The wind died down for a brief moment. In the short period of calm he heard the unmistakable sound of musket fire. It was quite unexpected. The French had not ventured out for a while. Still no one else gave any indication that they had heard anything.

"Corporal Rankin," said Stiles with a tone of urgency in his voice, "I can hear musket fire!"

Rankin looked unbelievingly at him. "I can't hear a thing apart from this damned wind. It's probably the fire spitting."

"But I tell you—" Stiles got no further. The door was flung open, and Tinsley was shouting, "There's a party of French approaching. They seem to be chasing a man who's running like hell towards us. They are firing at him but so far he doesn't appear to have been hit."

"Grab your arms and turn out!" ordered the corporal. He led the way down the narrow path, negotiated the abattis, and followed the track, which now ran between high banks, to its end. There, on the plain and coming at speed towards them, was a man. He was not approaching on a straight course but wove from side to side as he ran. Some seventy or so yards behind him was a party of a dozen French soldiers, who from time to time pointed their muskets at the fugitive and fired. The sound of the shots was now much louder, but still the man ran.

"Spread yourselves out and provide covering fire!" shouted Rankin. "Fire at will and take careful aim!"

They fired. The French hesitated before being urged on by an officer. Suddenly the man was down. Stiles had no hesitation. "Cover me!" he yelled at Burnside as he launched himself forward. The French switched their attention to him. Spurts of dust were raised near his feet and a ball hummed as it passed close to his ear. The man was now only a few yards from him and had raised himself on one elbow. A Frenchman, more bold than the rest, had advanced with speed way ahead of his companions, and Stiles could see that it would be a close thing as to which of them reached the victim first. 'I'll have to shoot him,' thought Stiles and he raised his carbine. The enemy soldier came to a sudden halt. Stiles squeezed the trigger. Nothing happened. He had not reloaded the weapon.

The obvious fear showing on the Frenchman's face was replaced first by a look of relief and then by deep hatred. He turned his musket towards Stiles.

"Get down!" That was Jim Burnside shouting. There were two shots, one slightly in advance of the other, so that the second sounded like an echo of the first. Stiles raised his eyes in time to see the French soldier sliding slowly to the ground with blood spreading across his chest. Stiles turned his head. There was Burnside, who must have followed him, grinning all over his face.

"That was a close call, Francis. I thought you'd had it! Now pick him up," he pointed at the fugitive, "and let's get out of here."

Stiles carried the man back to the foot of the hill.

"Who have you got there?" asked Corporal Rankin. As yet Stiles had not had an opportunity of finding out. The man's clothes were old and filthy, and he smelt abominably. There was blood on Stiles hands. "He must be wounded somewhere."

The bundle of rags propped up against a rock spoke. "Captain Henry Logan of the 24th Foot at your service." His voice, which could only be described as belonging to a gentleman, took them all by surprise. "It is by sheer chance that I found you," continued Logan. "It is imperative that I get to Lisbon without delay. I have important intelligence." With that he fainted.

"Let's get him back to the top," Rankin ordered. He picked out four men. "Captain Clark will be here with the relief soon. We'll see what he makes of him."

Clark arrived in time to see Rankin and his men reach the top of the path bearing what looked like a body. He listened to Rankin's report. In the meantime, they ripped the right leg of the captain's trousers to examine the wound, which was in the fleshy part of the thigh and was clean. Clark turned to Logan, who was now regaining consciousness, and introduced himself.

"You say that you need to be in Lisbon as a matter of urgency. If you are able to ride, we will get you back directly. Where precisely do you want to be?"

"Headquarters!" replied Logan. "I would have been there sooner if I hadn't run into a French patrol last evening. I thought I had made it through their lines and was careless enough to get caught. Fortunately for me their security was not what it should have been and I was able to escape. You know the rest. I will make it known of the brave conduct of your men and of these two in particular." He pointed at Stiles and Burnside. "I will be obliged if you will give me a note of their names. Now, if you can get someone to dress my wound and provide a little brandy – if you have such a thing – I will not delay you further."

Stiles was back at the base camp, on sentry duty, and was patrolling near the horse lines. The animals seemed restless, and

Stiles, who had heard of cases where for no apparent reason tethered horses had bolted, hoped that it wasn't going to happen while he was on guard. He thought that rats might be the problem, but on drawing nearer and having moved along the line he saw a crouching figure. He cocked and raised his carbine when a voice said with alarm:

"Don't shoot. It's me Banks!"

"What the bloody hell are you doing here?" asked Stiles, at the same time noticing that Banks was holding his haversack.

Banks replied, "I'm going. I've had enough. We're too near to Lisbon and I daren't be seen there. Anyway, I once told you that I'm not going to get myself shot by the French, so clear out of my way!"

"You're not going anywhere," Stiles replied. "These horses are my responsibility. Apart from that if you get caught, you'll be handed over to the Provost Marshal and hung. You'll be left to swing as an example to the rest of us, just like those two we saw the other day. Do you want that to happen?"

Banks was hesitating. Stiles saw that he now had him in two minds. Without any further conversation he turned on his heels and returned to his billet.

Orders to advance came to Lieutenant-Colonel Clifton on the 5th March 1811. It was a very foggy morning and the courier informed him that "Massena had taken advantage of the weather and had commenced his army's retreat. He might have got further away before his absence was discovered had not word been brought to his Lordship, by a very young Portuguese who swam across the Rio Major." Clifton opened his orders. The cavalry under Major-General Slade was to pursue the enemy. The Royals with the 14th Light Dragoons were once more to go up the road to Santarem.

General Jack Slade was feeling apprehensive. He was quite clear about his orders, which were to harry and maintain contact with the French. His anxiety arose from what might happen if they were to run in with a superior force. He was determined that he would not be disgraced but he was going to proceed with caution and would not be rushed into hasty actions.

The brigade, with the Royals leading and Slade and Clifton at the head, cantered up the Santarem road. As they filed across the bridge by the town, Lord Wellington with his entourage came towards them. Wellington ran an appreciative eye over the horses with their shiny, jet black coats.

"Good day, Slade. Clifton. I want you to make all haste along the Thomar Road."

It was clear that they were not pursuing an army but an undisciplined rabble. They started to come across stragglers who showed no resistance but who were genuinely relieved to be captured. For them the war was over. There were broken-down wagons, abandoned horses, and numerous mules which the enemy had hamstrung. If the men were angered at this, it was nothing by comparison to later events. Every building they came to had been ransacked and set alight. The remains of the contents, whether they came from peasant's hut or church, were scattered far and wide, giving the impression that the deed had been carried out by men in a frenzy. There were dead bodies everywhere, some showing evidence of torture. So desperate had the French been to find supposed hidden sources of food that they had resorted to these measures.

"Dismount and go and search those buildings," Clark ordered. He and Lieutenant Crosbie waited by the farm gate as the men began their search. They carried their carbines in case there was any enemy to deal with. What they found appalled them all. Stiles by now was no stranger to death and even months later could not obliterate the sight and smell from his memory. He couldn't believe his eyes. They found three men in the house. One was older, possibly the father. The other two might have been his sons. It looked as though they had been hacked to death with bayonets. There was blood everywhere and the bodies had been partly burnt. Burnside and some of the others meantime had made for the barn. A woman and two girls had been hung up, and the three naked bodies swayed gently from side to side on the ends of their ropes. Fires had been lit underneath them and Burnside was certain that they had been ravished. How could anyone do something like that to another human? They must be devils! One of the party expressed what till then had been an unspoken thought when he said, "I'll think twice in future before taking any more bastard Crapaud prisoners."

Clark and Crosbie were severely affected by the distressing scenes. The men were ordered to dig graves. In the village, thirty-six people had been found murdered in their beds, and one of the most macabre sights they saw was at the burial ground, where coffins had been dug up in search of buried treasure. It was difficult to know whether such primitive acts were the result of desperation, or whether the retreating troops were venting their anger on the populace at large. In any event it contrasted sharply with the enemy's previous courteous behaviour.

"They are a strange race," said Crosbie. "Do you remember just after last Christmas when they returned a lost cloak to one of the men?"

"Yes," said Clark. "There was also that occasion when we were in the lines and they told us not to worry if we heard one hundred and one cannon shots, as it would only be saluting the birth of Napoleon's son."

The advance through the devastated countryside continued. There were frequent skirmishes, but Slade, despite pressure from Clifton, would not allow his cavalry full rein. His overcautious attitude was complemented by Lieutenant-General Erskine, temporarily in command of Craufurd's Light Division, who had a similar outlook. As a result many opportunities were lost. Supplies became a problem, which, on top of Slade's many blunders, imposed a further burden. Clark and his fellows became more exasperated. Slade dithered when he might have advanced, using the excuse that he was waiting for more troops. He ordered out an enormous picquet of squadron strength and caused unnecessary fatigue to the overworked horses and men. Clark could clearly see that Slade, not a coward by any means, was becoming increasingly hesitant and that one day his hesitation might be the cause of great danger to the regiment.

Stiles and Burnside were hungry, as were all the others. It was the second day without bread and the third without corn. To further add to their discomfort, it was nightfall and raining. They tried to make the best of what shelter they could find under the trees, but the rain splashed down off the branches and it was not long before they were wet through. At last, they managed to light a fire, which because of the damp wood was giving off more smoke than heat and on which they were trying to cook a thin watery soup.

Burnside grumbled good-naturedly, "That skilly would taste better with some Brown George," referring to the standard issue army loaf. "They ought to shoot that bloody commissary," he repeated for the umpteenth time. "I keep hearing those bleedin' mules' bells jingling, but it's never anything for us. Why don't we go and throw stones at his tent again? It might wake the bugger up!"

Stiles demurred. On the previous occasion when they had bombarded the commissary's tent they had been warned of serious consequences if there was a repetition, and in all honesty it hadn't served any useful purpose. "It won't do any good," he said. More bells could be heard in the distance. As they approached, Stiles shouted, "Anything for us?"

"No," came the reply from out of the darkness. "We've rum, biscuit and corn for the 14th Light Dragoons."

"Bugger off!" yelled Burnside.

Eventually their turn came, yet they were told that the French were in a worse plight. By all accounts Massena's infantry were worn out; half naked and without shoes. Horse teams for his guns could only be found with difficulty and his cavalry horses could barely walk. The French general retired behind the Coa, and, in the process of following up, the Royals collected many prisoners, stragglers and foragers, in spite of Slade's attempts to hold them back. They also managed to capture several bullocks and sheep and to appropriate some for their own use.

Clifton led the Royals forward. They, with the 16th Light Dragoons and a detachment of horse artillery, were to assist Trant's Portuguese, who were in trouble. From what Clifton had been told, a French division from Almeida, the last French troops in Portugal had engaged the Portuguese. It seemed to Clifton that they were just in time, and the French commander, on seeing the cavalry and guns approaching, broke off the engagement. From the direction the enemy were taking, they were heading towards Barba del Puerco where there was a bridge over the Agueda. The cavalry pressed forward after them.

Stiles felt something tug at his shoulder, followed by a cry of pain from behind. 'Must have been a musket ball,' he thought. The French infantry formed squares and General Erskine recalled them. They rounded up the stragglers and passed them over to their infantry, which had followed up. Stiles then saw a dead French officer and he dismounted. He went through the man's pockets; they were empty. His watch, if he had ever possessed such an article, was gone. Stiles could tell by the paler round of skin on the man's finger that he had worn a ring, but it wasn't there now. He was just about to rise to his feet when he heard a horse approaching and saw that it was Captain Crosbie. 'I'm in trouble now,' he thought, but then saw that Crosbie was smiling.

"Can't you find anything? Here, let me show you!" With that Crosbie got down. "Get his coat off and give me your bayonet!" Crosbie ran the point of the bayonet up the centre seam of the coat's lining and put his hand into the opening he had made, just below the collar. "It is as I thought," he said and brought out a small chamois leather bag, which he shook so that Stiles could hear the rattle of coins. He placed the bag in Stiles' hand saying, "There you are. They often hide them there. Now be off with you and take up your position!"

Slade on Wellington's orders sent the Royals back to Barquilla, so that the regiment might be nearer its supplies and for a well-earned rest. The quarters were good and the district had escaped the attention of the pillagers. There was also enough grass to allow the horses to be turned out, and their condition speedily improved. This was as well, as, unbeknown to the regiment, they were about to take part in their first major battle.

Fuentes d'Onoro

Cornet Sigismund Trafford, with a draft of fifty horses and men, was almost at the end of his journey. He was making for Fuentes d'Onoro, where the Royals and the rest of Wellington's army were gathered. It was early on the 3rd of May 1811, and a passing rider had given him the news that Massena was advancing, possibly to relieve Almeida. Trafford's command had left the Home Depot at York some five weeks earlier, and he could now sense the heightened feeling among the men who had overheard the conversation. Trafford was seventeen years of age, very tall, and, apart from his height, was conscious of his bandy legs. He had a long pale face and staring blue eyes, wore a neckcloth and long jackboots outside his overalls. He was comfortably off and had advanced some money to Ben Cook, the new adjutant, before leaving England. As the group plodded on their journey, he was contemplating the profit he would make from his share in the scheme which Ben had devised.

At the main camp, Benjamin Cook was wondering what time Trafford would arrive. The draft had been sighted on the road, but as far as he was concerned Trafford could take as long as he liked. Anything to put off the time when he would have to pay what he owed him, although he couldn't wait to see the expression on Trafford's face when he told him the good news. Cook had been in the Peninsular for only a month and had made much better progress as he had not been encumbered with the draft. He was not known to the other Royals' officers when he joined the regiment in Spain, and if he'd appeared too familiar at a first meeting, he made no apology. What were Christian names for if not to be used? At least he'd made an impression. Favourable or otherwise, it mattered not to him, as long as he kept on the right side of the colonel.

It had been one evening in York, having seen Trafford quite free with his purse, that made him decide to broach a scheme which he had in mind but which until then had not possessed the wherewithal to put into practice. He knew that the Royals were desperately short of shoes. At one time in his life he had been apprenticed to a shoemaker and knew the trade well. He hadn't been sorry to leave that occupation, somewhat hurriedly as it turned out, when his master discovered that he was sharing his wife's favours. Cook had persuaded Trafford to advance him money to purchase one hundred pairs, which he thought he could buy for six shillings. They should, he had explained, be able to sell them for nine shillings and sixpence a pair. All had worked out as planned. The shoes were bought in Crediton, on his way down to Plymouth, and were snapped up on his arrival. Cook reflected that most of his brother officers had substantial private means, but in his case every little helped. His wife, who had been sent to the rear with the other wives at the first sign of danger, had two main failings – an explosive temper and, even under these conditions, expensive tastes. He looked up the road. There was no sign of Trafford. He decided to wait a while longer and adjusted his stance to take the weight off his club foot.

Trafford arrived during the afternoon. Cook, to the amazement of the onlookers, as soon as Trafford had dismounted took him to one side and began counting dollars into his hand. He prefaced this action by saying, "We've made three shillings and sixpence a pair profit." Trafford expressed his satisfaction as he put the money away. Privately, he thought that Cook had been right all along but it wouldn't do to become too friendly. Stiles and Burnside were within earshot and were pleased as Burnside put it, "Not to have lined those buggers' pockets!"

The battle started later that day but the Royals had to wait another two days before becoming involved. Stiles was on duty with Captain Hulton's squadron, when the French cavalry attacked at half past three on the morning of the 5th May. The enemy quickly came down on them and they might have fared badly if they had not been so alert. As it was, they were greatly outnumbered and Hulton got them into skirmishing order. The regiment was to the south of Fuentes, covering the road back to Portugal. Stiles and his fellows knew only too well the importance of holding on. They were well aware of the attempts made by the French, since the 2nd, to capture the town. Whilst they had not been in a position to witness the fighting, the sounds of musketry and prolonged cannonade were unmistakable.

Yesterday had been strangely quiet as each side collected its dead and wounded. Stiles hadn't liked the waiting. He knew that their turn would surely come and was pleased to be getting on with it. Today all hell had been let loose. It was at an early stage in the action that he had seen Burnside leading his horse to the rear, and from the way it was hobbling it was not going to be of further use.

The French continued to press. Clifton called the squadron leaders together.

"Gentlemen, I am going to give you an additional burden. The 7th Division are in trouble. They are holding positions at Nave de Haver and Pozo Bello, about a mile from here." He pointed in the general direction. "As you can see, there is not much cover, and with the superior force of French cavalry they are likely to be cut up. We are going forward with Craufurd's Light Division, Bull's guns, and the 14th, to assist them to retire. It's going to be confusing and damned dangerous, but we have got to try and get them out. Lord Wellington wants them to reform on the right of the line."

Major-General Houston, commanding the 7th Division, was at Nave de Haver. It was a fine day, with little wind, so that the powder smoke, as his men poured volley after volley at the French cavalry, hung in the air like fog. The division had not been more than a few weeks in the Peninsula, but for all their lack of experience, Houston was well satisfied with the performance of his troops. He could see that they were now isolated by an outflanking movement, which had cut their line of retreat to Fuentes, but somehow they must withdraw. In his opinion they might already have left it too late. He hoped that Lord Wellington would appreciate the situation and give them some protection. The French cavalry were milling around, and the last thing he wanted was to be caught in the open.

Friendly cavalry advanced in front of the Light Division, and Houston, seeing his opportunity, gave his division orders to retire. The Royals and the 14th charged with two squadrons forward and two in reserve. There was hand-to-hand combat and the air was alive with the sound of musketry and exploding shells. As each charge took place the men yelled like demons, and Stiles, not for the first time, was aware of the ineffectiveness of his sword. Although he was wielding it most ably, the French cavalrymen had their cloaks rolled across their left shoulders and it was difficult to inflict a mortal wound. During one of the brief lulls while his squadron was reforming, Stiles saw that the main onslaught was being directed against Craufurd's Division, but the guns of the horse artillery were continuing to harass the French infantry by constantly darting forward, unlimbering and firing. Gaps were occurring in the enemy's ranks. Stiles admired the gunners' nerve but wouldn't have changed places with them. The noise and the action became even more confused. The French were trying to stop the 7th, but slowly, only stopping to fire controlled volleys, they were nearing safety.

Stiles' squadron was going forward yet again, and the pace had picked up into a charge. Without warning he felt his horse stagger and the next thing he knew he was flying through the air. As he hit the earth, the breath was knocked out of him, but luckily he was not trampled on by the horses following. Looking round, Stiles saw his horse lying in a heap and not moving. He checked himself. Apart from a cut on the head, doubtless caused when he made impact with the ground, he did not appear to be wounded. He heard a shout,. "Get over here quickly man!" A sergeant of artillery was beckoning. Fortunately for him he was near to two horse artillery guns. The artillery men had been sheltering under the guns for safety, as each attack by the enemy cavalry had temporarily engulfed them. He had no sooner reached safety when the order was given to "Limber up."

Stiles wondered what was going to happen to him now. There was no sign of his squadron and it could only be a matter of minutes before the French renewed their attack. His only weapon was the sword, which was secured to him by the lanyard round his neck. He might have worried all the more if he had known that he and the gunners were in a pocket and already cut off from the British lines. His fate was decided for him.

"Mount that horse," he was told. An officer was pointing to one of a team pulling a gun.

"Hang on tight and touch nothing!"

Stiles quickly got onto the animal's back, and the team, drawing its gun and its limber, went off at a cracking pace. Stiles, from his new vantage point, could now see the danger they faced and grasped his sabre firmly in his right hand. The enemy were all around them. It seemed pretty hopeless when out of nowhere appeared a squadron of the Royals, his squadron, with some 14th Light Dragoons, and took up position around them. The combined force bludgeoned its way through the amassed French to safety, with Stiles on his unfamiliar mount, hanging on for grim death. Once within the lines, he found a loose horse and rejoined his squadron.

Lieutenant George Gunning had reason to feel pleased with himself. He had taken as his prisoner a lieutenant-colonel of the 13th Chasseurs. The enemy had badly mauled and captured a number of skirmishers of the 1st Division, which had been thrown out as further protection for the retreating 7th. Colonel Clifton had decided to launch a further squadron, and as its usual leader, Major Dorville, was with Slade (and by all accounts was not very happy about it), as it meant that he was away from the action. Gunning led Dorville's squadron in the charge. The result had been the release of twenty-five prisoners and the capture of Colonel Lamotte. Gunning felt aglow. He basked in the warmth of his success. All that he needed now to make his day complete was a woman. His thoughts switched to Mrs Alcock, (aptly named, so it was said), the housekeeper of the paymaster, Michael Byrne. On the few occasions they had met there had been no mistaking the message in her eyes, but he would have to wait his for opportunity.

The French cavalry continued to hover but it was obvious that they had lost their appetite and had no serious intent. The enemy preferred to conduct the engagement at longer range and the Royals were subjected to a particularly intense bombardment, which lasted four hours. Fortunately it was badly aimed and mostly went over their heads. It was Clark's squadron who seemed to be bearing the brunt of the enemy's activities, and as a result the bulk of the casualties.

Clark, mounted on his old horse, Jock, was speculating on the day's events and wishing that they could might get to grips with the French. Anything was better than sitting and waiting for the next shot. Still, the men were maintaining their nerve, despite the circumstances. In the meantime, some benefit might be gained in moving over to the right where a rise in the ground, between them and the French gunners, should give better protection. He was about to give the order to move when an unseen force, like some giant hand, plucked him from the saddle and simultaneously threw his horse to the ground. The cause was immediately evident as a shell exploded harmlessly a few yards away. Clark, who was unhurt picked himself up and saw Jock get back on to his legs, apparently uninjured. Soon afterwards the fighting died down.

That evening, having finished dinner, Lieutenant-Colonel Clifton prepared to write his report of the day's action. He could hear his Irish manservant, Simon, clearing away and cursing as he did so. 'The man's drunk,' he thought, but at the same time admitted to himself that Simon looked after him and his companion, Mrs Lamb, exceedingly well, as did Mr House, the commissary. They didn't usually want for food or drink, and Elizabeth Lamb looked after his other needs. It had been a most satisfactory, if tiring, day. The regiment had behaved well and he was particularly pleased with young Gunning. He was also going to recommend Eckersley for promotion, in his report to the commander-in-chief. 'Yes,' he mused, 'the day had gone very well; might even result in a battle honour for the regiment.' Their losses had been remarkably low – four men killed, one officer and thirty-six men wounded. Enough work there to keep Stead, the regimental surgeon, busy. More worrying were the seventy horse casualties; a lot higher than he would have wished. God alone knew where they would get the remounts from. He had witnessed Clark and his horse knocked over and smiled to himself as he recalled the look of consternation on Clark's face. He certainly would not wish to lose him and recalled his words to the startled officer, "It's not your time yet! We still have important work for you." Lord Wellington had been most gracious in his praise, saying that they had helped save six thousand men. He realised that he could no longer hear Simon, but more importantly that, as yet, he had not written a word.

Elizabeth called from the bedroom, "Don't be too long, Ben!"

In the act of refilling his glass, he replied, "Just got to finish this report, my dear." Clifton pulled the candle holder towards him and after a few moments' thought, he started to write.

In the scullery Simon Delaney had finished his work. Not a bad billet, this. He wanted for nothing and had all the food and drink he could lay his hands on, plus a shilling or two to be made out of his Master's housekeeping. To be sure, he'd fallen on his feet. After a while he heard Clifton pull his chair back and thought, 'That adulterous old bugger is off to his whore!'

Two days later on the 8th May, Captain Paul Phipps took his squadron out to reconnoitre. He discovered that the French were in full retreat. Massena had left Almeida to its fate.

Diversions

Following Fuentes, Massena decided to evacuate the garrison from Almeida. As a precaution he sent three separate messengers but only one was to get through. Unknown to Massena, the other two revealed his plan to the British before they were shot.

On the afternoon of the 10th May, General Sir William Erskine was at dinner. As far as he was concerned, eating was a supreme pleasure and meals were neither to be hurried or interrupted. His companions were Brent Spencer and Ned Pakenham. It was with great reluctance that he took a dispatch from his servant and only opened it after having been informed that it came from Lord Wellington.

"Listen to this," he said. "Massena has ordered the garrison at Almeida to explode the magazine and break out. I am commanded to secure the bridge at Barba del Puerco. Well, I will send a corporal and four men!"

"But William, that will hardly suffice," retorted Pakenham. "You might as well attempt to block up the bridge with a pinch of snuff!"

Erskine, who by now was quite drunk and feeling testy at having his dinner interrupted and his judgement questioned, said airily, "I suppose I had better write and instruct Bevan of the 4th." With that he scribbled out a note, which he placed in his pocket. His servant found it later, and at midnight Bevan received his orders but decided on his officers' advice that he need not march till morning.

None of this was known to the three squadrons of the Royals at Villa de Cerva. Stiles and Burnside had got their hands on some wine, which at first had seemed to be sour, but they had persisted. It was all they had, and having paid good money for it they were determined not to see it go to waste. Stiles, who had been asleep, woke with a griping pain. He was unsure whether to leave the comparative comfort of his blanket and the warmth of the stable to go outside to relieve himself. Eventually he was left with no option. On top of everything else, the fleas in the straw were biting. He threw back the blanket and went outside.

Burnside, who was in a similar condition, followed, saying, "I don't know about you but my guts feel as though they are on fire."

Stiles expressed the suggestion that "it might have been the wine."

Outside the barn it was as bright as day. The moon was full and they could clearly distinguish the road which ran away from the town. They walked on, with a growing sense of urgency, past the sentry. Burnside stopped, lowered his overalls, and squatted. Stiles went on a few paces before doing likewise. After a moment he felt better and as he regained his feet he couldn't believe his eyes. At first he blamed the wine. He thought he saw a large body of men moving along the road towards them. Then he was sure. It wasn't an illusion.

"Bugger my eyes, Jim, what's that?"

"Blast my eyes," came the reply. "It must be the French!"

Burnside all the time was struggling to fasten his braces. The pair hurried quickly back to their billet and shook awake the troop sergeant-major. Anyone else but these two he wouldn't have believed but he knew them to be completely reliable. In an instant the men were turned out. Boots were pulled on, arms gathered, horses saddled and mounted. Word was sent to the other troops and to the officers, who were more comfortably quartered elsewhere. This activity did not go unnoticed by the French, who clearly heard the preparations and swerved off to their left towards the bridge at Barba del Puerco, which was as yet unguarded. The Royals went in pursuit and captured two hundred prisoners and some baggage. The main body got away.

George Gunning had Mrs Alcock very much on his mind. Privately he would have admitted to being obsessed, and his desire was fired by Windsor's graphic description of her. Windsor's words echoed in his brain. He had seen her in a state of nudity that morning.

"By God, George," he'd said. "It was about three o'clock and barely light. She was standing by a window changing out of her shift. I can tell you, she is a big woman: plenty to get hold of there. Big firm breasts and a well-haired duff. Then she bent over and displayed her large and protuberant rump. I swear to you that I felt like mounting her instead of my mare, but duty called."

Gunning could wait no longer and, having seen Michael Byrne ride out of the camp with his servant, hurried round to Byrne's quarters.

Mrs Alcock, who had witnessed his approach, answered his knock on the door.

"Good day, madam, is Byrne at home?" Gunning innocently enquired.

"I am afraid not sir, indeed he will not return before tomorrow," she replied. She was looking at him in a way that told Gunning she had seen through his ploy. He entered the small, clean, sparsely furnished house and laid his hat on a table in the hallway. She led him into the drawing room. He noticed the dimples in her cheeks and groaned inwardly. How desirable she was!

"Please take a seat and I will get some port."

After what seemed an eternity she returned with a tray on which were a decanter and two glasses, poured two measures, and they toasted each other's health. They spoke of trivialities, and Gunning wondered how he was to advance his cause. All the while she looked at him intensely, which made him feel uncomfortable, but he could not leave without satisfying his desire. He heard her asking to be excused, and feeling somewhat flushed, George Gunning rose to his feet as she left the room. The swish of her skirt and a glimpse of petticoat added to his torment. His mouth was dry and he sipped his port. Then he heard her call from above. "George, will you please come up here." He was upstairs in an instant. Her clothes were scattered on the floor. She was wearing a peignoir, which was so transparent that it hid nothing. She was all that Windsor had described. With a shrug of her shoulders the flimsy garment fell to the floor. He stepped forward and took her in his arms. They kissed with passion and then he stood back and touched her breasts. The nipples hardened. He felt between her legs, brushing against her hair as he did so. She was wet and pushed herself against his finger. He could contain himself no longer and disengaged to take off his jacket and pull down his breeches. They fell onto the bed.

Colonel Clifton heard about Gunning's visit to Mrs Alcock from Cook, the adjutant, only one of a number who were ready to bring him any tittle-tattle. For the most part he ignored it. He didn't know what Cook expected him to do with the information and had thanked him coldly. After all, she was only Byrne's housekeeper. More fool he if he didn't keep her satisfied. Anyway, there were more pressing matters. That fellow Tomkyns, who had transferred in from the Life Guards last year, was in serious trouble. He looked again at the paper in front of him, which alleged that Tomkyns was responsible for the death of a Spanish mayor. Unbelievable! He supposed that he had better send for him.

Captain John Tomkyns was enjoying his evening meal when the adjutant arrived. After some hesitation and a great deal of hemming and hawing, he got himself round to telling Tomkyns that the colonel wanted to see him as a matter of urgency: "It has all to do with some mayor or other."

Clifton looked sternly at Tomkyns. Deliberately, he did not invite him to take a seat, and his opening words were, "I have been informed, sir, that you are responsible for hanging a mayor. Explain yourself, but understand that this is a most serious allegation which could result in a court martial. Give me the facts now and then write an account of the incident which I will pass on to the authorities."

John Tomkyns looked at his colonel in disbelief. How could he have found out? It had been weeks ago, and with each day he had grown stronger in his belief that the matter would remain a secret. He answered:

"It is true, sir, that I attempted to hang him, but the rope broke, and when he was sufficiently revived I gained his confession."

"Confession to what!" Clifton thundered. "Get on with it, man! From the beginning!"

"It was just under three weeks ago, sir, when Lieutenant Ross and I were bringing in fifty replacements and one hundred remount horses to make up for our losses at Fuentes. We stopped one night at a small town called Hoyos, and the next morning it was reported to me that some saddles, bridles, other horse furniture, and seven pistols were missing. I berated the men for their carelessness and we made a thorough but unsuccessful search. I sent my sergeant to get the mayor. He was a shifty-looking fellow if ever I saw one, and although he stoutly denied any knowledge of the affair I was convinced that he was lying. In the end I can only admit that my patience snapped. I ordered Parr, a farrier, to prepare a noose, and this was placed round the man's neck. He was given a further opportunity of admission but still maintained his innocence. We sat him on a horse and passed the rope over the branch of a tree and secured the end." Tomkyns omitted to tell Clifton that the Spaniard lost control over his bowels at that moment. "As the horse moved from underneath him the rope broke and he fell to the ground. On regaining his senses, sir, he confessed that the stolen property was in his house, and after a search we recovered all the stolen items."

Tomkyns, who by now was sweating profusely, concluded, "He was alive and well when we left."

"He died two weeks later!" said Clifton. "The Adjutant-General has had a letter from his wife demanding compensation. He has also ordered that I put you under arrest! Why was I not told of this affair? Your actions were extreme, too extreme by far!" By now Clifton realised that he was shouting. He continued in a quieter voice. "You have no right or authority to take the law into your own hands. It may be that we will be able to buy the woman off, but my mind is made up. I will offer you one of three choices – resign, transfer, or face a court martial. If you choose either of the first two, I think I can use my influence to avoid the third."

Tomkyns chose to resign.

After Tomkyns had left him Clifton wrote some notes on the paper in front of him. He still could not believe what had taken place. For the most part he was blessed with officers whose bravery was beyond question. Tomkyns was in that category, but he couldn't have him behaving like some latter-day Judge Jeffreys. One of these days he would have to deal with that fool Jones.

Early on the morning of the 6th June, 1811, Lieutenant William Jones was engaged in his favourite sport. He was lizard hunting with his dog, Toby, when he heard a trumpet sounding *Recall*. On his arrival back at camp, at Gallegos, he found a state of confusion. The picquets had been called in, the French were advancing, and he was ordered to take the heavy baggage to the rear. As soon as the hasty preparations were completed he led the procession of mules and wagons away from the camp.

He grudgingly admired those who might soon be engaged in fighting, but it was not for him. Neither was he concerned in the slightest that his fellow officers only considered him fit for this duty. He had once been put in charge of a picquet, at night, which turned out to be a terrifying experience. The position he and his men were allotted to had been near a gap in a wall, overlooking a wood. It had been very dark and after a while imagination had got the better of him, till he had convinced himself that the bushes were moving and that at any moment the enemy would fall on them. He had ordered a move to the other end of the wood, some two miles away, where a search party had found them two days later. Somehow they had still managed to draw rations from a supply cart. That incident had not gone down at all well, and although Clifton appeared to like him it had not prevented the colonel from suggesting that he take a transfer when a suitable opportunity arose. Still, his time with the Royals had been lucrative enough. He was well placed financially and his moneylending, at high rates of interest, was very profitable. He became aware of the sound of approaching hooves and shouting. For a moment fear gripped him. Was it the French? He turned in his saddle and saw Edmund Trafford riding towards him at a furious pace.

As he pulled up, Trafford asked, with a sarcastic tone in his voice, "Where are you going?"

"To the rear," replied Jones.

"Not that way!" said Trafford. "That's straight towards the enemy. Turn round before it is too late!"

Jones swiftly and meekly complied.

Back at Gallegos, Clifton was waiting for Slade. He'd received no orders and if the general did not appear soon, the French would be on them. He was about to give the order to retire when Slade appeared and the regiment was ordered to set off by echelons of squadrons, each squadron taking its turn to cover the withdrawal of the others. All went well until they reached Nave de Haver and were held up by a ravine and boggy ground. The men had, carefully, to pick a path to safety. Clifton could see that progress would be slow and he rode over to Dorville.

"Phillip, take your squadron and check the enemy."

Dorville gave the order, "Threes about," got the men into line and charged, scattering the French and enabling the regiment, including his squadron, to retire to safety. It was then the turn of the French to pick their way through the bog, but as they attempted to re-assemble they were hit by another charge and the skirmishers took their toll. Burnside was among the skirmishing party and happened to be near Captain Tomkyns. He heard him shout, "A guinea to any man who can bring down that officer."

Burnside followed the direction of Tomkyn's pointing finger and saw a splendidly dressed Frenchman. 'Must be a colonel at least,' he thought. The range was about fifty yards and the officer was urging his men forward. His target was getting nearer all the time. His carbine was loaded but he needed a steady platform from which to take aim. Burnside looked round and saw the remains of a tree trunk. That should suit his purpose. By the look of it, sometime in the past it had been struck by lightning and what was left of the trunk seemed to be at the right height. He rode over, quickly dismounted, pulled his carbine from its boot and as a preliminary tried out his position. It was a bit of a stretch but it would have to do. Burnside took aim, cocked the weapon, held his breath and squeezed the trigger. Almost simultaneously with the report came the vision of the man falling. There was much cheering and he heard Tomkyns shouting, "Well done, Burnside. Very well done!" He never did get his guinea.

Later that evening, Stiles, among a small party of men under Captain Clark, set out to find a missing picquet. They had not been seen since the previous evening. After the exertions of the day Stiles had looked forward to a rest but had barely time to dismount, water, feed, groom his horse, and snatch a bite to eat, before he and the others left the bivouac at Alfaites. It was starting to get dark and they had some distance to travel. All that Clark knew was that Sergeant Watkis and five men had been sent to picquet at Seradilla, and if they remained uncaptured they had to try and get them back. It was approaching midnight when they made contact. A horse was heard whinnying, and after a challenge Sergeant Watkis responded.

Watkis explained that in the morning the French had approached without warning, and in large numbers. The picquet secreted themselves in a small wood. They had been unobserved but had heard someone shouting, "*Ami! Ami!*" "I didn't notice till then that Banks was missing but saw him riding towards the French and calling out to them. They disarmed him and he rode off with them."

Stiles heard Captain Clark say in a strained but stern voice, "He has deserted, by God. If I ever come across him again, I will have him shot!"

On arriving back at camp, Stiles went looking for Burnside. Although it was early in the morning and he had to shake Burnside violently to wake him, Stiles first had to endure the story of how the French colonel had been shot. Finally, when he could contain himself no longer, he blurted out, "He's gone."

"Who's gone?"

"Banks. Seems he's deserted. Wonder if we'll ever see him again?"

"Only in front of a firing squad," replied Burnside.

Banks had been determined to get away and had seized his chance. He would never get a better opportunity than this. As he galloped towards the French he had a feeling of relief but this soon altered. He had only gone a short distance with them when he was roughly treated and then added to a party of prisoners, which was marched off towards the rear. His horse and equipment were taken off him, as were his clothes, apart from his shirt, overalls and boots. Judging by the state of his captors, he might not retain those items much longer. The French never asked, and he never volunteered, where he had come from, or who he had been with prior to his desertion. They marched for some days living on dry, hard brown bread and brackish water. At night they slept in the open.

On one of their overnight stops their escorts were attacked and butchered by guerrillas, a mixed bunch of Spanish, French, Portuguese and British deserters. One of them, an Englishman called Hawkins, told Banks their leader was a renegade French sergeant who was referred to as "Marshal Stockpot". By now Banks was certain that he had made the wrong move, especially when Hawkins pointed to the mutilated bodies of the former escort and described what they had done, adding, "You either join them or us!"

June brought long, hot, sultry days and an invitation for Clark to dinner with Major Jervoise, who had his quarters in a semi-derelict chapel. Clark guided his horse along a track, before he turned off at a wayside shrine and followed a narrow path. He approached the building which stood in a clearing. Some windows were broken and there was evidence of missing tiles. A vine had spread its way up the edifice. He mounted the three steps towards the large, iron studded, double doors. Mr Tom, Jervoise's Irish servant, must have been watching him approach, as one side of the door was opened just as he was about to knock. Tom took his hat and ushered him inside. Clark repressed an involuntary shudder as he exchanged the heat of the warm June evening, for the cold of the chapel interior. He could not think what had possessed Jervoise to make his home in such a place. What was even more bizarre was that Tom had laid out the food on the altar, which was illuminated by candles. Jervoise came to greet him.

"Good to see you, Alexander. Sit yourself down and have a sherry. Tom, see to Captain Clark." His fellow guests, Montague and Crosbie, were already seated.

After the meal, which, given the unusual surroundings, was excellent, they sat round drinking and smoking. Montague, who never hid his dislike for Catholics, or anything to do with them, looked at the altar and launched into a tirade.

"They say that their priests turn bread and wine into flesh and blood. How is that for superstitious mumbo-jumbo?" His outburst in front of Mr Tom was followed by an immediate crash of thunder, which shook the building, accompanied by torrential rain. Montague's face immediately turned white and Clark saw his fingers gripping the sides of his chair.

Bang! Bang!

Someone was ferociously knocking at the door. Tom opened it to find Montague's servant outside. He was ushered into his master's presence and he said:

"I'm sorry to report, sir, that something dreadful has happened. Your two goats have been struck dead by lightning!" Montague left the regiment a month later.

Stiles and Burnside were off duty. It was mid July, the sun was burning hot, and the pair had been down to the river to bathe. They were no longer in the same troop but continued to see each other as circumstances permitted. They had added to their enjoyment by taking with them a couple of bottles of wine, and all in all, they'd had a good day out. Now they were walking back to camp through the woods, which, being a mixture of cork and gum trees, offered little shade.

They were still some distance away from their base, but as Stiles put it, "You couldn't miss the place. Smells like a knacker's yard."

It was quite true. The stench was appalling. What had seemed ideal to start with had, with the passage of a mere two weeks, changed for the worse. The aroma, a mixture of horse and human excrement, hung on the hot, still air. They had tried to make the best of things; they had built huts, but the oppressive odour, the burning hot sun, the flies and ants, which their presence had attracted, combined to make life unbearable for man and beast. The ants got everywhere, even into their soup.

Burnside stopped to light his pipe. "You couldn't miss our camp, could you, Francis?"

"No," replied Stiles. "Not even in the dark. Did I tell you that they had caught a spy?"

"What spy?" asked Burnside. "Who told you that?"

"It was Tinsley. Seems this Spaniard has been going round the various encampments for a few weeks now, posing as a pedlar and selling needles and thread. When he was questioned, he admitted that he was in the pay of the French, so he was handed over to the Portuguese who shot him."

"I suppose if Tinsley told you, it must be true," said Burnside dubiously. He sniffed the air. "That's smoke unless I'm mistaken." Almost at once they heard the sound of crackling.

"Come on, the bloody place must be on fire!"

They broke into a run and as they neared the camp saw a number of huts ablaze and their comrades beating furiously at the flames with whatever was to hand.

"You two," shouted Corporal Phillips. "Over here!"

They needed no further bidding and joined a party of men who were attempting to form a fire break. Stiles felt the smoke sting his eyes, and the branches of the surrounding trees danced up and down as the heat from below grew in intensity, as though the scene was being conducted by some unseen hand. It was a hopeless situation. There was no water available and the fire was gaining hold. Eventually and by good fortune the wind direction turned and the fire moved away from the huts. It was still dangerous, as partly-burned branches, some sizeable, crashed to the ground, one only missing Stiles by inches.

"Corporal, move those men to safety!" ordered Captain Clark.

They skirted round the fire, and Stiles was relieved to see that his hut was intact. Later, when a semblance of order had been restored, he saw Burnside, who told him that he had not been so lucky.

"I've only got what I stand up in," he remarked gloomily. "All I have heard from Tinsley is that his journal is safe. I wonder what he writes in it?"

"I doubt if he refers to you or me," replied Stiles. Later, orders were given for the regiment to move to a site nearer the river.

Clifton had long been aware that the regiment's appearance left a lot to be desired. They had not received any new clothing for three years and he watched his men as they rode into their new camp.

"Just look at them, Jervoise," he remarked to his senior major. "No old London dustman ever wore so dirty an apology for a hat as the men are wearing."

Jervoise could only agree. "Look at that man, sir. He has got on what look like an old pair of yarn stockings, with a rusty spur at heel, and he is wearing, if my eyes don't deceive me, an old pair of shag breeches."

"Well," said Clifton, "something needs to be done and done soon." No one was more surprised than him when, within a few days, Quartermaster Shipley came to the rescue. He had obtained new hats, which were issued there and then, but they had to wait a while before getting overalls and jackets.

Burnside, ever the cynic, summed it up. "Frightened to give us the whole lot in one go in case we won't be recognised as the Royals but are mistaken for some new outfit straight from England."

"You do not have a choice," said Stead the regimental surgeon. "If you stay here, you will certainly succumb. Lisbon is your only hope." It was September 1811. The object of his remarks, Jervoise, had a severe bout of a fever, which had caused a high sickness rate in the regiment. Jervoise was one of the worse cases, and Stead wondered how much he understood. Sometimes he was quite lucid, at others his mind wandered. At the moment he was between the two states. If he got to Lisbon – and in Stead's opinion it was doubtful – he might recover. He doubted if Jervoise's constitution would stand the journey. The only means of transport was in the back of a bullock cart, and the patient's body would register every jolt as the cart traversed the potholed and uneven roads. Jervoise now lay with his eyes closed, and his once full face and corpulent body appeared to have shrunk.

Mr Tom sat in the back of the cart and hadn't left the major's side for two days as he required constant attention. "Stop!" he shouted to the driver. He fought to keep the tremor from his voice and added, almost in a whisper, "I fear it will soon be over." It was quite clear that the major was sinking fast. His breathing was shallow and noisy. Then it stopped.

A grief-stricken Mr Tom sought help. He couldn't just leave the body; the major deserved a decent burial. The driver was of no use and in fact he had cleared off as soon as the body had been laid at the roadside. He was getting desperate, but fortunately found an Irish sergeant who gave him the assistance he needed.

There had been a long period of inactivity and the Royals were in the village of Algeberea, when a fatigue party was ordered to dig a grave. Eventually the regiment gathered round the burial place, and Clark could not repress an intense feeling of melancholy. This was the second death in two days. First they had heard of Jervoise and now it was Crosbie. Clark wondered if it could be anything to do with that evening at the chapel. No, he decided, that was merely a coincidence. His thoughts were superstitious nonsense. Then there was Dorville, to whom Jervoise had sold his commission. Jervoise's untimely death meant that no one would benefit from this tragedy.

Clark turned his mind to Crosbie. Another case of bad luck. Only five and twenty years and dead because of an overdose of opium. True, he had been ill with dysentery, brought on by drinking new wine. Clark had enquired of Langman, the assistant surgeon, regarding Crosbie's condition, and had been informed "I have sent him to the rear and have advised him to stay with the baggage train and keep warm." They'd since learned that Crosbie had gone into hospital at Algeberea, and as he had seemed so much better an infantry surgeon had given him six opium pills with instructions to take one a day. Whether Crosbie had misunderstood or misheard they would never know, but he had taken all the pills at once. According to his servant, "The captain, who had been in high spirits, had lain down, fallen into a deep sleep, and died." To Clark it didn't seem that the regiment was blessed with the best of luck, on top of which they had a burden they could do nothing about – Slade and Erskine.

Stiles watched the ceremony with sadness. The colonel said a few words. The body, wrapped in a blanket, was lowered into the grave. A volley was fired and the fatigue party began filling in. Stiles remembered Crosbie for his kindness, and even after all these months he could hear his voice as he had searched the pockets of that dead French officer. Mr Crosbie had smiled at him and said, "Can't you find anything? Here, let me show you!"

Guerrillas

"Alexander, the colonel wishes your presence immediately."

Clark's first response was one of annoyance, his immediate reaction being directed at the bearer of the summons, Cook the adjutant. The fellow was far too familiar. Clark barely grunted in reply but strode, purposefully, off towards the headquarters building, leaving Cook limping along in his wake.

"He's got a civilian with him. A strange-looking cove," Cook called after him.

Clark entered the room. There was indeed a civilian, whose bulk filled the chair in which he was seated. He turned and Clark saw that he bore a scar, which showed white against his darkened skin and which ran down his forehead towards his left eye, which was covered by a black patch. His mouth was hidden by a very large moustache, which concealed his lips. He rose from his seat. Both this height and width were dominating.

"Alexander," said Clifton, "May I introduce Major Riordan from headquarters."

"My pleasure, sir." Riordan spoke with a faint Irish accent, and it soon became apparent that whatever was afoot had already been discussed by the colonel and the major.

"Major Riordan has a duty for you," said Clifton. "I will leave the explanations to him, but from what he has so far told me it could prove to be exciting and perhaps a little dangerous."

"Captain Clark. May I call you Alexander?" Riordan received a nod in reply, but Clark's senses told him that despite his jocularity this was not a man to be trifled with. "Alexander, you are no doubt aware of the important part that some Spanish irregulars are playing?" Riordan continued.

"I have heard, sir, that the guerrillas," – Riordan smiled at the expression – "are making life difficult for the French and are tying down troops which might otherwise be used against us."

"Capital!" Riordan replied. "My latest information is that they can no longer send a courier without the protection of a squadron of cavalry. Their importance to us is obvious, and I want you to meet with one of them. Colonel Clifton tells me that you are the man for the job."

"Your journey will involve danger!" As he spoke he unrolled a map which he laid on Clifton's desk, and with a "Do you mind, sir?" he placed two large glass inkwells on either end to hold it down. "We are here...," he said, pointing. "Your destination is here...," he jabbed at the map again. Clark read the name of the place indicated to him. It was Zalamea and the map told him it was located in the La Serena Mountains.

Riordan rolled up the map and handed it to Clark. "In five days time I want you to meet the guerrilla leader Don Julian Sanchez."

"How will I find him?" asked Clark. "Be in the vicinity of Zalamea and he will find you. You won't be travelling alone. I have discussed this with the colonel and we agree that you should take twenty men with you. Bear in mind that you will be behind the enemy's lines and that not all the irregulars are trustworthy. One group in particular is led by a renegade Frenchman who goes under the name of Marshal Stockpot, who is in it mainly for plunder. Mind you, this is also true of Sanchez, but he is a man of honour and was at one time a cavalry officer. Sometimes he has a thousand men with him. Other times he can barely raise fifty as they absent themselves to spend the proceeds of their raids."

'There must be more to this,' Clark thought, but he asked, "What is the *real* purpose of all this, sir?"

"You said he was nobody's fool, Colonel." Riordan shot a grin at Clifton. "The purpose is threefold, Alexander." He paused before continuing. "You are to deliver some arms, ammunition, and powder. Additionally there is a box, which to all intents and purposes looks like an ammunition box but which in reality contains gold coins. Apart from the colonel and myself – I packed the box personally – you and Sanchez are the *only* people in on that little secret. Thirdly, and in exchange, you can expect to bring back the latest intelligence. I have arranged for a team of mules, and the time for your journey and rendezvous takes into account that they will slow you down. You will leave after dark this evening. Are you clear on what you have to do?"

To Clark the details were clear, but they would need an awful lot of luck. He assumed that Riordan knew what he was about. He seemed confident enough. "Yes, I am quite clear," he answered.

"Pick your men carefully!" Clifton interjected.

"I would like to take Sergeant Horton and will give consideration to the remainder of the party," said Clark.

"They need be told only that it is a patrol and nothing else at this stage," said Riordan. "One more thing. If you must enter a village, stay only for the shortest possible time. On no account spend the night in one! Alter your campsite frequently. Above all, be vigilant, and good luck to you."

Just before dawn on the fifth day after they had parted from the regiment, Clark halted his party. He estimated that they were only one or two miles from Zalamea, and he sent Sergeant Horton on ahead, with two men, to find a place where they could safely wait away from the road. So far, their journey had been uneventful. He had obeyed Riordan's orders to the letter and the few peasants they had seen had barely given them a second glance. They were well used to seeing soldiers in these parts. The extra weight of one ammunition box had attracted attention. He had heard the men speculating what was in it and had been grateful when Horton had told them to shut up and get on with their work. He didn't hear the oncoming hoof beats until the last moment. If it had been the enemy, it might have been too late. Fortunately it was Horton and the men returning.

"I've found an ideal place, sir!"

Stiles lay on the crest of a hill, screened behind a large rock, one of a pair, between which ran a track from the village of Zalamea. His position gave him a good view. He could clearly see both ends of the small village; the river with steep banks, narrow in places, and the road which stretched uphill into the distance was empty. There was no sign of activity as it was the time of siesta. He wondered what might be going on in the houses on either side of the road. Eating and sleeping amongst other things, he guessed. Stiles ran his practised farming eye over the small patches of greenery which dotted the opposite hillside. A man would have to work hard to scratch a living. The inhabitants probably grew some produce down in the valley and there were quite a number of sheep and goats around.

It was very hot and getting hotter. The sweat ran down his back and felt like so many spiders crawling over him as he lay in the beating sun. His jacket, although fairly new, had rapidly become weather stained, and the once scarlet garment had assumed a brownish hue. He was also aware that his features were equally weather beaten after two and a half years campaigning, so, provided he didn't make himself visible against the skyline, he shouldn't be seen. By his side was his loaded carbine. A few feet away a lizard flicked out its tongue and caught a fly. Stiles thought: 'That's what sudden death must be like. Over quickly.' If he were to die, he hoped it would be over quickly, not slow and lingering as in the case of some of the poor devils he had seen. His mood of contemplation continued. It was now March 1812 and after they had buried Mr Crosbie the regiment had been involved in one or two minor brushes with the French and had then gone into winter quarters. Once they had been turned out on a false alarm, but it had been quiet until early March when they had been sent on the long journey south, leaving the regiment near Badajoz. It was from there that he and nineteen others had been detached on special duty, under Captain Clark, and why he was now on this hillside.

There was a movement behind him. He turned his head and saw Captain Clark making his way up the slope. He was, in Stiles' opinion, a good officer, particularly in a tight corner.

Clark crawled the last few feet before lying down beside him. "Seen anything?"

"Nothing, sir. It's all very quiet."

"Keep a sharp look out. As you know, we are expecting to meet the guerrillas here."

Now that they had reached their destination he had felt obliged to tell his men of the meeting. It would in any event have soon become obvious.

Clark returned to the foot of the hill. Other sentries had been posted round about and Sergeant Horton regularly inspected them. He had told Horton that he should detail Stiles to watch the village, as he was known for his excellent eyesight and dependability. Their position was well hidden, and while he could not afford to relax he felt secure. He hoped they were. There were no fires. He couldn't take the risk. It would have to be cold food for the time being. Clark leant back on the grass bank and looked about him. Horton had indeed found an ideal place. A steepish slope led up to the forward crest where Stiles kept watch, but the slope continued round, and although it fell away, it still gave good all round protection. They were some way off the road, and his only concern was the track which led straight to them from the village.

Stiles continued to watch. He thought about his own village, Northaw in Hertfordshire, where, unlike his present surroundings, there was an abundance of trees, which in summer provided ample shade under their huge canopies of leaves. He felt a pang of nostalgia and wondered what his parents would think if they could see their son now. Here he was hiding behind this rock, making sure he could see and not be seen. Still there was nothing... or was there? His eye detected a slight movement. A figure had detached itself from the shadow cast by one of the buildings. Could it be a villager returning to his work? No, his movements were too stealthy, and even from this distance he could make out that the person wore an odd assortment of clothing, which in no way resembled a peasant's dress. He was also armed and was waving a musket above his head. Other men were now riding towards the village. It looked to Stiles as though the first man he'd seen had been sent forward on foot to check that all was safe. Stiles took off his hat and, making sure he was below the hilltop, waved it in the direction of the sentry below him; the pre-arranged signal of a sighting.

The sentry's call sent Sergeant Horton racing towards the slope.

"No, Sergeant, I will go!" Clark countermanded. He quickly climbed the hill and asked Stiles what he had seen.

"Fifteen men have arrived," said Stiles, pointing towards the village. "They tied up their horses and entered several of the houses. Even at this distance I am sure I heard screams. I don't know what they are up to but the manner in which they approached was most suspicious."

"We will continue to watch," said Clark. "It does not seem likely that they are the people we are supposed to meet, and I cannot afford to take any risks."

Below the high bank of the river, where a depression had been formed by the flowing water gouging out the soil, Don Julian Sanchez was waiting with twenty of his men. Although he had ordered them to dismount he had remained in the saddle. They had followed the other party at a safe distance. He didn't know who they were but guessed that they belonged to that French renegade, and if God was good he might be among them. Sanchez had been in the area for twenty-four hours and had sent out scouts to see if there were any signs of the British, with orders to observe but not to be seen. He now knew that the cavalrymen were in the vicinity of that hill over there. He had been about to make contact when his scouts had also seen the bandits approaching the village and he wanted to dispose of them before contacting his allies. A few hours more, if it took that long, wouldn't matter. First things first. By standing in his stirrups he could just see over the top of the bank, and he looked towards the cluster of buildings. They had approached with care and he had sent Mateo on ahead to reconnoitre. Mateo reported having heard some screams but now all was quiet.

Sanchez spoke softly to his men but there was a touch of steel in his voice. "We must get them all. None must escape. Remember, use the knife and not the gun. Mateo! You will take half the men and flush them out of the houses on the other side of the road. The remainder will come with me to the other houses. Search the barns and stables. Kill them all, except one who must be kept alive. We must find out what he knows." He continued with his instructions and concluded by saying, "Go with God, and remember, no one must escape!"

Clark and Stiles, watching from the hill, saw a number of men rise from the river bank and move stealthily across the open ground to the houses, which they entered. All was silent. No shots were fired. After a short interval, from a window at the rear of one of the buildings, a man emerged and started to run in their direction. He was naked from the waist up, apart from the supports across his shoulders, which secured his overalls. As he got nearer they could see that he was barefooted, and although he cast a number of anxious glances behind him no one followed. He passed the last of the houses, left the line of the road, and took to the track. If he maintained his present course, the fugitive must pass directly by them. Clark's main concern was the security of the camp. He didn't want their position to be discovered. There were far too many people in the vicinity for his liking. Could it be coincidence?

He looked down the hill, the man was not as yet being pursued. There was no time to call up Sergeant Horton or any of the others. Well, he and Stiles ought to be able to cope with one man. He spoke to Stiles. "This is what we shall do. I shall go behind that rock on the other side of the track, it's set a little farther back than this one. Once he has passed your position, I'll attract his attention and you stop him. Don't fire any weapons, we don't want any more of his friends up here, but stop him you must! Understand?"

Stiles signified that he did, and Clark moved to the other side of the track.

Stiles remained well hidden and waited. The responsibility was his. He could now plainly hear bare feet pounding the earth, accompanied by heavy breathing and what sounded like a curse. The footsteps stopped. Clark peered round the rock and saw their quarry, whose back was towards him. He was tall, darkened by the sun, and had long matted hair. He turned his head slightly, and as he drew his head back Clark noticed that the man was sporting a long beard. Only twenty feet separated them. There was a shout from the village, and once more the man took to his heels. Clark waited and when he judged the moment to be right he stepped out onto the track. The fugitive, seeing the red-coated officer, came to a halt, turned as if to go in a diagonal direction, and was caught by a blow on the side of the head. He dropped to the ground instantly unconscious.

Stiles had hit him with the butt of his carbine and could hardly believe his eyes. The man lying on the ground and now groaning was Banks.

Aloud he said, "Sir, it's Banks."

"Is it, by God," replied Clark. "You certainly dealt with him. Well done! I am not so sure that he will be thanking you when he recovers his senses. Watch him closely. We will take him back to face the firing squad."

Banks groaned and opened his eyes. This must be a dream. His head throbbed with pain, and blood was trickling down the side of his face. He attempted to sit up when he heard a familiar voice. "Stay where you are, Tom!" He looked up and saw Stiles, who was pointing a carbine at him.

Sanchez left the village and put his horse towards the hill. He had seen a man running away in the direction of the British and hoped that they would take him alive. Unfortunately, his men had not obeyed orders and had killed all the bandits. Sanchez could not altogether blame them. He'd seen what horrors had been inflicted on the inhabitants.

It was Stiles who first noticed the lone rider. He sat his horse easily and had the look of a cavalry man about him. "Sir, there is a rider approaching." Clark looked down the hillside, swore under his breath, and thought, 'That's all we need'. "Keep Banks covered but also try to cover me. Banks, don't try to escape! If you move as much as a muscle, Stiles will shoot you! I will go a few paces forward and attempt to—"

The sentence was never completed as the rider called out, "Hello, Englishmen, Don Julian Sanchez at your service. I believe you are looking for me. Well, I have found you!" He approached, dismounted, shook hands with Clark and nodded at Stiles.

"Captain Clark of His Majesty's Royal Dragoons. Glad to make your acquaintance."

Sanchez looked down at Banks. "What have we here?"

"He came running from the village," said Clark, "and Stiles laid him low."

"I am pleased to see that he is alive," replied Sanchez. "Will you hand him over to me? He is one of a murdering band and what they have done in the village is a repetition of their dastardly deeds in many other places. I had hoped that their leader, Marshal Stockpot, would be present, but he was not. I have left my men to bury the dead. He," – Sanchez pointed an accusing finger at Banks– "with his brave companions," – he sneered as he said the words – "killed all the villagers after they had taken their pleasure."

Clark was in a dilemma. By rights, he should take Banks back with him to face a court martial. If he left him with Sanchez he would certainly die, eventually. If returned to the regiment and found guilty of desertion – and there could be little doubt about the verdict– he would be shot. Clark looked at Stiles, who was grim faced. He would have to trust him. He addressed Sanchez.

"This man is a deserter from my regiment. Before witnesses he quit his post, in the face of the enemy, about nine months ago. From what you now tell me he is a murderer, possibly many times over." He turned to Stiles. "I want you to forget what has happened here. So far as Sergeant Horton, or anyone else, is concerned, we have apprehended a bandit. For my part *I have not seen Banks and neither have you*. Is that understood, Stiles?"

"Yes, sir. I know nothing about this man."

At this Banks, who had been closely following the exchanges, yelled, "But, sir, you can't leave me here with him!" His protests were cut short.

Sanchez skilfully bound the prisoner's hands and feet and put a gag in his mouth.

Sanchez called up two of his men and Banks was carted away, slung over the back of a horse. Stiles would never forget the look of absolute terror in his eyes and the grunting sounds he made. It was arranged that the two parties would meet at the Royals' camp later. Clark told Horton that he and Stiles had captured an escaping bandit and that he had also made contact with the guerrillas. Eventually, Sanchez and his men arrived, bringing with them some sheep carcasses and wine.

Sanchez took Clark to one side and said, "He told me what I wanted to know. He didn't take much persuading, and I ordered that he should be put out of his misery quickly." This was the last reference made to Banks.

That evening Clark and his men had their first cooked meal for some days, and although they kept to their separate groups, largely because of language difficulties, there was much laughter and singing. Stiles, relaxing after a hectic day, felt the wine take hold of him. 'Well,' he thought, 'at least this night I won't feel the cold.' The heat from the blazing fire would see to that.

Clark handed over the arms and ammunition later that evening, glad to be rid of the mules. They would make quicker progress back to base without them. He indicated to Sanchez which box contained the gold.

"You will not have any difficulty identifying it from the others. It weighs more heavily."

"Mateo will guard it with his life!" Sanchez said in jest, as he pulled his stiletto from its sheath.

It was early next morning.

"Well, my friend, we have to complete our business." Clark took the proffered papers. "These are two dispatches which we intercepted," said Sanchez. Clark noticed that the seals were broken, and Sanchez, who had been watching him closely, said, "We also have to know what is happening, but I think they will prove most interesting to Lord Wellington. Now, I think it would be as well if we say our farewells and leave this place. Both of our parties have been here long enough."

They went their separate ways.

Maguilla

Clifton was pleased that Clark had returned safely from his detachment. Clark handed over the dispatches.

"I can tell from your appearance that all has gone well," Clifton remarked as he pumped Clark's arm.

"Exceedingly well," Clark replied. "We made contact with Sanchez, who is quite a decent fellow for a Spaniard."

Clifton waved Clark to a seat. "Sit down and tell me all about it. I shall of course need a written report for Major Riordan."

Clark related the train of events, omitting any reference to Banks. "The men did well. Especially Stiles. A candidate for promotion, I shouldn't wonder."

Stiles quickly settled back into the routine, but because he had been away ten days he felt that he was looking at his companions through the eyes of an outsider. For some reason there was a feeling of depression which seemed to be affecting their confidence.

Clifton was well aware of this and it was something which troubled him greatly. He had been a soldier far too long to miss the unmistakable signs, evidenced as they were by sullenness and an increase in the number of disciplinary cases with which he and his fellow officers were called upon to deal. When he had succeeded to the regiment, they had been short of experience but over the months had become a force to be reckoned with. In his opinion Erskine, aided and abetted by Slade, was to blame. There had been too many missed opportunities. Erskine was after all in command of the cavalry division but was quite plainly nervous, excitable, irresolute, and in constant fear of an attack on the cavalry screen. What did he think they were there for? He ordered picquets to be sent off in every direction except that from which danger was to be expected. On the slightest suggestion that the French were advancing he would, without waiting for confirmation, order the camp to be moved.

Slade was no better. On one occasion, with the French still some way off but supposedly moving towards them, he had given the order to turn out. He was hardly an inspiring sight. Clifton vividly recalled Slade running round the camp, shouting, "Bridle up! Bridle up! The first dozen men, for God's sake! God damn you, trumpeters! Blow, damn you! Haste! Haste! Gallop! God damn you, Corporal. Tell those men to turn out and never mind telling off! Turn out! Turn out! The baggage to Azinshal!" The result had been chaos, with equipment, food and corn lost. More important was the men's loss of confidence. They now firmly believed that the French were their superiors.

Clifton said to Dorville, "Phillip, we are going to pay dearly for the privilege of being commanded by Erskine and Slade. We have just had another example of their indecisiveness. Young Trafford and his picquet were almost taken at Llera, and without waiting to see what Lallemand's intentions are we have been ordered back. Phillip, take out your squadron and see what the French are up to."

Dorville advanced and sent out patrols. The message brought back was always the same: "No sign of the French." That was until Captain Nathanial Eckersley led his patrol on what, to start with, had been a fruitless journey to Valentia, where they found nothing. They moved on to Berlenga and had halted to feed their horses when he saw Sergeant Gibbs approaching with speed. He saluted his officer.

"Sir, a peasant informs me that the French are in Maguilla!"

Eckersley took his men in that direction and when he estimated that there was still a mile to go he held up his hand. "Halt!" he ordered. "Sergeant Gibbs, we are now about a mile from Maguilla. I don't want to advance further along this road. Take some men up through the woods and see if you can observe the French without them seeing you."

Dusk was falling as Gibbs and his group advanced through the woods on foot. There was a track but Gibbs told them, "We don't want to walk straight into them. They may have a picquet on it. Follow me!" He stepped into the undergrowth and, keeping the track to his right, headed in the direction of Maguilla. It was the smell of wood smoke, intermingled with a strong aroma of tobacco and onions, which confirmed their suspicions that the French were about. They had progressed for what Gibbs reckoned was half a mile when he signalled his men to halt. The sound of voices, punctuated by laughter, carried on the breeze towards them.

"We must be quiet," cautioned Gibbs. "Tinsley, you come with me. The rest of you stay here and no smoking." The two men went forward into the gloom, Gibbs counting under his breath the number of paces taken.

Stiles walked round the camp looking for Burnside. So far without success. He saw Tinsley writing in his journal and bearing, as he did so, a pained expression.

"John, have you seen Jim Burnside?"

"Not recently," Tinsley replied, "but I saw him earlier when he was going on picquet."

"What are you writing about now?" asked Stiles.

Tinsley held the page towards him. "Read it if you like!"

Stiles glanced at the page. He knew that Major Dorville's squadron had been in action, had been responsible for driving off a French brigade, and that Tinsley had been there. The entry, whilst no doubt accurate, was short. "Is that all that happened?"

"I can't write everything down but I'll tell you about it." Stiles having nothing better to do, sat on the ground, and Tinsley started.

"We were near to Maguilla when some of us were ordered by Sergeant Gibbs to enter a wood. Captain Eckersley had told him to try and find the French. After a while we smelt them. It was the smoke from their cooking fires at first and then the smell of their tobacco and onions." Stiles knew the smell only too well. "Gibbs halted the rest and took me forward with him. We hadn't gone far, Gibbs said thirty-five paces, when we saw their camp fires, just beyond the edge of the wood. The smell of the cooking made me feel hungry and we could hear the men jabbering to each other. There seemed to be a large number of them. We lay just inside the line of the trees, and it was just as well we did, as there was a sentry with his carbine on his arm only a few feet away. A bird suddenly flew out of a tree and the noise it made certainly startled the sentry. I saw him jump. Gibbs whispered that it must be the whole of Lallemand's Brigade so we'd better get back and tell the captain.

Back we went and picked up the others on the way. Captain Eckersley took us on a wide detour as he wished to avoid the enemy. When we got to Llera, Major Dorville, on hearing the news, drew us back behind a stream, put out patrols, and left a picquet in Llera. It was Sergeant Gibbs, poor sod, and five men.

At half past two in the morning seven squadrons came to surprise us. I heard the major tell Captain Eckersley that they must have thought we were still in Llera. They came through the wheat and corn and took the picquet – all save one, that is, who got away and raised the alarm. The French then attempted to cross the stream, but we charged and drove them back. Major Dorville got us to cheer and we made such a noise that I'm sure they thought they were facing the whole of Slade's brigade. They withdrew and we pursued them for a time. That's about the size of it."

"What are you going to do with this?" said Stiles, pointing to the journal. "Write a book?"

"Well," said Tinsley, "as you know, I've been keeping notes ever since we arrived in Portugal, and that's almost three years ago. If I survive, it will jog my memory when I think back to these days. Should I be killed, perhaps you would care to have it."

Stiles didn't reply. There was no answer to talk of possible death. Looking up, he saw Burnside, excused himself, and left Tinsley to his reflections.

Major-General Jack Slade raised his arms while his servant fitted his sword belt round his waist. He put on his hat and gloves and left the tent. Slade sniffed the air appreciatively. It was still fresh, but no doubt it would prove to be another hot and dusty day. Taking the reins from his groom, he mounted the big black gelding and rode to the head of the column. Earlier that morning he had ordered the brigade to bivouac in a wood between Hiniosa and Llera, and now there was news that the French were advancing in force. He felt confident in the men of the two regiments under his command – The Royals and The 3rd Dragoon Guards, which Lord Wellington regarded as the finest regiments of cavalry in the Peninsula. When a patrol had brought news of the enemy's approach, the horses had been unbridled and the men were cooking, but they were soon ready.

"Good morning, Clifton," said Slade as he came up to the head of the Royals' column. "We will conform to the original plan and ride towards Maguilla. Have you put out the skirmishers?" Clifton replied in the affirmative, disguising his doubts as to the wisdom of Slade's order, which committed the best part of a squadron to the task. If the men were needed as a matter of urgency, they could not easily be reassembled.

Slade merely retorted, "Good. Let us commence." A trumpeter sounded the advance, and the column moved off with the Royals in the van followed by the 3rd Dragoon Guards. It was the morning of the 11th June, 1812.

Stiles was with the skirmishers, who were well spread out and in front of the advance to Maguilla. So far, they had not seen the enemy. Stiles and another man climbed a hill. They were riding as point and with shortened stirrups, so that if necessary they could obtain better observation by standing up in them. Their carbines and pistols were primed and ready and they had removed their hats. Looking over his shoulder, Stiles could see back across the plain below. The brigade was still some way behind. The pair gained the crest, but although they could see for a fair distance they found their view of the forward slope cut off by the even ground of the summit. They put their horses forward across the ridge, to gain a better sighting and saw a large body of cavalry coming up the hill before them.

"It must be the French. It must be Lallemand's Brigade," Stiles shouted to his companion. They quickly retraced their steps to where they could be seen by their own forces and began circling their horses, quickly to the right, as a signal of a large body of cavalry approaching.

Slade saw the warning. He urged his men towards the summit, hoping that they would arrive before the French. The pace was picked up, but the steepness of the hill prevented anything more than a fast walk. They were just in time and had crossed the ridge before sighting the enemy, who were now going back down the reverse slope. Their commander must have ordered his men to retire as the opposing force, having faced about, had put out skirmishers. The pursuit started.

George Gunning, riding a horse's length in front of his men, had been thinking of other things, or to be more correct one other person–Mrs Henrietta Alcock. Since the first time they had experienced each other, their feelings and friendship had blossomed, so that now he was certain that there was no one else for him, or not while this war lasted. Perhaps that was unfair of him, but by God he could do with her now. His sergeant's voice pulled him back to the present.

"Skirmishers signalling the approach of enemy cavalry, sir!"

At that moment Slade ordered them forward. His was the leading troop, and as he came abreast of Stiles he was told that the enemy had turned about. Slade came up. "Get after them, man!" Gunning, who now had his mind firmly fixed on the task in hand, took his men off in pursuit. Stiles, temporarily separated from his own group, joined them. At first all went well. Stiles enjoyed the chase and there was many an anxious Frenchman looking over his shoulder as the heavy Royals' troopers came crashing down the hill. Stiles and his fellows cut and thrust till their arms ached, killing, wounding and even taking some prisoners, but the French, realising that their pursuers were few in number, turned a squadron about and it was the Royals turn to be attacked. After a few minutes the only survivors were Gunning, Stiles, and half a dozen others. Their salvation came from Slade who led the main body forward. The French broke off the action and resumed their retreat.

Slade put his pursuing brigade into a hand canter. They passed through Valencia de los Torres in fine style, moving all the time towards Maguilla and capturing prisoners on the way. Still Slade did not order a charge and he missed several clear opportunities of closing with the enemy, until they reached uneven ground by a river. He could not have chosen a more unsuitable place when he ordered two squadrons of the Royals to charge with the 3rd Dragoon Guards in support.

"What went wrong? Why did the men run?" Clifton asked. It was now evening, and the regiment was twelve miles back in Hiniosa. He had no doubt that the commanding officer of the 3rd Dragoon Guards would be asking the same question. Clifton looked round the group. It had been a disaster. Thirty-two killed and wounded; Lieutenant Windsor and forty-seven men missing. Many, he dared to hope, would be prisoners. If that was not bad enough, there had been almost one hundred and fifty horse casualties. He looked at each of his officers with a stern gaze – Radclyffe, Eckersley, Hulton, Clark, and Gunning.

Radclyffe broke the silence. "We were chasing the French towards Maguilla and at one of our brief halts I approached General Slade. Nathaniel," he nodded towards Eckersley, "joined me, and we both pressed the general not to let Lallemand gain the unfavourable and hilly ground about Maguilla before charging, but he was not responsive to our suggestion. Is that not so, Nat?"

Eckersley took up the story. "It is exactly as Charles has said. And indeed, General Slade waited until conditions were least favourable before ordering the charge. By then we had covered twelve miles. We were disordered and our horses were blown. As you are aware, sir, they have been fed largely on green barley and are mostly too fat for really hard work. Initially the charge was a great success. Both ourselves and the 3rd Dragoon Guards cut down many of the enemy and captured a large number of them. There was a cry of 'Look to the right'. I do not know from whence it came, but on looking I saw some French cavalry, which must have been left as a reserve. I am certain they did not intend to counter-attack but merely cover the retreat of their fellows. Do you agree, gentlemen?" They nodded assent.

"It was then," said Clark, "that matters really got out of hand. There were some shouts of alarm at the sight of the enemy's reserve, and our once victorious troopers were transformed into an undisciplined rabble. Admittedly, we were all exhausted by the extreme heat and disordered by the pursuit and the charge. I heard someone give the order, "Threes about", which was generally taken up, and for a while the two opposing forces were running from each other. We tried to check them, but our men would have none of it. Unfortunately the French were the first to reform."

"Well, Hulton," said Clifton, "you had the reserve squadron and I presume you saw what happened?"

"Yes, sir, it looked like a rout. Our two squadrons with the 3rd Dragoon Guards rode furiously towards the rear. There was no order and the regiments were intermingled. When the French came after our men, I ordered my squadron to charge and we checked them. I had hoped that General Slade would restore some order and that we might get some support, but no help was forthcoming. In the end, faced with superior numbers, I had no option but to yield to circumstances and put threes about. We followed the rest to Valencia and it soon became obvious that some had pushed their mounts to the limits of exhaustion in their desire to get away. There were a large number of fallen horses and their riders must now be in the hands of the French."

There was a pause, which seemed endless. Even the ebullient Gunning was muted as he shared in the deep sense of shame.

Eventually Clifton spoke. "If no one has any more to add, I can only say that this has been the worst day since we commenced the campaign. Whilst there is no doubt that the men behaved badly, if there is any mitigation, it is because their confidence has been undermined these last few months by our superiors." At this there were murmurs of assent. "It is the regiment's reputation that concerns me most and hopefully we shall have an early opportunity of redeeming ourselves. Thank you for being so candid, and now go and have some rest."

Three days later, fifty men, twenty-five of them from the Royals, rode back to Maguilla. Stiles was one of them. It had been reported that the French were holding some of Slade's wounded there. General Erskine ordered the sortie and placed his Austrian ADC, Lieutenant Strenowitz, in command. They arrived in Maguilla only to find that all but four of the wounded had been removed. As Strenowitz was making arrangements for their transportation he heard the sound of hurrying footsteps behind him. He turned and saw a sergeant accompanied by a Spaniard.

"Sir, this gentleman is the mayor and he says that there is a French detachment approaching. Could be as many as one hundred men."

Strenowitz looked at the mayor and wondered if he could trust him. He supposed that he would have to, if for no other reason than that the man had sought him out. He thought about his own force—fifty men. Given the right circumstances and a well chosen position, they might well pull it off. Strenowitz spoke to the mayor.

"I am greatly obliged to you for the information. Which direction are they coming from?" The mayor, in a state of agitation, pointed towards the other side of the town. "We will attempt an ambush," said Strenowitz. "We haven't much time. Do you know of a suitable place?"

The mayor led them through the town and out the other side. He pointed to a wall which ran parallel to the road and was placed above it on a slight embankment.

"The French will come from that direction, señor," said the mayor, pointing up the road. "You and your men will not be observed from behind the wall." The mayor hurried off.

Strenowitz ordered the men to dismount, and the handlers led the horses away. "We will spread the men out, about three feet apart," he said to Bridges, who was in charge of the Royals' detachment. "I will take the end farthest away from the town, and you take the other. Now, all of you behind the wall! Sergeant, space them out. Keep hidden and wait for my order to fire. They won't be expecting us, and a well-controlled volley should quickly reduce their superiority of numbers. Does everyone understand? Good, to your positions!"

The men moved off enthusiastically. Hopefully there would be an opportunity of retrieving some of their lost honour. Charles Bridges was not so sure that this was a good idea. During the campaign so far, he had managed keep out of harm's way by pretending to be involved but he felt that one or two of his fellows had their suspicions. There was always someone who wanted to play the hero. That was fine by him, provided it did not involve him in danger. Why couldn't they do just what they had come here for and take the wounded back? What had seemed a straightforward duty now bore all the hallmarks of danger. Although he tried not to show it, he was petrified with fear.

Crouched behind the wall and two places from Bridges was Stiles. 'The lieutenant doesn't look too well to me,' he thought. 'Still, that's his worry'. They had loaded and primed their carbines. All they had to do now was wait.

Strenowitz heard the slow hoof beats and the jingling harness of the column coming towards them. There was much talking and laughing among the enemy troops. They seemed relaxed, which was all to the good. The surprise, when it came, would hit them all the harder. Peering through a gap made by a missing stone, he could see an officer riding in front with his chin slumped to his chest. The men behind were in threes and riding well closed up, so that he should be able to bring his full fire power to the length of the column. He just had to wait until the last men were abreast of him.

At that moment a horse reared and crabbed sideways towards the wall. Strenowitz held his breath as its rider dug in his heels and fought to control the rearing animal. Hoots of derision accompanied his display. The horse and rider were getting ever nearer to the wall, and Strenowitz was on the point of giving the order to fire when the beast submitted and moved back into the column. An order was given. The French troopers stopped talking and straightened themselves up.

In the end it was easy. The last man was passing as Strenowitz rose to his feet, came waist high to the wall, and shouted "Fire!" A volley rang out and simultaneously men and horses fell. Some lay groaning, others including the officer were immobile. Stiles had got him. Perhaps half a dozen ran off in the direction from which they had come, as did the riderless horses. Strenowitz and his men leapt over the wall, sabres in hand, but although a few shots were fired in their direction there was little resistance.

"Anyone seen Mr Bridges?" asked Strenowitz. Stiles had seen Bridges go but, like the others, professed ignorance. Bridges had gone off towards the horses as they had climbed the wall. They went through the pretence of looking for him but he could not be found.

Later, back at Hiniosa Clark met Strenowitz. "Hear you have had a successful day."

"Indeed yes, but we seem to have lost Charles Bridges. Couldn't find him anywhere before we left Maguilla. Later, I discovered that he had taken his horse from his handler."

"He's been here a good two hours," replied Clark. "Said he had escorted back a wounded man."

Return to Portugal

Clifton woke to see his servant Delaney standing by the bedside, candle holder in hand.

"'Tis time, sir," he whispered, before putting the candle down and padding off.

Clifton eased himself from the bed, careful not to awaken Elizabeth Lamb, who slept on with a serene look on her face. He gently eased the bed covers up across her shoulders, covering her exposed left breast. It was still one and a half hours to daylight, on another wet morning in November 1812. He moved into an adjoining room, where his portable washstand had been set up, and he commenced shaving.

It was to him a necessary habit, a form of discipline and an example to the others, even though the Royals and the army were involved in an arduous retreat. He wanted to satisfy himself that the dismounted men, under Trafford, would be on the road in good time. Elizabeth Lamb would ride with him when he led the remainder of the regiment westwards.

The summer, although still blackened by the memories of Maguilla, had seemed full of promise. The weather had been extremely hot, even for Estremadura. The sirocco, accompanied by stifling heat, the usual shortages of water, and always the troublesome ants and flies, had, at times, made life hard to bear. Despite all these difficulties, they had eventually advanced as far as Madrid, but when Soult and Joseph Bonaparte had united at Almanza at the beginning of October with a combined force of a hundred and twenty thousand men, Wellington, who had at his disposal seventy-five thousand, had been obliged to raise the siege of Burgos and evacuate Madrid. The retreat had continued and he hoped today they would reach their destination. The Royals and the other cavalry, who were the rearguard, had been little troubled by the enemy. Their opponent was the weather. It hadn't stopped raining for days and there was almost a complete lack of food and forage.

By now Clifton was dressing. He considered himself most fortunate in having a roof over his head, unlike most of his men. This, he readily acknowledged, was due to Simon Delaney's talents. He might be a rogue, but he had an unfailing knack of finding good quarters. If asked, Delaney would have said that, "it was as much in his own interests." Clifton's clothes were still damp, and although he did not expect a full breakfast table he was sure that Simon would manage to find him something.

Stiles paraded with the other dismounted, which now accounted for almost half the regimental strength. There was just over an hour to daylight and he was wet, hungry, and tired from the fatigues of the last three days – three days which, on reflection, seemed to run one into another. After the continuous marching – if you could call it that, more like slipping and sliding – he had begun to believe that there was no other existence. His leg muscles ached and there was a pain across his shoulders, no doubt caused by marching with his head tucked into his chest as he tried, in vain, to avoid the worst of the weather. There had not even been the prospect of a warm fire and hot food to look forward to at the day's end. They had become so desperate that they had eaten acorns and leaves. It was hard to recall what it was like to have a full stomach. To eat until you could eat no more was certainly a far-off memory. His stomach rumbled and hunger pains shot through him. His clothing was mud splattered. Mud caked his boots and overalls to the knees. He had a haversack, sabre and carbine to carry. Fortunately, his saddle and other equipment were being conveyed on a baggage wagon. To make matters worse, it was raining and it hadn't stopped for three days. Constant rain that fairly deluged the earth.

Three days ago Stiles had been forced to shoot his mare. God only knew what had happened to the supplies, but there had been no corn for the horses. He had gone to the horse lines to find his mare, by then a skin and bone relic lying down, and despite all his efforts and kind words of encouragement he had been unable to get her to stand. His mount was only one of a number similarly stricken. She had looked at him with pleading eyes. The farrier sergeant's inspection had confirmed his worst fears – she would have to be shot. Stiles, who would have had no compunction had it been one of the enemy, had to steel himself as he held his carbine close to the mare's head. It was soon over.

They were called to attention. The commanding officer had arrived. He quickly ordered them to stand at ease. Stiles knew that the colonel didn't have to turn out, but there was a strong bond between him and the men.

Clifton spoke. "Only one more day, my lads – bear that in mind. Once across the Agueda, and all of this will seem like a bad dream. There will be rations aplenty. We haven't lost any stragglers yet. Now, off you go!" Cornet Trafford gave the order to march.

They marched, Trafford at their head, with a party under Provost Sergeant Else at the rear. Stiles had taken up a position in the left, outside rank, towards the head of the column, where he hoped to find firmer ground. Many had travelled that route before, and the beaten track, which passed for a road, resembled a bog. The mud pulled at his feet, threatening to pull off his boots. Every step became a supreme effort to remove his boots free from the thick, clinging liquid. All the while, the heavy rain continued. It was running down his face and neck and soon he was soaked to the skin. There was no talking, which in itself was a bad sign. Each man devoted all energy and effort to pressing on with a mechanical resolve. Now and again the non-commissioned officers would urge their charges on, but the intervals between the rows of the column inevitably lengthened.

Although concentrating on his progress, Stiles found that he was able to think of other things. This was certainly a country of extremes in the weather. He would always remember that time at Albuera, back in the summer, when the brook had become a trickle and they'd dug holes in search of water – foul putrid water at that, contaminated by the decomposing bodies of English and French soldiers. There was the never-to-be-forgotten twelfth of July, when the sirocco wind, which had been blowing for some days, reached an increased level of intensity. Man and beast alike had suffered agonies. It had been hotter by far than standing near to Bill Thomlinson's blacksmith's forge and there had been no air to breathe. He, like the others, had lain under the belly of his horse, where he had remained panting for air. Many had suffered heatstroke, and it had not been until after midnight that a change of wind to the north had brought relief.

Yes indeed. What a country! Plenty of poor people and many rich. The Spaniards had no idea of fighting as a disciplined force but their guerrilla bands caused the French many problems. There was no doubting their hatred of the enemy, and when the regiment had passed through Corpis de Montalban and Toledo there had been much celebration. The effigy of Bonaparte had been burnt, accompanied by deep-felt cries of 'Death to the French!' At the end of October they had spent three hours in Madrid, and although the residents had expected the Army to make a stand, it had been from there that the retreat had begun.

There was a cry from beside him and, on looking, Stiles saw Will Venning stagger and fall to his knees. He would have fallen face downwards in the mud but Stiles managed to catch his coat collar. Jim Howell, who was on the other side of the stricken soldier, and Stiles each took an arm and raised him to his feet.

Venning, who was as white as death and whose eyes seemed to have sunk into their sockets, gasped to his helpers, "It's no good. I can't march another step."

Stiles, hoping that the colonel was right and that this would be the last day's march, said, in mock anger, "You've got to go on. Anyway, we are not going to leave you here. Give me your carbine and haversack. Can you manage his sabre, Jim?" Having relieved the man of his burdens and catching him under the elbows, the three resumed their sluggish progress and forced their way back into the column, which until then had swirled round them.

Clark was among the more fortunate. He still had his mount, Jock, who carried him now as he had done for the past ten years. He'd seen the resigned looks on the faces of the dismounted men when they had assembled that morning. He was, in his opinion, justifiably angry. He would admit that the condition of horse and man had deteriorated, due to the atrocious weather, but his anger was directed at the inexcusable bungling of the quartermaster general. Clifton had informed his officers that supplies had been sent by General Gordon along the wrong road. How were the Royals and the other regiments expected to perform their duty in the face of such inefficiency? It was not as though they had the French snapping at their heels. Once the error had been discovered, surely the supplies could have been redirected! As it was, nearly twenty men had died. It was as well that the men knew nothing of this. The conditions had already provoked outbursts of insubordination.

He wondered what Phillip Dorville would have made of it all? He had last seen him in July, when Dorville was suffering from fever and delirium. It had been proposed that he should be sent to hospital in a springless bullock cart, a conveyance hardly likely to improve his condition. On hearing of this, Dorville had declared, "He'd be hanged if he was going to be left to die in a bullock cart. Look what had happened to Jervoise! Bugger that!" In spite of his illness, he had ordered his horse to be saddled and then ridden seventy miles to Badajoz. There weren't many as tough as old Phil and it was as well that the regiment had its characters, some of whom were noted for their eccentricities and others for their steadfastness under physical danger. Clark noticed the distance between himself and the rear of the preceding troops was lessening. The column came to a halt. They had almost reached their destination.

In the last days of December 1812, Clifton was in the house assigned to him at Sorez, only eighteen miles from Alcantara. He looked across the room to where Elizabeth Lamb was sitting by a blazing fire. He studied her fair hair, her profile as she looked intently down at her embroidery, and he watched her deftly moving fingers. What a pillar of strength she was! He doubted if he could have coped without her. He was aware that she could twist him round her little finger, but she never took unfair advantage and was never unreasonable. It was well known that if any one felt they had been badly done by, a word to Elizabeth was all that was necessary, and provided that she was convinced of the justice of their case, she would come to him. 'Damn me!' he thought to himself, 'she is desirable'. A pity that Benjamin Cook, the adjutant, was coming to see him or he would take her here and now.

She became aware of his gaze, looked up, and smiled. "A penny for your thoughts, Ben."

"I was thinking what a dreadful year 1812 has been," he lied. "Be glad to see the back of it. I know nothing is accomplished by dwelling on it, but as if Maguilla was not enough, we are still encumbered with Erskine and Slade." He felt his former mellow feeling slipping away but his good spirits were soon restored when Elizabeth replied in her soft voice:

"Be patient, my dear. Things can only get better. I am sure there will be an improvement soon. Do you realise how much I love you?"

He rose from his chair to kiss her when there was a knock at the door.

His servant, Simon, entered the room. 'Damn fellow!' thought Clifton, despite being told several times to knock and wait, he had, yet again, ignored the instruction. A few minutes later and they might have been caught in a compromising situation.

"Well?" he enquired testily. "What is it?"

"The adjutant is outside, sir."

"Show him in!" Clifton ordered.

Elizabeth stood as though to leave the room. "I'll go."

"No, stay. It is only Cook, with the returns for me to sign."

Simon opened the door and ushered the adjutant into the room. Cook entered, carrying a file of papers, and crossed the room to where Clifton was seated. He bade Mrs Lamb, "Good evening," and was acknowledged. As Cook walked, Clifton noticed the way he limped, despite the fact that he was wearing a built-up boot. "The returns, sir," said Cook in an unctuous tone, which to Clifton's annoyance he reserved for occasions when he addressed his colonel. He laid them on the desk.

Clifton ignored them for the moment, invited Cook to sit, and asked solicitously, "How is Mrs Cook?"

"She keeps well, sir."

Clifton wondered if that were so. By all accounts they often caused injury to each other and the sound of him shouting and her screaming was plainly heard on numerous occasions.

Clifton at last looked at the papers on the desk and read. "Twenty-six men died on the retreat," he said out loud. "Sixty men are sick, twenty-six held as prisoners of war, and one hundred and thirty-five detached. How many effectives do we have?"

"There are ten officers, five staff, and three hundred and seven other ranks," replied Cook.

"What about the horses?"

"As you will see, sir, we have lost one hundred and forty and there are only one hundred and seventy fit for work."

There was a silence. At the fireside Elizabeth Lamb had heard the exchanges and knew that Ben, despite his stern exterior, would take the news badly. She would need to comfort him. She heard him sigh and then the sound of the quill as it scratched across the paper. He was signing his name: "Benjamin Clifton".

To France

"The commander-in-chief desires you and the men to know that the retreat does not put an end to our endeavours in the Peninsula." Clifton was passing on a message from Slade, who had impressed on him Lord Wellington's command. Clifton had called his officers together. He was mindful that the regiment had suffered great hardship and knew that it was of paramount importance that morale should continue to improve. He continued, "You will already detect a lightening of spirit since food and comfortable quarters became available. Impress on the men that this year, 1813, will be better. We are already back in Spain and achieved this when we crossed the little frontier stream of the Ella. Tell them that the French had to move such a large part of their armies to force us back that the guerrillas are playing havoc with their rearguard."

It was early January and the Royals were cantonned in Alcantara and its environs, with excellent quarters and forage. Clifton, having dismissed his officers, sat alone. They still had to make up for the large number of horses lost, and consequently there were still a large number of dismounted men. Fortunately they were likely to be in Alcantara for some time yet and he should have sufficient breathing space to get the regiment back to something approaching normality. Rumour had it that the 4th Dragoon Guards were about to be recalled, in which case the Royals would get their remounts from that quarter.

There was a clattering of saucepans followed by raucous laughter and then singing. Who was making that noise? Clifton opened the door. The singing stopped and he heard, "The old bugger is an adulterer and she is no better than a whore." The words, though slurred, were clear and echoed round the hallway. The very familiar voice belonged to none other than his servant, Simon.

Clifton stepped into the hall and saw Elizabeth, looking pale, who had come from an adjoining room.

"What on earth is Simon up to?" she asked, hoping that Ben would not discover the whole truth.

Clifton was now beside himself with anger and roared, making her start as he did so, "Simon! Simon, damn you, come here!" Simon knew only too well why he was being shouted at but he hoped that Mrs Lamb had kept her promise not to tell the colonel. For some time he had been filled with lustful thoughts and earlier that morning had decided to put them into action. The mistress had soon put him in his place and had warned him against a repetition on pain of being reported. Then he had started drinking. So he wasn't good enough for her. He'd show them!

Clifton heard the sound of approaching, unsteady footsteps. Simon stumbled into the hall, bottle in hand – a bottle of Clifton's best claret – and said in an insolent tone, "You want me, sir?"

" I do, sir!" Clifton replied. "What were those remarks you were making?"

Simon took a generous swig from the bottle before replying. "I said you are an adulterous old bugger and she...," pointing to Mrs Lamb, "is no better than a whore!"

Elizabeth thought that Ben would have a seizure. The veins on his neck stood out; his eyes bulged from their sockets and his fists were tightly clenched. She expected him to shout but when the words came, although spoken softly, they did not disguise the anger behind them.

"You will leave this house at once and you may regard yourself as no longer being in service! If you were one of my soldiers, instead of a civilian, I would have you flogged! Go this instant! Collect your belongings and leave." With that, Clifton strode purposefully to the door and threw it open, dramatically raised his arm, and pointed to the outside.

Simon, taken aback, dropped the bottle. It broke as it struck the tiled floor, the glass and liquid spreading in all directions. He shambled off to his quarters without so much as a word or gesture.

Shortly afterwards there was a commotion in the street outside the house. A small crowd had gathered, and Simon, although not repeating his insults, was regaling the onlookers at the top of his voice. "Can you find some pity for a poor servant who has been cast out without so much as his wages? He hasn't even given me my passage money back to England."

Elizabeth, peering from behind the curtain and fearing what else might be said, turned to Clifton. "Ben, I fully appreciate your feelings in this unsavoury matter, but would you, as a kindness to me, provide some money so that we may be rid of him?"

Clifton, who could refuse her nothing, summoned Provost Sergeant Else and, having handed over some coins, told him to ensure that his erstwhile servant left immediately.

Tinsley wrote in his journal: '19th January at Brosa we received our helmets'. The entry was not altogether correct. Whilst some of the men were adorned in their new headgear, Stiles and Burnside still had their old bicorne hats and would continue to wear them until further supplies arrived. They had very little money and decided to walk round the town. There were many others from the regiment proudly wearing their new helmets, which had a black skull and peak with a brass crest and edge, surmounted by a long flowing mane of black horse hair, a thistle tip in front, and secured by a brass chinstrap. The newly-adorned drew many an admiring glance from the Marias, Conchitas, and other women.

Burnside was his usual randy self, but, lacking the wherewithal, complained to Stiles, "Are there no charitable women in this town?"

"There probably are, but you might get more than you bargained for," replied Stiles. "Anyway, I thought you were accommodated in that department?"

"I *was*, until her husband returned home," was the reply. They had walked the length of the town, and after some two hours, with only a little wine for comfort, decided to return to their quarters.

It was after midnight when Provost Sergeant Else and his henchmen woke the sleeping troops. Some were in a deeper sleep than others and there was much cursing. Stiles, on coming to his senses, was convinced that the French must be nearby. On being turned out, the two troops at Brosa were informed that the proprietor of a cantina had been assaulted by three men and there would be an identification parade at nine o'clock that morning. At the appointed hour they were assembled, in a long single line which stretched up hill. The senior troop leader, Clark, was accompanied by Troop Sergeant-Major Austin and a small, rotund Spaniard, who bore a black eye, a swollen lip, and a grazed left cheek.

The examination commenced with the Spaniard scrutinising the face of the first man. He peered for what seemed to be an eternity and then passed to the second and so on. Stiles watching, from the corner of his eye, saw the Spaniard coming towards him, felt nervous, felt the guilt of the innocent, met the man's gaze, and then he was past. At the end of the line the canteen owner stopped and came back again. He pointed to three men, Hubble, Taylor, and Sims. All three were wearing the new helmets.

The sergeant-major was not to be outdone. He asked Clark in a whisper, "May I speak with you, sir?" They drew to one side and Austin continued, "I am certain in my own mind that the guilty parties have been identified, but I ask you to consider what will happen to them if we rest on the present situation. I am not suggesting that they escape punishment, but floggings will not be beneficial to morale. Can we suggest to him," he pointed to the innkeeper, "that we wish to be certain in view of the seriousness of his allegation. If you permit, I will fall the men out, get them to change places, and at the same time order the three to change headgear with those not wearing helmets. We will see if he repeats his choice."

Clark and the Spaniard agreed. The changes took place and this time three different men were selected. Clark and the Spaniard left, the latter casting baleful glances over his shoulder and issuing what were, if the accompanying gestures were to be correctly interpreted, threats.

The sergeant-major had not finished. "You three," he said, pointing to Hubble, Taylor and Sims, "are in the shit. I am taking you before the squadron leader for punishment."

Hubble, a corporal, was reduced to the ranks and all three suffered loss of pay.

The room was darkened against the daylight. Behind the drawn curtains, which fluttered in the draught coming through the partially open window, Breedle, Sir William Erskine's valet, removed a flannel cloth from his master's brow, passed it through a basin of cold water, wrung it out, and having folded it into an oblong placed it back one the patient's forehead. Erskine was suffering from fever and delirium, and whilst occasionally lucid, he soon lapsed back into his ramblings. Most regarded him as mad in any event, and if others could see him now they would be confirmed in their opinions. Breedle would agree with that view, which he had heard was shared by Lord Wellington. God, how dark it was in the corners of the room. A solitary candle and the flickering firelight were the only sources of illumination. His master had been confined to bed these past three days and Breedle had enjoyed very little sleep. The only other visitor had been the doctor, who tut-tutted and instructed that Sir William be kept warm. He continued with his ministrations, thinking that he would soon have to get some fresh water, when Erskine spoke: "Is that you, Clifton?"

Breedle was too tired to humour him and replied, "No, it's me, Sir William – Breedle," and let him ramble on.

Erskine continued, "I should tell you that I have no regard for you, or that damned regiment of yours. Much prefer the 3rd Dragoon Guards. What is that, sir? Speak up!" Then, in a quieter voice, "The damn fellow is walking away. Come back! Come back, I say!" Breedle was halfway to the door, water pitcher in hand, as Erskine finished this address to the imaginary Clifton. His voice trailed off and was followed by the sound of deep, regular breathing. He was asleep. He ought to be all right to leave for a moment, thought Breedle.

A voice called, "William. William, are you there?" It was his mother. Strange that she should be here, but he had heard her calling. She must be outside. "I am coming mother!" Erskine sat upright and put his feet to the floor. She must be in the garden. If only it were daylight. He heard her voice again. "William. Father and I are waiting!" He crossed the room towards the window, pushed through the curtains, muttering to himself, "Damned window is almost shut." He pushed it up, got onto the sill, and stepped out.

"Erskine is dead!" The news spread round the regiment like wildfire. Clark received an account from Strenowitz, who had been Erskine's ADC and who was on his way to inform Clifton.

He told Clark, "His man left the room and it seems that the general threw himself from a window which was two storeys up. When the valet returned and found Erskine missing, no one at first thought to look outside. The interior was thoroughly searched and on not finding him, the grounds were carefully examined and he was found. The general, fortunately for him, was unconscious. He had fallen onto an iron palisade and had torn and broken his thigh, by all accounts in a most terrible manner. He died two days later." If he were honest, Clark could not find it in his heart to have any feeling of regret. He, like many others, thought that the regiment had been sorely used by Erskine, and now there was only Slade to contend with.

Stiles was at last remounted. It was the end of March 1813, and since the previous November, although he had used various troop horses, he'd not had a permanent mount. The regiment had moved to Las Narvas as there was more food and forage available there, when they received one hundred and eighty-seven remounts from the 4th Dragoon Guards, who were going home. Stiles ran an appreciative eye over his new steed. Probably getting on for fifteen hands high, he estimated, and must weigh something over a thousand pounds. He carried on grooming the animal, giving her an occasional pat. She certainly looked in good condition. Hopefully, there would be no shortages of fodder and water. He recalled an old sergeant telling him when he was a recruit, "Look after your horse and it will look after you. In normal conditions a horse should have a daily ration of twelve pounds of hay, ten of corn and eight of straw. In cool weather it will drink five gallons a day."

"Let's hope we will both be lucky," Stiles said out loud.

"What did you say?" asked Tinsley.

"Just talking to my mare."

They both laughed.

"First we were delivered of Erskine and now Slade. He's been sent home." Clifton had just returned from a meeting with the new brigadier, Major-General Sir Alexander Fane, who was Slade's replacement.

"What type of man is he?" asked Elizabeth. The spring sunshine shone strongly into the drawing room of the house in Seradilla, which had been their home since the end of April.

Clifton paused before replying. "He is a tall, strong featured man, who has seen plenty of action. He was in command of an infantry brigade at Vimiero and later had charge of Hill's cavalry, but had to return to England in 1810 due to ill health."

Elizabeth could not help but feel sorry for Slade, who had only discovered the news of his transfer in General Orders. He had always been charming to her and she said so. Clifton was not in the least surprised that he had been replaced. "Last time I saw him he was very depressed and apprehensive of being superseded to the extent that he had paid several visits to headquarters and had obtained reassurances. Lord Wellington has never forgiven him for Maguilla.

I am only sorry that he has lasted so long. If anything is to be said in his favour, Slade did show partiality to his old regiment. We are now nearer to General Hill, and with Fane in command of the cavalry, I am certain that this will help further to improve the men's spirits."

The regiment marched on the 21st May; the cavalry providing a broad screen for the army, which had become compressed owing to the nature of the terrain. Stiles urged his horse up the incline of the mountain pass, on the slopes of which large boulders perched precariously. There was evidence of rock falls. Rocks of all shapes and sizes littered the roadside. It was now the 25th May and the surrounding peaks of the Sierra de Bejar were covered in snow and would remain so all year round. The squadron would soon be nearing the town itself. The thought had hardly left his mind when he saw Bejar, which straggled out along a narrow platform of rock, with ramparts along its southern end. It was as well that the enemy were not defending the place. As far as he knew, the French were still retreating and were some way ahead at Salamanca.

Some days later they caught up with Vilatte. The Royals splashed their way across the Santa Marta fords with a renewed sense of purpose. Stiles, who was with the right hand squadron, felt an enthusiasm which had been absent for some time. If he had been asked to explain this feeling, he would have undoubtedly replied, "This time we are going forward. This time there will be no retreating. We are going to win!"

Captain Hulton watched the French under their commander, General Vilatte, who were caught between the cavalry and Lieutenant-General Sir Victor Alten's brigade, which he knew had crossed the river at Salamanca and was coming up towards the enemy's rear. The enemy cavalry had been scattered but there was no denying that their infantry were veterans. They marched steadily, in large moving squares, which, although occasionally hit by random fire, soon closed ranks, and their discipline defied him to order his men to charge. Clifton galloped up and told him not to attack unless a clear opportunity presented itself. He had just observed Purvis' squadron attack a square and receive a volley. Both Purvis and Cook, the adjutant, had had their horses shot from under them.

Stiles was one of those who hovered on the enemy's flank waiting to pounce. Some horse artillery guns had come up, and although their shelling was effective and caused many casualties, the French veterans promptly closed ranks. It was hot; very hot. Many of the French were dropping and Stiles could only surmise that it was the combined effects of the heat and their exertions. The main route of escape was approaching a narrowing in the road with an embankment on either side. A French ammunition wagon overturned, causing an immediate blockage, and Hulton, with the Royals' Right Squadron, charged. The trapped French troops put up little resistance.

Those who did not were cut down and many more were taken prisoner. Stiles was curious. The attitude of the captives was strange. True, it was hot and they had been harried for ten miles, but many were reeling about. He was one of those dismounted to secure the prisoners' armaments. One Frenchman offered him a bottle, which he refused. The man was drunk, as were many others. Stiles caught his horses' reins from Tinsley and remounted. The prisoners were shepherded together and the march back began.

The cavalry was brought forward by Fane late in the afternoon of the 21st June and was halted in a small wood. Nearby, a line of hills ran all the way to Vitoria and were occupied by the French, who made the most of the situation, as they overlooked the surrounding countryside. Captain Paul Phipps halted his men, gave the order to dismount, and handed the reins of his charger to his servant. It was good to have both feet on the ground, even though the French artillery was firing at them. From time to time a cannon ball ripped through the trees, so far without causing injury. Phipps saw Clark nearby. Since the brush with Vilatte, the regiment had performed more marching than fighting, and even now the prospects of real action looked bleak. He repeated his thoughts to Clark, who replied, "It looks as though we will not be required. It is likely to be another infantry battle and I fully expect that we will be told the terrain is unsuitable for cavalry."

Phipps agreed and added, "'Tis a pity we cannot be positioned nearer to Vitoria where we could be more effective at getting at their retreating forces. At the very least we could harry their rearguard, and as I am told that General Graham has deprived the enemy of the use of the Bayonne Road, they will have a hard time going by way of Salvatierra to Pampeluna."

At that precise moment, Phipps, troop sergeant-major, came hurrying across. "Beg pardon, sir, but Wright, the trumpeter, has had his foot carried off by a cannon shot. I ordered some men to take him to the surgeon."

"Very good, Sergeant-Major," said Phipps, then to Clark, "I had better get back to my men."

Clark's opinion was borne out. They were not used and spent the night a little to the east of Vitoria along the Salvatierra road.

Daylight unveiled a scene of chaos. Clark viewed the road, which was scarcely passable. The French had left cannon, ammunition wagons and carriages, complete with their mules and harness. There were carts, which on examination revealed the enemy's accumulated plunder, consisting of casks of brandy, barrels and boxes of dollars and doubloons, wearing apparel, silks, laces, satins, jewellery, paintings and sculptures. The French, in their haste to escape, abandoned it all along with a large herd of cattle, sheep and goats. Clifton received orders from Fane to secure the discarded weapons, baggage, and other material.

Stiles approached one of the carriages. It was dark blue in colour and had a broken shaft. There were two large leather boxes strapped to its rear and the curtains were drawn. 'Better have a look inside first,' he thought, and leaning forward in the saddle pushed the curtains with the tip of his sabre, to one side. There were more boxes and what looked like a discarded cloak, on the floor between the seats. He got down, secured the reins to a wheel rim, and pulled the door open. It was then that he heard a soft whimper. At first it was difficult to know where the sound came from, but then he saw the cloak move. Very gingerly he picked it up and got the surprise of his life. There, huddled on the floor, looking at him through tear-stained, wide blue eyes, was a pretty fair-haired little girl, who, on seeing Stiles, cowered back.

He spoke softly. "Don't be afraid, my pretty one, Francis won't hurt you! What are you doing here? Where's your mother?" He realised that she didn't understand a word he was saying and that she was most likely French. The child said nothing and as he reached inside the coach to pick her up she pulled further back so that he had to climb inside the coach to reach her. All the time he kept repeating, "Don't be frightened!" and on lifting her, he cradled the child in his arms and stepped back onto the ground. She didn't struggle but only stared straight into his face. Her earlier tears remained on her cheeks.

Clark saw Stiles leave the coach but from a distance he could not distinguish what he was carrying. His orders were clear – there was to be no personal looting. Everything recovered was to be shared for the common good. He rode nearer and called out, "What have you there?"

Stiles turned, and if Clark had expected to see a look of guilt, he was disappointed. Stiles looked at the captain and his face bore a grin which ran from ear to ear. "Some unexpected baggage, sir!" He held out the child, who commenced struggling. He explained where he had found her and concluded by saying, "What do we do with her, sir?"

'A good question,' thought Clark. "We cannot leave her here. I think this is a matter for the colonel." He addressed the child in French, asking her name, but she did not reply. "Give her to me!" Stiles offered her to Clark and immediately she started to cry. "You had better come along as well," he said to Stiles, who on mounting was greeted by the sight of the child holding her arms out towards him.

Clifton was with General Fane when he saw Clark and a private approaching with what, from a distance, looked like a bundle. As they got nearer he could plainly see that the bundle was indeed a child. After Clark had given his explanation, Fane turned to his ADC and ordered him to take the child to his headquarters, but then as an afterthought asked Clifton, "Is Mrs Lamb in the vicinity?"

"She is about five miles back, sir."

"Could you please send someone to ask her if she would be good enough to accompany the child? I will put a carriage at her disposal and we will endeavour to trace the mother." Clifton could only agree on Elizabeth's behalf.

Clark then intervened. "If I may say so, sir, I think it would be as well if Stiles went along, at least until Mrs Lamb is located. The girl seems to have become attached to him." There was agreement to this. Clark went back to Stiles, who he had left a little way off, and told him what had been proposed. "Don't worry," said Clark, "I will ensure that you get your share of the prize money.

Having acted as nursemaid, Stiles, on his return had to endure some good-natured ribbing from his comrades and the deed was entered in Tinsley's journal. Stiles was eventually told by Clark that the mother had been found in Franco two days later. The mother, a French lady, had struggled to keep up with the retreating French army and had been unable to carry both her children. She had carried the youngest one in her arms and was obliged to leave the little girl, who was called Claudette and was three years of age, in the carriage.

Clifton paced the room with a degree of agitation. He had a very fine house in Villafranca but the regiment had been too long in the town. As usual the period of inactivity had led to indiscipline, with an increase in court martials and the inevitable floggings. It was January 1814 and the regiment had not seen any fighting since the previous June. The Pyrenees was not a place for cavalry, but once the enemy had been forced back into France, no doubt their turn would come. A regimental court martial had just sat and dealt with another offender. A man, who had been drunk at the time, had stood accused of striking a sergeant and had been found guilty. The sentence awarded was three hundred lashes and this would be carried out later that day, before the whole regiment. The man had shown bravado when sentenced, but Clifton had seen this sort of attitude before and knew that usually a culprit's demeanour changed when he saw the "triangle". He wondered if this would be so in Sadler's case. Clifton detested this form of punishment but authority had to be upheld. He was thankful for the recent order from the Horse Guards limiting the number of lashes to three hundred. That would spare him having to witness another marathon beating. Private Watts, he recalled, had been sentenced to nine hundred lashes and received seven hundred and ten before being taken down.

Clifton stopped pacing and sat down. He would need to speak to Cook, whose treatment of his wife was becoming more outrageous and was becoming the talk of the regiment. By all accounts, Mrs Cook gave as good as she received, but that was hardly the point. The most recent episode, where it had been necessary to put Mrs Cook in the guardroom for the night to keep them apart, had been the last straw. Originally he had told Cook that he would have to get rid of his dangerous companion, but a word from his wife, to Elizabeth, had caused him to change his mind. Elizabeth had seen the unfortunate woman, who at the time was sporting a swollen lip. On enquiry Mrs Cook had replied, "Ben Cook did it. Beat me with his fists, and that's not all." She had drawn back her hair and disclosed a bloody wound, stretching from above her right ear and down almost to her jawbone. "Tried to cut off my ear, he did. Took his sword to me, but I got a stick and beat him soundly." Elizabeth had added that there was a rumour that Mrs Cook had fallen in love with a French prisoner, a trumpeter. Whatever the reason for this behaviour, Clifton wanted an end to it and would tell Cook so.

George Gunning lay in bed with Henrietta Alcock. There was nothing new in this. They had been lovers for sometime. Gunning had decided to take advantage of Byrne's absence and they were in Byrne's bed. Henrietta lay sleeping with her left arm across his chest and was holding his left leg between her thighs, as though trying to retain the memory of their more intimate contact for as long as possible. He felt spent but glowed with a warm, satisfied feeling. Gunning had no particular duties to attend to, and though it was well after eight in the morning, he was quite content to lie for an hour or so longer. She was breathing deeply and steadily, as well she might. Neither had got much sleep. As he had continued to make demands of her, she told him that he was insatiable. He would agree with that as far as she was concerned. Without waking her, he tried to make himself more comfortable by withdrawing his leg. Her nearness and the thickness of the bedclothes made him hot. As he moved she gave a sigh, opened her eyes, and smiled at him. Just then a door slammed and there were footsteps on the stairs. Henrietta sat upright; alarm showed on her face and in a trembling voice she said, "It's Michael!"

Michael Byrne's business at Brigade had finished more quickly than expected. He had enjoyed his night away, had been well entertained, and had caught up on the latest news. On his return to Villafranca he visited Cook, the adjutant, to inform him he was back and told him that the regiment was likely to be in Villafranca until February.

Cook in turn informed him, "There is to be a flogging at two o'clock this afternoon and all officers must be present. The men will be marched from the town square. Assembly is at one."

Byrne, who had spent the night carousing, felt in need of sleep, and he decided he would go to bed for a few hours. Like many others he found flogging distasteful but an order was an order. He opened the door and entered quietly, so as not to disturb Henrietta, but the wind took the door from his hand and slammed it shut. There was no sign of her, she must still be in bed. Well, he would join her and perhaps... He climbed the stairs, opened the bedroom door, and saw Henrietta, bare breasted, sitting up in bed with George Gunning at her side. He stepped back in amazement and in a hoarse voice managed to say "What—" before Gunning interrupted him.

"You might indeed say "what", sir. What," and he laid emphasis on the word, "do you mean by invading my privacy? Can you not see that I am engaged? How dare you? You are a rogue and a scoundrel!" Gunning had decided to brazen it out. Henrietta had urged him to hide but there was no time for that. Anyway, he was not going to skulk about. He was comfortable, and if Byrne did not like it too bad. Attack, in his view, was always the best means of defence. His words fixed Byrne to the spot. He looked from one to the other; no words would come.

Gunning decided to go for the kill and said, "I am so outraged by your insensitivity that I challenge you to a duel. Let me know who your second will be so that arrangements may be put in hand."

Byrne's mind raced. Gunning was quite aware of his lack of prowess with either sword or pistol. He'd had his suspicions for some time about these two, and now they were confirmed he was not too sorry. Better to cut his losses and be rid of her. Nowadays she scarcely paid him much attention. At last he replied. "I will not fight you, sir." He turned to Henrietta. "You have caused me much pain and I expect you to leave this house as soon as it is convenient for you to do so." He turned on his heels and went downstairs. A minute or so later the door slammed, for the second time that morning.

Henrietta threw her arms round George's neck and burst into floods of tears. "What am I to do now, my love?" she sobbed.

Gunning stroked her hair and kissed away her tears. "Do not be sad. I am posted to Lisbon to clear all the malingerers out of the depot. You will come with me." He also had a scheme in mind for getting himself back to England, but for the moment did not mention the subject as he felt the need for her growing once more.

The men marched in order of their troops, with the officers riding at the rear. It was shortly after half past one and they were on their way to witness the flogging. Their destination was a large barn-like building on the outskirts of the town, which had been adapted as a riding school. Stiles marched with the rest. He would be glad when it was over. He knew the man in question, Luke Sadler – a man with a nasty temper, which wasn't helped when he had been drinking. Stiles had seen him on one occasion with swollen bleeding knuckles, the result of his having deliberately punched a wall. When it came to a fight, Sadler was one of the best and could take on men much bigger than him and win. Not more than five feet seven inches in height, he had shoulders as broad as a barn door. Stiles shuddered inwardly at the thought of having to see and hear the lash striking that back.

They arrived at the riding school, were halted, and marched into the building in files. The men were squeezed in along three sides of a square, with the officers in front. The fourth or open side held the triangle where the farrier-major and his assistants waited. Just before two o'clock, Clifton, the surgeon, and the adjutant entered and took their places to one side of the three crossed halberds, the triangle. Sadler was marched in under escort. The party halted; the adjutant read the charge and the findings of the court martial. Sadler was seized, lifted up, and tied by his wrists to the top of the triangle and had his shirt ripped from his back. Clifton nodded to the farrier-major as the sign to begin.

"One," cried the farrier-major in a loud clear voice, The cat-o'-nine-tails came crashing down on the victim's back. Stiles saw the lash fall and the man writhe, but Sadler did not utter a sound. So the punishment progressed in a slow rhythmical manner, until after what seemed an eternity, the count of one hundred was reached. Still Sadler made no sound. Steed, the regimental surgeon, held up his hand to halt the flogging, stepped forward and felt the man's pulse, and then signalled for the punishment to continue. Stiles had the abstract thought that a fresh tormentor took his turn after each twenty-five strokes, as another farrier-sergeant took over.

Stiles heard the count reach, "One hundred and ninety-seven, one hundred and ninety-eight, one hundred and ninety-nine." Sadler gave a convulsive jerk and then hung limp. The doctor instructed the sergeant to stop the beating, and what would have been the two hundredth blow was diverted away from what was now Sadler's bleeding and tattered back.

Having taken the man's pulse, Steed turned to the colonel, "Sir, he can take no more."

Clifton was as relieved as any by the news. "Take him down and attend to him," he ordered, which was followed by an audible sigh as the onlookers collectively released the breath they were holding. Sadler was untied and handed over to Steed's orderlies. Stiles and his much subdued comrades, having been ordered to form up, gladly left the building.

Clark and some other officers, including Hulton, rode back from Saragossa towards the regimental headquarters at Tausta. They rode along the valley of the Ebro, with the river to their left, and at Alagon would part company with Hulton, whose squadron was detached at Ravillinas. It was March 1814 and the riders, with their heads bowed, were facing into a penetrating north-easterly wind, which came at them from the snow-covered Pyrenees. They had bundled themselves up against the cold, but Clark could feel the wind coming through his clothing, and his ears, nose, hands and feet had lost all feeling. He stole a glance at Hulton and felt concerned. George Hulton, the senior captain, had not been well of late and the weather would not help his condition. They'd had a pleasant trip to Saragossa but Hulton had not joined in the banter and merriment, as was his usual style. Clark pulled his cloak more tightly about himself and peered at Hulton in the half light. His appearance did nothing to suggest that his state of health was improving. The quicker they got out of this wind the better.

They arrived at Alagon and halted in the lee of a building. Clark turned to Hulton.

"George, I feel we should attempt to find some accommodation. You look about all in and I am sure that you would find a rest, out of this damned wind, to be beneficial to you."

Hulton looked at Clark with gratitude, and with a supreme effort to stop his teeth chattering said, "It is a kind thought but I must get back to my squadron. It should not take me longer than two hours and I will be better off in my own bed."

"Are you certain?" enquired Clark anxiously.

"Absolutely. I will see you two days from now." Hulton bade all of them farewell and rode off into the darkness. The wind blew with renewed vigour.

A horse and rider trotted along the track to Ravillinas. The rider, Stiles, had a dispatch for Captain Hulton. He was quite content to be on his own. He didn't feel at all lonely and regarded his mission as an opportunity to get away from the others, if only for a short while. His temporary freedom would soon be over, but there was still the return trip to look forward to. He guessed that it must be about eight o'clock in the morning and his only discomfiture was the bloody wind, which had not let up since he had left Tausta.

Captain Clark had sent for him just as he was about to leave. "Be sure to find out how Captain Hulton is. You can say you are enquiring on my behalf. Come and see me immediately on your return!"

Stiles breasted a hill and saw a wayside shrine. Then he saw a riderless horse, and a figure lying face upwards on the ground. He rode nearer and saw that it was Captain Hulton. Stiles got down. The captain was unconscious and his face was deathly white. He put his ear to Hulton's mouth. Yes, he was still breathing but making rasping sounds. Stiles took off his cloak, wrapped it round the recumbent form, then, quickly mounting, went on at a gallop for help.

Later Stiles made his way back to Tausta. They had got Captain Hulton to his quarters and sent a horseman for the surgeon, but it had all been in vain. Hulton died before Stead arrived. Stiles had been in Hulton's troop when held joined the regiment, back in 1804. He had always been a kindly man who had taken an interest in his men. What a tragic loss of life! On returning to camp he reported to Clark.

Clark had been aware that all was not well with Hulton when the messenger had galloped in, seeking the surgeon. The news, brought later by Stiles, had not come as a surprise, but it was still shocking. If anyone had emerged with glory from the nightmare of Maguilla, it had been Hulton. They would all miss him, and it was noteworthy that Lord Wellington never passed the regiment without speaking to him.

They had ridden since two o'clock that morning. Their destination was Aire and they were well within France. It was the 19th March, and since leaving their base at Tausta, on the 2nd, Stiles and the others could sense that the war was nearing its end. There had not been any sign of the French and they had drawn their camp equipment at Irun, which had excited much comment.

"We haven't had a tent in the whole of the Peninsula," Stiles had said to Tinsley. "Who are they trying to impress?"

The regiment had crossed into France on the 11th March and had halted at St Jean de Luz, which had been memorable only for its bad cider, although, to be fair, Burnside had developed a taste for it. Stiles had likened it to vinegar, and in a bantering way had accused Burnside of having no taste. Stiles looked up and saw they were approaching a town. Perhaps this was Aire. The regiment halted in the market place and had no sooner done so when the officers' call was sounded.

Purvis, in command in the absence of Clifton, was waiting at the head of the column. "We are to continue to advance," he told them.

The men received the news with groans. Of course they had to obey orders and they did. To Stiles, as they ascended the narrow and hilly road, had come the feeling that he had seen it all before. He didn't know about the others, but he was tired. Not just tired physically but tired of the war. He rode in a semi-stupefied fashion, having to steel himself to prevent sleep overtaking him. He could tell that the column was lengthening and was not surprised to learn later that it extended two and a half miles from front to rear. It was long after dark when the camp was reached, and after all their endeavours they were not used on the morrow.

At last the war was over. It had come to an end on the 13th April. Stiles and his fellows couldn't at first believe the good news. It had begun to feel, despite all of the recent positive reports, as though it would go on for ever. The French in their immediate vicinity took some persuading that hostilities were at an end and had to be approached under a flag of truce. The regiment was now at Villefranche, with food in abundance and excellent wine available. Stiles, who did not consider himself a good correspondent, decided that it was about time he sent a letter home. He could not remember the last time he had written, but as it was plain to see that they would be leaving Villefranche shortly he felt that he ought to put pen to paper. He was in his billet and had borrowed paper, pen and ink from Tinsley. He sharpened the quill with a penknife, dipped the instrument into the ink, and wrote:

Villefranche

29th day of May, 1814

Dear Mother and Father,

I am sure that by now you know that this war is over. We shall all soon be coming home and are getting ready to leave here any day now. Presently, the cast horses are being sold at prices which are considered to be extremely low. The dismounted men, women and children and the regimental hospital are being sent to

Bordeaux two days from now. The rest of us are to march across France to Calais.

Towards the end we didn't see much fighting. The ground around Toulouse was not suitable for our horses, there were too many waterways. We celebrated fit to bust at the end. Some of our young gentlemen disappeared for a few days and the provost sergeant was sent to look for them. He brought them back in a wagon.

It is hard to believe it is all over after five years. There were times when we thought the weather and lack of food would beat us, but we never thought the French would.

Hope that both of you and my brother and sisters are well. I trust I will see you all soon.

Your loving son

Francis.

Stiles laid down the pen and read the letter. "That should do," he said to himself. He folded the paper, addressed the front, and on the back wrote, 'From F. Stiles, Pte 1st Royal Dragoons'. He held a small piece of sealing wax to a candle flame and sealed the letter.

He reached Calais on the 17th July and crossed to Dover on the 19th.

He was back in England.

The Great Bath Road

"Mail coaches for London leave from the Boar's Head," said the man in response to Stiles' enquiry. He gave the information without asking his unspoken question as to why a soldier would want to know. Instead he pointed into the distance, where a sign hung. "That's the entrance to the yard. You will find the booking office on the far side."

Stiles thanked him and walked on. Two weeks today it would be the beginning of September and he would walk this way again, but on that occasion it would be to catch the coach, at the start of a month's furlough. Not for the first time in his life he was wishing the time away. He wished he was going today.

As he walked he thought back. Since they had returned from France they had been at Sevenoaks; Richmond, where they had been reviewed by the Duke of York, an occasion of much cleaning of man and beast; Newbury; and now Bath. Each move had taken him further away from home. Earlier this month they had all received five month's back pay and many had tried to spend it all at once, on drink. He admitted to himself that it had been an enjoyable time but as often happened some had gone too far and had been incapable of performing their duties. That had resulted in the regiment being paraded on Clifton Downs to witness the subsequent floggings. He had kept the greater part of his money, and having heard about the mail coach, he thought of it as the means of a quick passage home.

Stiles paused at the entrance. The sign, which hung high above, displayed the words BOAR'S HEAD, and the boar had what could only be described as a fearsome set of tusks. The archway now before him was high enough to allow laden coaches to pass through. On either side of the entrance, like a pair of sentries, were large granite bollards, and as he walked under the arch and momentarily out of the bright sunlight the temperature noticeably dropped and there was a smell of damp. On emerging into the yard, it was as though he had entered a small township, a place where everyone had a job to do and purposefully went about their duties.

It was a hive of industry. The stables were to his right and he saw the coach horses, some being exercised in the yard and others being groomed by the ostlers. There were separate shops for the smiths, farriers, wheelwrights, and harness makers. Above the stables and continuing round the other sides of the yard were what he presumed were the bedrooms. These opened on to galleries overlooking the yard, and when he brought his eyes back to ground level saw a paved and covered way to lead passengers to and from the reception hall.

Chambermaids, barmaids, cooks, waiters, and boot-boys were all employed here. A maid came towards him carrying clean and sparkling white bed linen, piled so high that she had to peer round the bundle to check her progress. Stiles saw that her mop cap was awry, her cheeks were flushed, but most of all that she was pretty. She smiled as she passed with a cheery, "Good morning, sir." He walked on across the yard and entered the booking office. He was going to travel like a lord – it was the quickest way and he could afford it.

A fortnight later, with his dream about to become reality, he was back at the Boar's Head. He had arrived at the inn just after thirty minutes past the hour of four o'clock, giving himself plenty of time to catch the coach but beforehand had spent most of the day resting. Once on the coach, he had no doubt that if he went to sleep, he might run the risk of falling off the vehicle. The coach, when eventually driven into the yard, presented a grand sight. Stiles, in his excitement at going home, took in all the detail. The doors and lower panels were painted maroon, upper panels black and wheels red. On the doors were displayed the Royal Arms and the words, ROYAL MAIL, with the names of the two places at either end of the journey, lettered on the door and lower panels. "London to Bath", he read. "Yes. This is it." He spoke the words out loud, without realising that he had done so.

Equally impressive were the driver and the guard. The former was a resplendent figure in his smart box coat, with a posy in his buttonhole and black beaver hat. He greeted Stiles:

"A cavalryman, I see. Don't get many on this coach! Which regiment are you with?"

Stiles replied, "The First Dragoons, lately back from France."

The guard was even more grandly dressed with a tall black hat, a scarlet coat, cut military style, and frogged with gold braid. As he approached, Stiles saw that he carried a blunderbuss, two pistols and a timepiece in a locked box.

Following his gaze, the coachman said, "We're closely timed on this run. Will, here," he pointed at the guard, "hands the clock in at certain stages so that the time can be entered on a bill. Heaven help us if we're late."

Then Stiles was introduced to the guard, who told him that he might as well get up. The mail was put into its box, the lid of which formed the footrest below the guard's seat. "We'll be starting soon," he said.

Stiles, having climbed up, put his valise under the seat, and surveyed his surroundings. The place still bustled and his excitement was further heightened by the fact that he was going home.

The booking office door opened and the booking clerk, who had attended to Stiles when he had booked his seat, ushered the other passengers towards the coach. There were two women. One young and pretty. The other much older, who was very stern faced, must be the chaperone. They were followed by two nondescript-looking men, who obviously wanted nothing to do with each other. All four got inside the coach. His travelling companions, "outside", were a horse dealer, who sat on Stiles' right and lost no time in trying to engage him in conversation, and one, who by his garb was a minister of religion but whose nose by its colour suggested that he had other interests, who sat by the driver. Except for a nod of acknowledgement, to Stiles' relief, he gave no indication of being friendly.

The booking clerk was staring at him and enquired, "What is your business, sir?"

"I am travelling to London and have purchased a ticket for that purpose," said Stiles, waving the ticket.

"You are supposed to check in at the office first of all," said the horse dealer.

"In which case, I apologise," said Stiles. "I am new to this mode of transport."

The guard interrupted the exchange. "I told him to get on board."

The dealer introduced himself as Ned Latham, and Stiles hoped that he would hold his tongue, wondering at the same time where he kept his money. He didn't relish unlimited chatter all the way to London, a journey of over one hundred miles and still thirteen hours away.

The coach started with a, "Right, driver," from the guard and a cautionary, "Mind your heads," as they neared the arch. It was at this point, as they passed into the streets of Bath, that the guard blew his post horn, the sound of which was amplified by the enclosed space. Passers-by stopped to stare at the coach and its passengers. As the speed increased, Stiles found that he had to hold on to the slim rail at his side, at the same time bracing his feet so that he could remain in his seat.

The mail coach, pulled by its team of four, matching grey, horses, climbed slowly up the hill out of Marlborough, one of the many stops to change horses. A new driver and guard had also taken over. The way ahead ran through a tunnel of trees, formed by the great wood of the Savernake Forest, which closely bordered the road on each side. The coach was by now some three and a half hours into its journey to London. It was a clear moonlit night; the heat of the day had given way to a crisp chill, and Stiles pulled a flask from his pocket and took a generous swig of rum. It was getting colder so he drew his cloak ever tighter about him. The carriage creaked and groaned. He could hear the sound of the straining harness and the horses blowing as they hauled their heavy load. The weather had been dry for some days, and the dust kicked up by the horses' hooves tickled his throat. A slight breeze fanned his face and would increase once the horses reached level ground and put on speed. Latham had not uttered a word for some time, except to curse and cry out in alarm as the coach had lurched and swayed. Stiles was wide awake and felt he could relax until they gained the summit. His curiosity in one respect had been satisfied. He now knew where Latham kept his money. He wore a money belt, which he had felt when Latham had lurched against him.

The driver, broad shouldered, and skilful in the management of his horses, occasionally gave them a word of encouragement, but otherwise kept silent and looked straight ahead. The coach was picking up speed and starting to sway. Stiles thought the coachman would be pleased that it was a moonlit night. It must be difficult in mist or snow, no matter how familiar he might be with the route, but tonight it was bright enough to pick out the milestones at the road's edge.

At about the same time but on a road heading north, Captain Alexander Clark was speeding along in a hired post-chaise. The chaise, drawn by two horses, was making good time. He enjoyed the luxury of this mode of travel, in the yellow wheeled and bodied carriage, whose postillion was dressed in clothes of similar hue. In the course of his journey Clark would stop only at the best inns. He was relaxed, had settled himself snugly in the interior of the chaise and had his long legs resting on the seat opposite. His servant, seated in the corner, diagonally across from him, was having great difficulty in keeping awake. Clark was going home to Dumfries, and now at thirty years of age was contemplating marriage. Colonel Clifton, who had just rejoined the regiment, after an absence of four months, had expressed the opinion "Time you were married. Nothing like marriage to round a man off."

Clark was unsure as to whether that had been an observation or an order, and had thought it was all very well for the colonel, who had Mrs Lamb in Bath with him. If there was a Mrs Clifton, he had never seen the lady, but he had replied, "I can assure you, sir, that the subject is very much in mind." Clark turned his thoughts to Harriet Rebekah Randall. He had met her when the regiment had, all those years ago, been stationed in Ipswich. A brother officer, Purvis, had been invited to spend the weekend at the Randall's house at Darsham and had taken him along. Harriet had seemed attracted to him from the first and he certainly had been to her. They had corresponded regularly since then. The last he had heard was that she was still unmarried and he vowed he would call on her father, in Suffolk, as soon as he had seen his Aunt Jane and finished his business in Scotland. The war was over and Napoleon was in captivity. The regiment, as far back as could be remembered, had only served in Europe and was not likely to be sent to India, Canada, or the West Indies. There should now be a few years peace. Yes, he would get married after a respectable period of engagement. The chaise slowed down and pulled into the yard of an inn.

Meanwhile the mail coach had reached the King's Head at Thatcham. The guard told the passengers, "Twenty minutes, ladies and gentlemen, then we must be on our way."

The parson dismounted, without a word, followed by Stiles and Latham. As his feet touched the ground, Stiles saw the inside passengers alighting. The two men got off first, but framed in the doorway, lit by the lamps hung about the yard, was the young woman. Blonde curls peeped from under her bonnet and Stiles saw that she was staring anxiously at the ground. Despite the wooden steps placed to assist her, she still seemed to be having difficulties. Stiles took her hand and she lowered herself onto the cobblestones.

"Thank you, sir," she said, rewarding him with a smile.

"'Tis a pleasure, miss," was all that Stiles could mumble.

The girl, followed by her companion, whom he similarly assisted and whose only acknowledgement was a sniff of disapproval, went into the inn.

Stiles did not follow but passed through the yard and round the back of the stables. He left the light of the yard behind but the moon yet shone brightly. The cobbles gave way to an earthen path, which muffled his footsteps. Having relieved himself, he retraced his steps and could see his breath on the cold night air. He then heard a voice which brought him to a halt.

"Are you both ready?" There was a murmur of assent. "Let the mail get to the second milestone from here, as we planned, and then approach it from the rear. Your job is to take care of the guard. He is well armed but won't be reckoning with me. I'll force the driver to stop. I don't think the passengers will give us trouble. Not if I threaten to blow the driver's head off, although there is a soldier up top who might be a problem." Stiles smiled to himself. "Is Tom out there with the spare horse?" the voice continued.

"Yes!"

"Good. We'll need to be quick, the down coach will be due round about Woolhampton. We'll take more than the mail. There's a young woman who, by the look of her necklace, is worth a bit. We might as well rob the passengers while we are at it. Now be off with you!"

Stiles heard the sound of movement and looked round the side of the barn. He was just in time to see the parson turn the corner. He could also see the imprints of his own footsteps on the dew-covered grass. It was as well that they were not observant.

Stiles hurried back to the yard looking for the coachmen. They were standing talking. The changed horses were restless as though they were impatient to be on their way, scraping their hooves on the

cobbles and tossing their heads. The parson had disappeared –
'probably inside the inn and doing better than me,' thought Stiles. At
that moment two men rode out of the archway. The driver saw Stiles.

"It's the soldier. I knew *you* would be ready on time."

"I must speak to you," said Stiles and related what he had
overheard. At first the pair were incredulous. Highway robbery had
died out in comparison to a few years ago.

"Are you sure?" asked the guard.

"Certain," said Stiles. "What are you going to do?"

"We can't stay here," the guard replied. "Including the parson,
there are four of them, you say. I think we should go on as normal.
What do you think, Dan?"

The driver nodded in assent and added, "Whatever we do we shall
be in trouble. If the mail is late, we shall be reprimanded. If we fail
to stop them and lose the mail, that will be even worse. If we
succeed, we might just get away with it. You never know, they may
even give us a reward."

The guard turned to Stiles. "With your help we should be able to
manage them. What's your name, lad?"

"Francis."

"Well, Francis, hold on a minute." He got up onto the coach and
rummaged in a box. "Take this pistol and prime it. Here's the
necessary." He gave Stiles powder and shot. "Hide the pistol under
your cloak. I'll go and have a word with the landlord."

The guard returned from inside the inn. "All fixed Dan," he said
to the driver. Stiles wasn't too sure what that remark meant but knew
that he could rely on them. The tooting of the guard's horn
reassembled the passengers, and the young woman smiled at Stiles as
she passed. 'Just as well she doesn't know what's afoot,' he thought.
The driver, having made sure that all were settled, climbed up onto
the box seat, picked up his reins, gave them a flick, and once more the
coach was on its way.

Stiles kept a watchful eye on the clergyman. He probably had the
pistol under his topcoat. The man was casting glances all round and
once or twice looked over his shoulder. No doubt he was feeling
nervous. By contrast Stiles felt calm, although he could feel his heart
beating a little faster than usual. In some ways it was like waiting to
go into battle, but at least he was prepared. The coach was moving up

a slight incline and the road shone white into the distance. He saw the first milestone. It wouldn't be long now.

Stiles, watching his man like an eagle, saw a movement. The parson had reached inside his coat. At the same time the guard shouted, "Two riders coming from behind. One on either side of the road!" Stiles saw a pistol barrel glinting in the moonlight. The hammer clicked as the weapon was cocked and in a flash it was pointing at the driver's head. The parson yelled, "Coachman!" but that was the only word he was able to utter as Stiles, without hesitation, caught the parson a vicious blow with the butt of his pistol, followed by an almighty push in the back. The man, taken by surprise, lost his seat, teetered momentarily as he tried to regain his balance, his pistol fired and he was gone. The pistol shot, if anything, acted as a spur to the horses, which, having reached level ground, strode out as the driver urged them on.

The guard shouted in Stiles' ear, "Those two riders have pulled up. Don't think we'll get any trouble from them. You got rid of the parson all right!"

The noise and the coach's sudden turn of speed caused consternation among the passengers. Latham had hardly believed what he had seen and stared at Stiles with fear in his eyes following the unceremonious departure of the clergyman. Stiles could almost read his mind as Latham's hands clutched his money belt. He was sure that he was about to be robbed. From inside the coach there were cries of alarm. One of the men leant from the window to enquire of the guard and was quickly reassured.

The driver, who had now slowed down his team, half turned his head. "The innkeeper from Thatcham will take care of that lot. We'll keep going until we reach the Angel at Woolhampton. Never known anything like it in all my life!" Stiles didn't comment. He was aware that highway robbery had declined, but it wouldn't be surprising if some men turned out of the Army, by the reductions taking place now that England was once again at peace, should turn their hands to robbery. Provost Sergeant Else, more renowned for his brawn than common sense, had on leaving the regiment joined a gang of burglars in Birmingham. He had been caught and hung. Stiles shuddered at the prospect.

The coach entered the yard of the Angel, and the guard hurried off to inform the innkeeper. Stiles dismounted and stood by the coach while the driver told the passengers the tale and how the young soldier had been of assistance. The young woman looked at him with warmth and with the others offered her thanks. There was no doubting her beauty, and Stiles, despite the early hour and his recent experiences, felt stirred as he gazed at her. He was very taken but at the same time was realistic enough to admit to himself that she was far above his station in life.

The coach continued on its way. Stiles enjoyed fitful sleep between stops, punctuated by the sound of the guard's horn. Reading, Twyford, Maidenhead, Slough, Colnbrook, and Hounslow, with its notorious heath and the gibbets now mere stumps, where the bodies of highwaymen had once hung in chains, all passed. He guessed as they approached Brentford, a narrow mean looking place, that it must be a little before six o'clock in the morning, and by the look of the sunrise another fine day was promised. There was now much more activity on the road. They passed wagons, farm carts, and carriages, which had all given way as the guard blasted his horn. Stiles suddenly felt ravenous. It was a long time since he had last eaten and he produced some rye bread and cheese from his pocket. It was then that he realised that he still had the guard's pistol and returned it to its owner. He took out his knife and cut off slices of bread and cheese, pushing them into his mouth as he did so. He felt a tap on his shoulder. The guard was holding out a flask.

"Try some of this." It turned out to be brandy, which burned the back of his throat.

Chiswick, Hammersmith, Kensington and past the Halfway House, "A one-time haunt of highwayman's touts," said the driver, pointing with his whip. Hyde Park Corner, Green Park, with its grazing cows, and finally to their destination, The Swan With Two Necks, in the city.

The guard looked at the timepiece in the wooden box and announced, "Just after seven o'clock, ladies and gentlemen."

A crowd gathered, some to meet the coach, others out of curiosity. The guard informed his superintendent of the happenings near Thatcham. "Fortunately this dragoon overheard their plans." He looked round but the object of his conversation was nowhere to be seen. Stiles, more intent on getting home and anxious to be away from pickpockets or the many other sources of danger, which lay in wait for the unwary, had melted into the crowd.

Northaw

The city at seven in the morning was busy. Stiles merged in with the crowd and was soon out of sight of the coach. The press around him eased and he was able to lengthen his stride. He walked with purposeful steps and found that oncomers got out of his way, as they saw the tall, tanned soldier bearing down on them. It was unlike the day when he had come down to enlist and had been pushed into the path of a wagon. Stiles soon lost the stiffness which had overtaken him after so many hours sitting. Despite the night's excitement he did not feel tired as he headed in the direction of the Great North Road. Now to get home. It was too early in the day to expect to meet Dan Smith, who had brought him to London all those years ago. Anyway, he might no longer be doing the job.

He had not walked far when he heard the sound of slow, plodding hoof beats on the road behind him. A voice enquired, "Would you like a ride, soldier?" He turned and saw a bewhiskered man, who addressed him from his seat on a wagon.

"Where are you going?" Stiles asked. "Barnet eventually. I've some feed to deliver to a big house in Highgate Village. You may find it's a slow journey, but it will be better than walking! The name's Davis. George Davis."

Stiles introduced himself, put his pack under the seat, and got up beside the driver. George asked him where he'd come from, how long was his furlough, and what regiment he belonged to. Answering these questions preoccupied him for some time but they did not stop him from noticing that in the ten years since he had last travelled along the road, the city was sprawling out from its centre.

Now they were passing through fields, and the road, which for a while had been running slightly uphill, rose sharply ahead of them. Stiles knew that at the top lay Highgate Village.

"Time for us to walk and spare the horses," said George. For the first, but not the only time on the journey, they dismounted. George pointed to his right. "We won't have to climb this hill much longer." Stiles' eyes followed the pointing fingers. Men were labouring away by digging into the hillside to the right of the old road. "They are pushing a tunnel through. Mind you, it will still be a long climb to the Woodman but not so steep. It should be easier on these two." He affectionately patted his team.

They must have stopped in the village for an hour. Stiles gave George a hand in unloading the sacks but couldn't manage as well as the carter, who was well practised. Stiles didn't begrudge the time spent. The urgency had temporarily gone, as he was, if the need arose, well within walking distance of home.

"We'll quench our thirsts," said George. "Let's go round to the Flask." It was much later when they left the tavern and passed through the toll gate. The road now descended and climbed repetitiously – over Finchley Common, through the village of Totteridge, and finally up the last steep climb of Barnet Hill.

The wagon came to a halt outside the Red Lion in Chipping Barnet. George tossed the reins onto the seat behind him, jumped down and called over his shoulder, "Must see to the horses first. There's a pump in the yard round the back." He took two buckets, which still swung gently on their hooks, underneath the wagon and went round the side of the building. Stiles followed. When the two horses had been attended to, Stiles went into the inn, called for two flagons of ale and took them outside. George was sitting on the ground, eyes closed, back to the wall and with his legs stretched out in front of him.

Stiles said, "Here's your ale," and handed it over before sitting down. It was another hot September day and the sun's glare made him squint.

"Your good health," said George, taking a long drink and then wiping his mouth with the back of his hand. "I'm almost home and you haven't got far to go. When I get back, I'll load the cart for the morning and see to these two," he said, pointing at his team.

"Another early start tomorrow?" asked Stiles.

"Yes, but I'm used to it after thirty years. How much longer have you to serve?"

"I've been in the Army ten years and enlisted for as long as they want me. The regiment had its numbers reduced when we came back from France, but I'm still in. I'll just have to see what happens." Stiles had finished his ale and got to his feet. "Have another?"

The carter said he would but must then get on.

Stiles watched the wagon as it pulled away from him. It turned off the road and entered a track. He was hot and had long since abandoned wearing his tunic which he carried draped over one arm. He adjusted his hat, picked up his valise and started to walk. Only about five miles to go; the City of London now lay far behind.

Later he left the Great North Road and turned right into a leafy lane. Not far to go now. His boots stirred up the dust. It couldn't have rained for some time by the look of things. Now he was really shaded from the sun's rays as he passed under the thick canopy of oak leaves and crunched over the fallen acorns. Young children noisily played outside some cottages. They stared with curiosity at the tall weather-beaten soldier. Now he approached Northaw House, which stood on higher ground to his right. The building was bathed in the light of the early evening sun and reflected its light of fiery red, from its many windows. His sister, Anne, was in service there, as far as he knew. On the other side of the road, where the ground fell away, was Nyn Park with its woodland which stretched northward to the Great Wood. His course now ran slightly downhill before climbing again. He could see the top of the church tower; almost there. Now he was hurrying, oblivious of rounding the final bend and passing the Sun. There, opposite the church, in the far end cottage, was home.

The door was open. His mother, who had her back to him, was stirring a pot which hung over the hearth. She hummed a tune. His body, framed in the doorway, cast a shadow across her and she turned to see who it was.

"It's me, Mother!"

"Francis," was all she said as she rushed towards him and flung her arms around his neck. He bent down and kissed her cheek.

"It's good to be home! How are you?"

"Oh, I'm all right." She dismissed his enquiry as though it was of no account. Her only immediate response was to hold him even more tightly. "I expect you are hungry. Your father will be back soon and then we'll have something to eat. It's rabbit stew." Stiles felt the juices rise in his mouth. Apart from the bread and cheese that morning, he had not eaten.

"Is Anne still at Northaw House?"

"Yes she's lady's maid to Mrs Strode and gets home at the weekends for an hour or two."

"Any sign of her getting wed?"

"No, she has had one or two suitors. I keep telling her she'll end up as an old maid." Stiles looked at his mother. She appeared a little older than he remembered and had a few flecks of grey in her otherwise dark hair. Mary Hollis, as she had been, had married his father when she was seventeen. His older brother John had been born a year later, followed by himself two years after. Then had come his sisters, Anne and Lucy. Both John and Lucy were married and lived in nearby villages.

"I can hear your father coming! Will," she called, "we have a visitor." William Stiles entered the cottage and embraced his son.

"This calls for a celebration," said his father. "Mary, pass that jug and I'll get it filled at the Brewers. Do you want to come over with me, son?"

"Not if you don't mind, Dad. What I need most of all right now is to get this dirt off me." He knew that once in the hostelry, which lay across the road, they could be there for some time. He was tired and hungry, but a wash would freshen him up. He took a bucket of water from inside the back door and went outside.

He slept well that night and woke to find the sun blazing into the room. It must be late. It had been quite an evening. The meal had been as tasty as it smelt. Rabbit stew with thick pieces of bread, washed down with ale. They hadn't been left alone for long. News of his return soon got round, due to his father's visit to the Two Brewers and there had been a succession of callers. Eventually, Stiles had been persuaded to go across to the pub by Bill Thomlinson, the blacksmith, where he had been made to feel most welcome. The hour had been late when he and his father returned home.

'It's time I got myself up,' he thought. He rose and dressed in a shirt and trousers belonging to his father and went downstairs.

After he had eaten, his mother asked, "What are you going to do today?"

"Thought I'd go and see Granfer Hollis. How is he?"

"He keeps well. Over eighty, you know, and as independent as ever. Won't let me help him but I go round from time to time and tidy up a bit. He moans but I think he appreciates it. I'll come with you!"

George Hollis, now in his eighty-third year, was working on his vegetable plot. Tall, lean, and bearded, he grunted as he stooped to lift the potatoes and searched the ground with his fingers to ensure that none were left behind. Despite his age he was in good health and had lived on his own since Mary had married William Stiles. His wife, Maria, had died giving birth to their daughter, almost fifty years ago. He was a joiner by profession and still did odd jobs but he could turn his hands to most things. He had a passion for clocks, which chimed and ticked their way through the days and nights inside the cottage. Clock repairing earned him enough for tobacco and beer. Looking up from his work, he saw his daughter.

"I suppose you have come to tidy up? Can't find anything for days after you have been here! Who's that with you?"

"It's Francis," she said as she came forward and pecked her father on the cheek.

The old man greeted his grandson with a gruff "You're home, then!" shook hands with a firm grip and pumped his arm. "Good to see you, boy."

"You too, Granfer. How are you?"

"I'm fine." He motioned towards a bench. "Let's sit down while your mother gets to work."

"How long are you home for?"

"Till almost the end of the month." The old man lit his pipe and looked closely at his grandson's face.

"You've filled out, but by the look of you you've seen some hard times. Was it bad?"

"Not all the time. I've been to places I never knew existed. True, we had our bad times and suffered from heat, cold, rain, snow, lack of sleep, and shortage of food. It's hard to explain, but when you are part of a group the hardships are somehow shared between everyone. We could usually find something to laugh about. If anyone suffered, it was the horses. It would have made you cry to have seen the state of them at times, with their bones sticking out, when there was no feed for days and no grazing either. Still, I'm in one piece."

138

'The boy's wiser than when he left us,' thought George Hollis. "How old are you now, Fran?"

"Eight and twenty."

"Any signs of promotion?"

"There's been some talk of it but nothing definite. It's going to be hard to get used to peacetime soldiering, and if I am ever to consider marrying I could do with a step up the ranks."

Mary, who had been busying herself inside the cottage, only caught the last part of the conversation as she came out to join them. "What's this about marrying?" she said. "Have you met someone or got some poor girl into trouble?"

"Neither. Mother. We were talking about promotion. I don't think it is a good idea to be married and be in the Army. A soldier's life is hard enough, without having to worry about your family. If the regiment goes abroad, only six wives get to go. The remainder have to stay at home, fend for themselves, which probably means turning to the parish. We all know what that means – the workhouse. Those that do go are a worry for their husbands, and it can be dangerous for the wives. I've seen them when we have had to retreat, clutching their belongings and trying to drag the children along. No, I'll not marry even though we are at peace and Napoleon is confined!"

"Been a lot of changes, I hear," said Stiles to his grandfather, realising that he would get him on to his favourite topic and pet hate – William Strode, Lord of the Manor.

"It's all to do with that damn fool Strode," said the old man as he relit his pipe. "I prefer things as they used to be. Bad enough that the big house in Nyn Park was pulled down and its stones used to build Northaw House, standing up there on its hill. What with that and the land hereabouts being enclosed and robbing ordinary folks of their grazing and rights to kindling. I'm sure he's lost his senses!" Stiles nodded. This was now old news.

"Keep your voice down, Dad, if you please," said Mary Stiles, "you don't know who may be listening."

"I'm not saying anything which isn't the truth!" was the angry retort. "Do you know what he's done since you've been gone?" The old man hardly paused for breath and puffed furiously at his pipe. "Only pulled the old church down in '08 – said it wasn't big enough. Then he's had a new road cut from the village to the hill below Newgate Street. From there another road has been built. He calls it

The Ridgeway, which connects with the turnpike. He only did it to impress his rich friends who come up from London. We'll have all sorts of foreigners passing through, and you know what foreigners mean – trouble!" He spat contemptuously. "I don't like change."

Despite his daughter's previous warning, he had continued to talk too loudly for her liking. She rose.

"We'll have to go now, Father.

We'll see you at the harvest celebration tomorrow. Goodbye, and don't go upsetting everything once our back is turned."

"Will I see you later at the Brewers, Granfer?"

"You might, after I've been to the Bowling Green," said the old man, referring to the Sun by its old name.

Saturday dawned and the fine weather still held. Stiles went off to visit his sister, Lucy, who lived at Goff's Oak. He walked across the fields now shorn of their wheat crop, and the stubble tore at his boots. In his mind's eye he could see the men harvesting; cutting the wheat with their scythes as they advanced, in a line across the field. They would have been followed by the women and children gathering the cuttings into sheaves, trying to avoid the thistles as they stood them in stooks to dry. In the old days there would have been the gleaning, but the practice was another victim of the enclosures. What was a hard life had become even harder.

Having made his reunion and finding all to be well, Stiles returned home but took an alternative route which would bring him through the woods to the Hook, by way of a bridle path. The track ahead, through the trees and dense clumps of ferns, was dappled in sunlight. He was in no hurry. In places brambles and nettles combined to bar his progress. He was about a mile from home when he saw a movement ahead. A girl in a white dress stepped out onto the path and came towards him. She had a basket over her arm.

"Hello, Francis," she said. "Do you remember me? I'm Margaret Hicks!"

Stiles found it difficult to hide his surprise. Last time he had seen her she had been a child. Her father was a gamekeeper at Nyn Park. Now she was a fully grown, shapely young woman, whose auburn hair accentuated the paleness of her skin. Her arms were bare and freckled.

"Well, say something!" she commanded.

"I'm sorry, but I didn't recognise you," he replied. "It's been a long time. What are you doing?"

"I could say I was waiting for you, but Mother sent me for some blackberries. I think I have enough now." He could see the basket was almost full. "Don't take too many!" she said as he reached out and took some.

"Are you going home?" he asked. "If so, I'll walk with you."

They walked along, talking as they went. In places where the path narrowed they had to move closer together and he could both smell and feel her warmth. They seemed to find conversation easy between them. Then she dropped a bombshell, although he didn't know why the news should disturb him so much.

"I am to be married next spring when I will be one and twenty."

His heart sank. "Who will be the fortunate man? Is it anyone I know?"

His heart sank even further when she replied, "It's Tom Bates." Tom, always a bully, and he had been boys together. He had disliked him then and had no reason to alter his opinion now. They were soon back to the village, having walked the last part in almost total silence.

At Stiles' door she asked, "Will I see you later?"

"I expect so," he said.

Darkness came early. Black clouds had gathered which acted like a blanket and held in the day's heat. It was still, ominously calm and sultry. Stiles, with his parents and grandfather, joined the procession of other villagers going towards the field, near the Great Barn. The men wore their best smocks, and the women were adorned in home-made dresses and bonnets bedecked with ribbons and flowers. The stillness was broken by excited chatter as the inhabitants made their way along the farm track. As far as Stiles was concerned, a depression hung over him and he didn't care whether he went or not.

Stiles had met the vicar the day before, who told him that the population now stood at over four hundred. Judging by the long column of people, most of them must be present. They entered the field. On adjacent log fires, which glowed red in the gathering gloom, a pig and an ox were roasting. The long-handled spits were being slowly turned by the cooks, and the aroma of cooking meat hung on the still air. At the field's edge trestle tables had been set up and were laden with pies, puddings, tarts and other delicacies. In the middle of the spread was the pig's head with an apple in its mouth. Behind, on their cradles, were the beer barrels.

"This is very generous of Mr Strode," said Mary Stiles.

"The bugger can afford it!" said old George.

"Hush, Father! I wonder whether our Anne will be here? She did say she hoped to be. You can cheer yourself up as well, Francis! I don't know what's wrong with you but you have been out of sorts ever since you got back this afternoon."

The torches were lit round the flattened square of earth which was to serve as the dance floor. The fiddler, who had finished tuning his instrument, turned to his companion, who was holding a wooden flute, and said, "I'm ready when you are." They began to play a lively jig, and the dancing started. At first only a few couples took part, but soon an increasing number were kicking up the dust with their pounding feet. Stiles' mother and father joined in and even his grandfather with old Widow Crutchley. Stiles, who was not much for dancing, walked across to the barrels and helped himself to a drink. He was exchanging some banter with his friends when he saw his sister, Anne, standing on the edge of the watching crowd, anxiously scanning the faces. They had always been close, and although he had been up to Northaw House she had been busy with her duties. So, apart from a brief greeting, they had not had an opportunity of talking together. By her side were Margaret Hicks and Tom Bates, who on seeing him scowled, said something to Margaret, and pulled her into the dancing throng. Stiles hurried over to his sister, who as he bent to kiss her put her arms round his shoulders and gave him a hug.

"Francis, I've been looking for you. Come and dance!"

The musicians, stamping their feet in time with the music, were playing with increasing vigour. The dancers, growing in number by the minute, spilled out beyond the square onto the grass surround. Stiles saw Mr Strode, an extremely large man, with a nose to match, bushy eyebrows and a florid face, looking benignly on. The light cast by the torches reflected on a gold watch chain spread across his ample stomach. A young man, in militia uniform, stood by his side and bore a look of condescension. Foppishly he dabbed at his nose with a handkerchief, which was probably perfumed, as though he was afraid of catching some infection from the common folk. That must be Strode's son. Making up the party were two ladies, dressed as though they were off to a ball, the vicar, Mr Heathfield, and his wife.

By now, Stiles had changed partners a number of times. Strode's presence undoubtedly meant there would be an interlude with a speech or two. 'I'm off till they are over,' he thought and feigning tiredness he left the dancing. He went over to the barrels, refilled his pot, and, pausing only to pick up a portion of pie, he walked outside the circle of light. He was just in time. The music stopped and he heard the vicar shouting to make himself heard.

"Mr Strode, our benefactor, would like to say a few words."

He had not gone far when he heard a woman's voice.

"Francis, wait for me!"

He stopped and turned – it was Margaret.

"Where's Tom?" he asked.

"With his cronies; he'll be drunk by now. He's always the same – one or two dances with me, then onto the drink. What are you doing out here?"

Stiles thought that he could well ask her the same question but simply said, "I just wanted to get away for a while." He took a gulp of beer. "Would you like some of this?" he said, holding out the pot, which Margaret took from him and gently sipped. "I've also got a piece of pie." Lightning flickered in the distance followed by a faint rumble of thunder. "We had better not go too far away with the storm coming," he said. "There are some straw bales over by the barn – let's sit there."

Raucous laughter came from under the oak trees.

"That'll be Tom and his mates," said Margaret. "He's jolly now but his mood will soon change for the worse." Then wistfully she added, "It is good to see you again!"

Stiles looked at her and remembered the little girl. What a beauty she had become! He wished he could pluck up the nerve to kiss her.

"It's good to be home and all the more since I've seen you! How come you've got mixed up with him? Tom of all people!"

"He's not so bad at times," replied Margaret defensively. "My mother kept nagging me to find a man and get married. If I had known that you were coming back..." Her voice trailed off, leaving Stiles wondering, as she realised that at last Mr Strode had stopped speaking and he heard the vicar calling for three cheers. The storm was getting nearer and the crowd made its way towards the refreshments amid a happy buzz of conversation.

A figure reeled towards them. It was Tom Bates.

"There you are, Meg! Who's that with you? Oh, it's the hero," he sneered. "I'd stay away from him if I were you. By all accounts he has been to foreign parts, and you never know what he's brought back with him. Come here, girl!" Margaret did not move. Tom Bates now walked menacingly towards Stiles and jabbed him in the chest with his forefinger. "In case she hasn't told you, she's *my* intended. Too good for the likes of you! I suppose you have been filling her head full of fancy tales of your doings. You and your family have never amounted to anything. Margaret, come here! Do you want folk to think you are a slut? Get over here!"

A crowd had gathered. Stiles felt his temper rising and, while not wishing to cause Margaret further embarrassment, it had reached the point where he could no longer ignore the insults. The steel in his voice surprised Bates and all who heard the reply.

"Don't speak to Margaret like that. If we have a difference to settle, how about you and I going round the back of the barn?"

Tom walked off, attempting to be precise in his step. "I'll settle you all right!" he snarled. Stiles, conscious of many eyes watching him, followed Bates to the rear of the barn. Bates turned, as if to take him by surprise, swung a wild punch, but Stiles saw it coming and ducked. The missed blow brought Tom towards him, and Stiles thumped him in the stomach with his left fist and caught him with a right to the jaw as he doubled over. Bates fell to the ground, where he lay sprawled and unconscious. Stiles had put all of his frustration and bad humour into that final punch, and as he pushed his way through the crowd he felt better already.

His leave was almost over. Tomorrow he would be on his way and a local carter would take him back to London. He had enjoyed being home in the company of his family and friends, all of whom had seemed like strangers to start with. He now knew that it was *he* who had been the stranger. Looking back, he had divided his time between his family, numerous visits to the Brewers and going down to the Smithy. He liked watching Bill Thomlinson at work. He was a powerfully built man who had a gentle way with horses. He could not stop thinking about Margaret. He hadn't seen her since that night. He had deliberately avoided her and didn't want to cause any more trouble. If it hadn't been for him there would not have been a scene at the harvest celebration.

Stiles decided on a last walk round and went into Nyn Park. The sun shone fitfully but was still warm, even though September was drawing to a close. He noticed that the oak leaves were beginning to look jaded, as were the ferns. It would soon be winter. He was aware of the bird song, interrupted by the cawing of the rooks, as they clattered round the tree tops. All in all, he was feeling nostalgic, and while at the moment he was taking in the sights and the sounds, he wondered how much he would remember when the reality of army life took over again. The ground fell away as he neared the lake. Then he heard a cry for help.

Breaking into a run, he sped along the path and could see the water before him. Thirty feet or so away was a young auburn-haired woman who appeared to be drowning and was waving her arms about and calling for help. Without thinking he drew off his boots and still fully clothed dived into the water. On surfacing, at first he could not see her but on looking behind he was just in time to see her disappear into the ferns at the water's edge. Realising he had been hoaxed but not feeling displeased, he struck out for the bank. Some discarded clothes lay in a heap and a voice called, "I am over here." He forced his way through a barrier of ferns and there, lying in a small clearing, as naked as the day she was born, was Margaret. She lay with one leg drawn up. The water glistened on her body and had darkened the colour of her hair. She spoke.

"I thought I should give you some encouragement. Don't stand there gawping with those wet clothes on. Take them off and come over here!"

Afterwards they lay in each other's arms.

"Will you come back for me?" she asked.

"You know I will! But what about Tom?"

"He's been taken care of. My father told him that if you hadn't thrashed him the other night, *he* would have. When Tom tried to argue Dad said that if he came anywhere near me again, he would shoot him! He wasn't joking either!"

Stiles lay, feeling the sun's warmth on his body. It hadn't been such a bad last day at home after all, and it wasn't over yet. Once more he pulled her closer to him.

The wagon which was to take him away from Northaw drew up. Having taken leave of his family, Stiles climbed aboard amid repeated calls of farewell. The wagon lurched forward, and some of the villagers who had turned out to see him off gave a cheer. Stiles back in uniform returned their huzzahs with a mock salute. He looked at his mother, who had cried before he left the cottage, his father and grandfather. As the wagon passed the church he caught sight of a solitary figure, who was both waving and dabbing her eyes. It was Margaret. They had said their goodbyes earlier. Stiles looked back over his shoulder and waved till the bend in the road took him out of view. He wondered when he would see them again.

Cornwall

His leave over, Clark returned, almost reluctantly, to Bristol. Any doubts he'd had as to how Harriet might respond to his proposal of marriage had soon been dispelled. He had been warmly received by her father, John Randall, and Harriet had accepted him readily. The days spent in each other's company had sped by, and the evening of the engagement party, the only stipulation made by Mr Randall, had drawn near. He had insisted that there should be a formal celebration, at which the engagement would be announced. Clark well remembered that evening at her father's house. As he had entered the large hallway, Harriet had been descending the stairs. Clark had thought he had never seen anyone more lovely. She wore a white gown, edged with gold; a diamond pendant hung about her neck, and her fair hair was piled up above her head. As they embraced, her blue eyes sparkled and he led her by the hand to just inside the doorway, where they were to receive their guests. He had never felt so warm and proud and had whispered to her as they walked, "I cannot wait until we are wed!" The pressure of her fingers on his hand had signified agreement.

As Clark waited at Clifton's Bristol house, that evening seemed an age away. The colonel was late for their appointment, one of the privileges of his rank. Clark paced up and down the drawing room. He heard voices in the hall and Mrs Lamb entered the room.

"Alexander, how good to see you!" She held out her hand, and Clark raised it to his lips. "Ben will be with us directly. He is giving instructions as to the care of his new carriage. I understand that you have some news for him. Ah, here he is!" Clifton came into the room.

"There you are, Clark. Good to see you! Been waiting long? Elizabeth and I had some duty calls to make. You must have a look at my new carriage before you depart. It is a very fine carriage, if I may say so!"

Clark said he would certainly be pleased to inspect the vehicle and was about to launch into the reason for his visit when Clifton continued:

"The latest intelligence is that we may be bound for Canada. What do you think of that?" Clark's immediate thought was that was the last thing he had wanted to hear. How would it affect Harriet and their wedding plans? Before he had the opportunity of replying, the colonel spoke again. "I will tell you what *I* think of the idea in one word – nonsensical! I can see no good purpose in putting a regiment of heavy cavalry in that godforsaken country. It's full of copper-coloured savages, not to mention the extremes of weather!"

Clark, although not overjoyed by the news, was becoming increasingly anxious to get to the reason for his calling on the colonel. Elizabeth Lamb detected his anxiety.

"Ben, Alexander has something to ask you!"

"Sorry, my boy, but I got somewhat carried away. What is it you want of me?"

"Sir, I would formally request your permission to marry." Clifton gave his consent immediately and Elizabeth, though equally delighted, felt an inner sadness at the thought that it could never be so for Ben and herself.

Clifton rang the bell for his servant. "I have a fine bottle of Madeira which has been waiting for an occasion such as this. Do be seated, and inform Elizabeth and myself about your intended."

"Corporal Stiles, get the men dismounted and let them eat some biscuit if they want to. There's to be no talking or smoking!"

"Yes, Sergeant," replied Stiles, not yet accustomed to his rank. He gave the order and got down himself. The regiment had moved further west in November and his troop was stationed at Truro. It was five in the morning in early March 1815 and a thick fog had descended in the last hour. Stiles had got his promotion the previous month and he with fifteen men of Number Seven Troop, under Sergeant Horton, were reinforcing the revenue men. They were lying in wait for smugglers on a track which led up from Polperro. The army contingent had come across from Truro the day before and had met the excise men at a prearranged rendezvous. Although they had endeavoured to be as discreet as possible, it was well known that almost everyone in Polperro was engaged in smuggling – or free trading as it was known in these parts – and their presence might well have been detected. Even excise men were susceptible to bribery, and Stiles knew that if he and his comrades had been stationed here, a barrel of brandy might have been left for them to look the other way.

He took a sip of water. In the last few months they had performed similar duties with little success. Now his party had halted and covered the road to Talland, whose churchyard was said to be haunted by devils. If Stiles knew anything, the devils would bear a striking resemblance to local villains. It was rumoured that a consignment of brandy was being brought ashore that night. Some of the gangs were well armed and protected by guards but Stiles hoped that he and his companions had surprise on their side. When they had halted, they had drawn off the track into a gully and were well hidden. All they had to do now was wait.

Sergeant Horton came across. "I shouldn't think it will be long now, or at least they don't seem to think so," he said, jerking his thumb in the direction of the revenue men. "We'll let them pass and ride them down before they get to the church. It's said that the parson is in on it and the squire, but I don't reckon that we'll catch them doing the hard work. Mount up the men and keep those horses still!"

Stiles didn't care for this form of soldiering. There was too much hanging around, often with little result. If they were supposed to be a deterrent to free trading, they didn't seem to be very effective; smuggling went on just the same. Still, orders were orders. The army and the revenue men were at a disadvantage because the locals knew the ground. Any suspicions on their part and they would anchor the brandy barrels below water level and draw them up when the coast was clear. Stiles hoped that if they took that action, the barrels would have to be left for so long that they would become impregnated with seawater. That would serve them right. The contents would change into a foul-smelling liquid. What did they call it down here? Yes, he remembered – stinkibus.

A party of smugglers led a long file of packhorses, each with barrels slung either side, up the long, steep, winding hill from Polperro. They had been delayed by the fog. Some of the men wore a harness, which held two barrels, one of which was carried on the chest and the other behind. The horses' hooves were muffled with sacking to deaden their tread, and apart from the sound of panting from both man and beast all else was silence. On reaching a fork in the road, the majority bore to their right towards Talland, while the remainder headed for the Punch Bowl Inn at Lanreath. The fog, thicker than ever, swirled round, and soon both parties were lost to the sight of each other.

Another hour had passed and it was still dark. Sergeant Horton had placed a picquet some two hundred yards away, in the direction of Polperro. Thomas Hall was the sentry and he had, on the sergeant's instructions, removed any part of his equipment which might rattle and alarm the smugglers. He had been chosen as he could, when occasion demanded, put on a fair turn of speed and he always easily won the regimental foot races. He also possessed an acute sense of hearing. Sergeant Horton's parting words echoed in his brain: "Don't go giving the game away. As soon as you hear them and make sure you are certain, come back as though Old Nick is behind you. Make sure you don't lose your way in this bloody fog. Count the number of paces you take!" Hall lay on the damp earth. It was dark, but through the swirling fog he could just see the track through a gap in the bushes. All was deathly quiet. 'Just as well I'm not superstitious,' he thought, as the silhouettes of the objects around him took on strange shapes and seemed at times to move. He wondered how much longer his vigil would last.

The smuggling party, having left the village behind, considered themselves safe. They were feeling more relaxed and were inclined to be talkative. "Be glad when we gets to the church, Sam," said one to his companion. The reply at first was a grunt of assent followed by, "Won't be long now, John," as he adjusted his harness, the straps of which were cutting into his shoulders. "It's as well that this fog wasn't around earlier when we started to unload the cargo, else those Frenchies wouldn't have seen the signal and we would have turned out for nothing. Still, this fog should keep us safe from prying eyes!" His words were hardly out when the sound of a galloping horse was heard coming towards them.

Thomas Hall had heard the smugglers and was just about to dash off and warn Sergeant Horton, when the lone horseman approached at what was a fast pace for the conditions. It must be someone very familiar with the area to ride like that, he concluded. Hall couldn't see the rider but he heard him pull up and shout in a high thin voice, "Scatter all of you. There's revenue men and soldiers about!"

"Bugger," said Sergeant Horton. "Let's get after them!"

They spurred their horses up onto the road just in time to see vague, indistinct shapes speeding off in all directions. Some had discarded their precious barrels, which lay on the ground. Somewhere a shot was fired. One or two merely stood open mouthed and were soon rounded up. The Dragoons and revenue men fanned out in pursuit of the remainder. Stiles was the first to reach the road and was in time to see a lone rider racing away from him. He urged his horse forward at as fast a pace as he dared. The fog was now patchy and the sky was beginning to lighten. His quarry appeared to be dressed in black and was casting anxious glances over his shoulder. Stiles followed for about a mile, by his reckoning, without gaining ground, but he felt, more importantly, that the gap between them wasn't widening. It was then that the other horse stumbled and threw its rider.

Stiles looked down at the prone figure, sprawled face down and softly moaning. His victim's hat had come off and lay some distance away. Stiles found himself looking at blonde hair, tied by a blue ribbon at the back.

"Come on you. Up on your feet. You're not badly hurt. Just had the wind knocked out of you. Come on. Move!" His captive rose unsteadily at first and knelt before standing upright, then turned and saw the pointed sabre. Stiles was taking no chances but then he saw that it was a woman and knew at once that he had seen her before. He lowered the sword. "It's *you*!" was all he could find to say before the words rushed out. "You were on the London coach back in September."

The woman looked up at the tall dragoon who had dismounted but still towered over her. A flicker of recognition showed in her face, and when she spoke her voice had that husky tone which made Stiles tingle. "Well, sir, I suppose this time instead of protecting me I am to be placed under arrest?"

Stiles decided to play her along. "Yes. First it will be the local jail, until you are brought before the magistrates, who will refer you to the assizes. You will be held in custody meanwhile, and if you have never seen the inside of a prison before, you are in for a rude awakening. Eventually, if you are fortunate, it will mean transportation." His prisoner reacted angrily and without a trace of fear. A red patch appeared on each cheek. Now she stood, feet slightly apart, with hands on hips, and this time spoke with venom.

"If that be so, my man, then do your worst!"

Stiles thought that the joke had gone far enough. He had only meant to teach her a lesson but could only wonder at the change from the defenceless, apparently helpless girl who had descended from the mail coach to the aggressive person standing before him. He was certainly seeing her in a new light and hoped that he had gained his objective by impressing on her the seriousness of the situation.

"I was but jesting, miss. I wouldn't want to see you treated as a common criminal - not someone, if you'll beg my pardon, as young and pretty as you. I only ask one thing of you." A look of alarm spread across the girl's face. He continued. "Never get involved in this sort of thing again. Will you promise me that?" The girl nodded her head. "You may not be so fortunate if there is a next time! Now, what are you doing here?"

"I'm staying with my uncle, Sir Richard Trelawney. One of our servants was walking to Polperro and discovered the trap set for the smugglers. He returned to the house full of alarm." Several thoughts crossed Stiles' mind. It would have been an unusual hour for a person to be abroad. It seemed more likely to him that the servant was one of the gang. He held his tongue and let her continue. "I decided to ride out and warn the free traders. I thought it would be an adventure."

"I suggest you get home, miss, before someone else comes looking." As he spoke he gathered her horse's reins and handed them to her. "I'll just feel his legs and make sure that he's not injured." Having done that and found all to be well, he cupped his hands so that she could help herself into the saddle. It was her turn to look down on him.

"You are a remarkable man, Corporal. It is the second time I find myself in your debt. My name is Jane Trelawney. I am sorry I did not introduce myself earlier but I am sure you will agree that you did not grant me the opportunity."

"I'm Francis Stiles," he replied, "and don't worry - your secret is safe with me." Anxiously he scanned the horizon. The fog had cleared completely. "I really think you ought to be on your way!" he said with reluctance, not at all wishing her to be gone.

152

"If you think that is the wisest course, then I will go. Thank you, Francis Stiles." Gently she urged her horse forward and rode towards the skyline. Stiles, gazing after her, saw her turn and wave. Then she was gone.

On rejoining the others Stiles reported to Sergeant Horton that he had lost his quarry. "He had too much of a start on me. Must know the country like the back of his hand." He looked at the captives, who stood with their hands bound behind them and looking thoroughly dejected and miserable. He couldn't bear to think of her in that situation.

"Corporal," said Horton, "I'm marching the prisoners to Bodmin Gaol. I'll leave you four men to gather the discarded barrels, but you will have to wait until a wagon arrives and then you will escort it back to Truro. Horton, who was nobody's fool, had his suspicions about Stiles' yarn but knew that he couldn't prove anything. 'That'll teach him to come back with some cock and bull tale,' he thought as he dismissed them.

Sir Richard Trevelyan nervously paced backwards and forwards across the hallway of Talland House. The heels of his riding boots echoed as they struck the stone floor. It was daylight and Jane had not returned. He had not been aware of her absence until his manservant had entered his bedroom and shaken him awake, with a note of extreme agitation in his voice as he feared what his master would say.

"Sir Richard, Miss Jane has ridden off to warn the smugglers."

"Smugglers, man! What are you saying and how is my niece involved? Now calm down and tell me."

The servant related how Price, the gardener, had come running back to the house and had excitedly told that the revenue men and soldiers were lying in wait. "Miss Jane heard the commotion and appeared in her night attire. On hearing the news she ordered a horse to be saddled and in the meantime quickly returned to her room to dress. We tried to stop her but she would have none of it. She took a hat and a cloak belonging to one of the grooms and galloped off."

Sir Richard looked at his watch yet again. Jane had been gone well over two hours now and her prolonged absence could only mean trouble. He hoped she had not been taken. What was that? He heard hoof beats crossing the cobbled yard. Was it her? He rushed to the door and was just in time to see his niece dismounting.

After leaving Stiles, Jane Trelawney had returned to Talland House by a roundabout route. As a precaution she had thrown away the hat and let down her hair. If challenged, she would say she was out for an early morning ride. What should she tell her uncle? He would be furious and quite rightly so. Everyone in these parts was aware of smugglers, and although Uncle Richard did not discourage them he would scarcely approve of her involvement. He was like a father to her and had provided parental love and guidance since her parents had died in a coaching accident when she was but a small child. Jane had told her uncle about the dragoon who had saved them all on the London-bound coach. What a coincidence that he should turn up again! Francis Stiles certainly had a way with him. She thought back to how he had teased her, and if truth be told she had been very frightened at the prospect of being transported. In retrospect, she was ashamed that she had thought that he was suggesting something quite improper. She would have to tell her uncle the truth, but overriding everything was a mental picture of the face of Francis Stiles. She knew that she would very much like to meet him again but next time in the right circumstances.

"Jane," her uncle cried with a note of relief in his voice. "Where have you been? I was beginning to fear the worst. What has detained you so long?"

She related her tale and described her flight across the moor. "I was pursued by a corporal of the Dragoons until my horse stumbled and I was thrown. He told me to get up, and as I turned towards him I did not at first recall his face, until he identified himself as the soldier who saved us all on the London mail coach! I am unsure who, of the pair of us, was the most surprised!"

"He let you go free?" her uncle interrupted. "Yes, after threatening me with arrest and deportation, in an attempt to dissuade me from further adventures."

"Does he know who you are?"

"I had to tell him my name and that I am your niece."

Sir Richard's blood ran cold and he looked out of the window expecting at any moment to see the revenue men and dragoons appear. "What do you know of this man, and can we trust him?"

"His name is Francis Stiles, a corporal in the 1st Dragoons, stationed at Truro. That is all I know."

"But can we *trust* him, Jane?"

154

"I have implicit faith in him," his niece replied. By the look in her eyes Richard Trelawney was quite sure that whilst she might trust him, she was certainly smitten.

An hour later Sir Richard, his doubts unresolved, sat in his study deep in thought. He did not like threats to the security of his family, particularly when he was not in control of the situation. Finally, he made up his mind. There was no point in worrying – as always, if there was a problem the only way to meet it was head on. He raised the window and called, "Price. Will you come in please? I want to talk to you."

Price knew only too well why his presence was required. He wasn't accustomed to entering the house except at Christmas time when his master entertained the staff and their families. Apprehensively, he scraped the mud off his boots, entered by a side door, and walked along a passage which led to the hall. The door to the study was open and Sir Richard was waiting.

"Come in and close the door!" Sir Richard was seated behind his desk, and Price, hat in hand, stood before him. "Take a seat!" This was unheard of. Price selected a cane bottomed chair, conscious that his clothes were not clean, and sat. "Price, you know of my niece's involvement with the free traders earlier today?"

"Yes, Sir Richard."

"Well, I have reason to believe that she may be in danger, which may have implications for all of us." He paused to clear his throat and continued. "Miss Jane was apprehended by a corporal of Dragoons, and it is sufficient for you to know that he let her go free. The man's name is Francis Stiles and he is barracked at Truro. You have been in the King's service?"

"Yes, sir. With the 32nd of Foot."

"I am going to Truro within the hour and I'm taking you with me. I will leave it to you to make discreet enquiries concerning the corporal. You will know the soldier's favourite haunts. Find out what opinions others hold of him and most importantly is he trustworthy? We will lodge at the Red Lion, so if you consider it appropriate you may bring him to me. Be extremely careful and do not raise suspicions!"

Two days later, Clifton, at his Exeter headquarters, received some disturbing news. Napoleon had escaped from Elba and landed in France. He summoned the officers immediately available. Dorville,

Radclyffe, Clark, and Phipps presented themselves. Clifton informed them of Napoleon's audacity and continued, "Twelve regiments of cavalry are being sent to The Netherlands as a precautionary measure but I regret to tell you that the Royals have not been included in their number. It remains to be seen how successful 'Boney' will be. Much will depend on how many regiments which have sworn allegiance to King Louis go over to him. One thing I can tell you is that we are no longer in danger of going to Canada."

"Sir," said Phillip Dorville, "can you not make representations for us to be sent to The Netherlands? It does not sit well with me that the regiment, veterans of the Peninsula, should be employed as excise officers and constables when there may be real work ahead!"

"I fully intend," Clifton replied, "to write to the Adjutant General to ask that he request His Royal Highness, the commander-in-chief, that the Royals be sent to The Netherlands."

Stiles entered the guardroom at Truro Barracks just as the clock over the main gate struck one in the morning. A faint fetid smell greeted him – a combination of stale sweat and tobacco. He had returned from visiting the sentries, who, while not due for relief for another hour, needed checking on from time to time to ensure that they had not skulked off for a smoke. After all the years he had spent in the army he knew all the dodges, and many a time, particularly in cold weather, he had found temporary shelter away from his post. This night was mild but windy and all had been in order. He had ensured that his steps rang out loudly as he went on his rounds. Sergeant Horton, the guard commander, was asleep and snoring in a chair, which was precariously balanced on its two back legs. He opened one eye. "All well, Corporal?"

"Yes, Sergeant," Stiles replied. "Another hour yet," referring to the next guard change. He took a seat behind the table. The fire in the grate had burnt low and the relief guard, dimly illuminated by the light of the candles, were asleep on their cots, fully attired. Their carbines were held in nearby racks. No alcohol was allowed during the duty and they had eaten their supper earlier. One prisoner was in the cells, a man named Watkis, who had returned drunk and had easily attracted attention. Sergeant Horton had ordered him to be locked up, but if previous experience was anything to go by he would be released before the guard dismounted about five hours from now.

This always seemed to be an eerie time of night. It was almost as though time stood still and yet it was still less exhausting than four o'clock when the final two hours of duty commenced. Thinking back to when he'd been a private, it didn't seem to matter that you had been asleep for the preceding four hours, limbs seemed slow to move and the brain was numbed. Stiles could recall patrolling the barracks in a dream-like state.

For some reason he could not get Jane Trevelyan out of his mind. He was certain that he would never see her again, but that's what he'd thought the first time. He'd dearly like to see her, but what was the point? She certainly wouldn't entertain him as a suitor, and although his understanding with Margaret wasn't formalised he felt guilty. Was he being unfair to her? He had no doubt that Jim Burnside wouldn't have any such inhibitions. "Make hay while the sun shines" would be his attitude, and with his charm he would get away with it. Then there was Napoleon's escape from Elba, and what was proposed was a disgrace to the regiment. Why should they have to remain in the West Country when there might be fighting to be done? He realised that his preoccupation had lasted for almost an hour. He rose and shook the sergeant, who without prompting said, "Get the relief ready."

Price had become familiar with his hiding place, in the alley, opposite the barrack gates. He had spent a lot of time there since his arrival in Truro. The sentries were alert and spoke to no one except when addressed by a superior, which was only to be expected. He had to find a way of making contact with Corporal Stiles. As each day passed, Sir Richard was becoming more anxious to meet him, and he might even have to throw in the name of Miss Jane. He could hardly send Stiles a note. He must have a favourite drinking haunt. Patience was required. Well, he had plenty of that but time was all important.

A group of soldiers emerged through the gate, and Price decided to follow them. Eventually they entered an inn, and Price trailed behind them. The group seated themselves and called for ale. Price did likewise, having taken a seat nearby so that he could listen to their conversation. They were discussing Napoleon. "It's a bastard us being stuck down here when we could be in Belgium," said one. There was a general murmur of agreement followed by a thoughtful pause.

Price took his chance. "My old regiment is there!"

Six pairs of eyes focused on him. "You're an old soldier then?" enquired a large weather-beaten private. "What regiment might that be?"

"The 32nd. What else, if you're from these parts? They were one of the first to go. I served with them for nigh on twenty years before being invalided out."

"Come and join us!" The invitation came from the soldier who had spoken to him. "The name's Jim Burnside." He introduced the others.

Price ordered more ale all round, thanking his luck that Sir Richard had given him an advance against such expenditure. "What's it like in your lot?" he enquired.

"Boring!" seemed to be the consensus. "Nothing but playing excisemen being stuck down here," said Jim.

"Yes," they agreed on enquiry, "they had known worst places, but having spent five years on active service in the Peninsula – not that that had been exciting all the time – was much better than what they were presently doing.

"Just got back from Polperro," said a tall ginger-haired lad.

"Right muck-up, that was," said another. "We were after smugglers and were dashing round in the fog looking for them."

Price was pleased no one thought to ask him from whence he came.

More ale followed and tongues became looser.

"Watch yourself, Jack!" said one soldier to another. "Sergeant Horton and Corporal Stiles are not in charge of the guard tonight. If you have too much, you could spend some days 'inside'."

Price, hardly believing his luck, pricked up his ears. "Corporal Stiles, you say? *I* was once a corporal. What sort of man is he?"

"Firm but fair," was the common feeling. "With us in the Peninsula, he was," said Jack. "Jim here is a friend of his and has known him as long as he's been in the regiment. Since his promotion he can't be seen in public with us. He's in the town today and usually goes to the Angel."

Price ordered more ale and then, feigning urgent business, said, "Time for this old soldier to be on his way. See you again, lads." Amid shouts of general farewell he left to find Stiles.

Stiles sat alone a table in the tap-room of the Angel. He wasn't thinking about much in particular, when a man, whom he took to be in his fifties, short in stature and slightly stooped, came to sit nearby.

The newcomer put the flagon to his lips, took a hearty drink, and said, "That's better!" He then looked at Stiles as though he had just noticed him.

Stiles, more to pass the time, said, "Been hard at work then?"

"Not today," replied the stranger. "I'm a gardener and work for Sir Richard Trevelyan over at Talland House near Polperro."

The information came as a shock, but Stiles was not left wondering for long. The man continued. "If you are Corporal Stiles, I have a message for you." He saw the look of surprise on the corporal's face followed by a narrowing of his eyes.

"How do you know of me?" said Stiles.

Price didn't answer the question but said, "Sir Richard would like to meet you." Then he lowered his voice to a conspiratorial tone. "I believe you are acquainted with his niece, Miss Jane. If it suits you, we can go now to the Red Lion, where he has taken rooms."

Warning bells sounded in Stiles' head. He heard himself saying, "What does he want with me?"

"Nothing to worry about," said Price, "but will you come?" Stiles agreed, swallowed the remainder of his drink, and followed Price as he left the room.

They entered the Red Lion by a back door which led from the yard. "It will enable us to avoid the public rooms," explained Price. He led the way along a passage, up a flight of stairs to the first floor, and turned to his right. Price stopped and knocked.

"Come in," boomed a deep voice. Price motioned Stiles to wait, then opened the door and entered the room. Stiles heard a rumble of voices but was not kept waiting long before he was ushered in.

A large, florid-faced man bore down on him and vigorously shook his hand. "Good to meet you, Corporal. I am Richard Trevelyan. My niece has told me about you. Please take a seat!" He waved towards an armchair. "Would you care for some refreshment?"

Stiles wondered what Jane had told her uncle. He declined further drink. It was time to keep a clear head. They exchanged a few pleasantries.

"I am deeply indebted to you, Corporal," Sir Richard began. "You have protected my niece on two occasions and I would like to know if there is some way I can show my appreciation?" Stiles noticed that Richard Trelawney's hand moved in the direction of a leather bag, which unmistakably held coins, and immediately his face hardened.

"There is no need for that, Sir Richard. On the first occasion all of us on the coach were in danger. The other morning, when I caught Miss Jane, I told her – and I will say it again now to you – that her secret is safe with me. I was glad to be of service!"

Richard Trelawney realised that he had misjudged and thereby offended the young man and he now looked him straight in the eyes and said, "You will appreciate that not having made your acquaintance previously, I could not be certain as to your character, but I now know that I have misjudged you. You are undoubtedly an honest and thoroughly trustworthy young man! Nevertheless, are you certain that there is no way I can help? Not necessarily now but perhaps in the future. What will you do when you leave the army?"

"That could be some way off, sir," replied Stiles. "I was a farm labourer before I enlisted, but I have no desire to follow that trade again."

"Well, Stiles, if and when the time comes and you find yourself in need of employment or a testimonial, do not hesitate to contact me. I shall not forget you and neither will my niece, who by the way has asked me to give you this letter. I hope we will meet again." With that they made their farewells and Stiles left the inn to return to the barracks.

For what must have been the tenth time he reread Jane Trevelyan's letter. After thanking him for his gallant action she concluded by saying:

> *I do trust that your generous deed has not been a source of trouble. You will recall that I turned to wave to you and I am certain I saw, for at least a moment, a horseman, who might have seen us together.*
>
> *I will always remember you with affection and hope that some day we may meet again.*
>
> *Yours*
>
> *Jane Trevelyan*

Stiles guessed that the mystery horseman could have been Sergeant Horton. That would account for the sergeant appearing to disbelieve him. But he didn't care. Horton had said no more about it. She hoped to meet him again. He hoped so too.

Clifton at last received what turned out to be a disappointing reply to his letter. He sat reading the response and having digested the contents threw the letter angrily on the table.

"Bad news, Ben?" asked Elizabeth.

"Yes, my dear," he replied in a despondent tone. "The Adjutant General says that the Royals cannot possibly be spared. He says that the coast duty is too important, particularly in Cornwall. What is wrong with the man? Let us pray he has a change of heart!"

His prayer was answered when, late on the 21st April, orders were received for the regiment to proceed immediately to Canterbury and prepare for immediate embarkation.

Belgium

They had sailed at four o'clock in the morning from Ramsgate Harbour, and although he could not yet see the Belgian coast Clark felt that they must be getting near. For the past half hour or so some heavy-looking boats, with huge lug sails, had put in an appearance, which was surely an indication of an imminent sighting of land. He stood on deck, towards the prow, holding onto a stay for support and conscious of the water thrusting under the ship's bows. Clark could clearly see the other vessels carrying the remainder of his squadron and Colonel Clifton with his headquarters. They had been the last of the regiment to leave England.

Clark drew his cloak more tightly round him. The day was overcast with a chilly breeze, and the sea, which was rough, reflected the gun-metal greyness of the sky. He thought of Harriet and her letter, now in his pocket, which he had received two days since. She had urged him to be careful for her sake, an instruction with which he fully intended to comply, but his safety was not entirely in his own hands. By all accounts the French Army had given Napoleon its full support after his escape from Elba, and had reinstated him as Emperor. Even Ney, who had promised King Louis that he would bring the traitor back in chains, had once more fallen under his spell. Clark heard footsteps on the deck and, on turning, saw George Gunning lurching towards him as he moved quickly from one hand-hold to another.

"I have been talking to the Mate," said Gunning. He estimates that we should soon see the coastline and should reach Ostend by two o'clock."

The first sighting was hardly inspiring. A long line of sandhills stretched as far as the eye could see, behind which lay the grey buildings of Ostend, with the spires of Mittlekirk and Nieuport rising above the dunes. Clark didn't rate the place and said as much to

Gunning, who readily agreed. As the ship neared the coast, as if to disprove his comment, through gaps in the sandhills could be seen a rich green level countryside, with numerous villages, farms and small woodlands.

Gunning excused himself with, "Must go and ensure that the men are ready to disembark."

As there was nothing that Clark could usefully accomplish by going below, he decided to remain on deck. The ship was now approaching the harbour entrance and Clark saw the port before him. A long mole, to his left, ran out to a small fort, behind which was a long, curving sandy beach. Straight ahead lay a dense mass of shipping, so dense in fact that it appeared to act as a bar to further progress. Where were they to berth? His unspoken question was soon answered when the vessel was quickly turned and the ship was driven hard and fast onto the sands.

Stiles, quite naked and up to his neck in water, could hardly credit it. No sooner had the ship beached, when a naval officer with some sailors had boarded and, without so much as a 'by your leave', the horses had been hoisted out of the hold and dropped into the sea. The expression on Captain Clark's face had been a picture. First a look of complete amazement, followed by a colouring of his features as he saw what was happening. Anyone who had served under Clark would have recognised the danger signals, and his mood had been evidenced by the tone of his voice as he spat out his words, icily at the navy man.

"What is the meaning of this outrage, sir? What are you doing?"

Stiles guessed that the sailor had heard it all before. "Can't help it," he had replied. "No business of mine. The Duke's orders are positive. You are to be off-loaded as quickly as possible." Despite Clark's further protests the unloading had continued. It was then that Clark had given the order: "Over the side, men!" Stiles and the others had stripped off their uniforms and gone down a rope ladder into the sea.

The waters of the North Sea, even given the protection of the harbour, broke in waves over them and were icy cold. The horses, having suddenly been removed from a warm hold, kicked and thrashed about.

"Put your backs into it!" Stiles shouted and on taking a pace forward disappeared from sight. He had stepped into a deep hollow in the sand. Stiles surfaced, coughing and spluttering, to be greeted by hoots of laughter.

A voice called down to him from the ship. It was Lieutenant Gunning. "Corporal Stiles. Now that you have provided us with entertainment, will you be so good enough to get the horses onto the beach!"

Stiles and the others managed, by grasping the horses' bridles, pushing and cajoling, to get them ashore, where they stood shivering with matted coats. Certain of the men, deputed as horse handlers, were almost pleading for their garments as the cold wind whipped round their half frozen bodies. They had to wait until all the animals and equipment had been recovered. By then the tide had receded and the arms and clothing removed from the ship. Fires made from collected driftwood were lit, and as he dressed Stiles felt his blood begin to circulate again.

Colonel Clifton came over to Clark, passing, as he did, groups of women and children in search of their husbands and fathers, but not daring to leave unattended their heaps of belongings. Clifton wondered, not for the first time, about the advisability of bringing families on campaign. Most of the time they would suffer hardship and were often exposed to danger. Still, the alternative did not bear thinking about. Apart from the lucky (if that was the correct word) six wives and any children, the Army washed its hands of the remainder once a regiment left England and the dependants were left to fend for themselves.

"Not the best of receptions, Alexander," he said to Clark. "Get one of your horses saddled and come with me. We should ascertain where our accommodation lies. I would wish to be settled before nightfall."

Later they rode along the quay, which was thronged with troops, wagons and horses, and into Ostend, which was crowded with army personnel. After enquiry they found the town commandant. They were not surprised to hear that there was no accommodation to be had and were advised to ride the seven miles to Ghistel.

"You will need to draw rations before you depart," the officer informed them. "I would suggest that you send your quartermaster to the commissariat and give him your requirements." They returned to the beach, and after a wait of four hours the rations arrived. In darkness, through steadily falling rain, Clifton led them along the Rue

Madeleine, where a solitary lamp cast its light on the glistening cobbles. It was through a nearby gate that they passed into the countryside.

The sun shone from an almost cloudless sky. It was a splendid day for the review of the entire British Cavalry. The Royals' horses had recovered from their rough handling when being disembarked at Ostend; they had lost their troublesome coughs and their black coats glistened in the strong light. All forty-eight squadrons of Cavalry were on parade. Household troops, Dragoon guards, Dragoons, Light Dragoons, and batteries of Horse Artillery awaited inspection by Lord Wellington and Marshal Blucher. Clifton sat motionless on his horse in front of the Royals, who were drawn up in review order. They were the right hand regiment of the Union Brigade. By inclining his head to the left he could see Hamilton, commanding The Scots Greys, and, further on, Muter, of the Inniskillings, similarly positioned in front of their regiments. The brigadier, Sir William Ponsonby, had recently ridden onto the parade ground, past the Household Brigade.

Clifton was happy that conditions had improved in the last ten days. The men were in good heart and ready for battle, wherever and whenever it should come. He was perfectly satisfied that they would acquit themselves well. All now enjoyed comfortable quarters at Ninove, and Elizabeth Lamb had joined him. He was certain in his own mind that her presence would not interfere with his military duties. In fact, apart from the obvious advantage, he was glad of her company at the many balls and race meetings which had been arranged. What more could a man possibly ask for? Clifton mused on. There was nothing the Army, with its Prussian allies could not accomplish. He was damned if he would accept the arguments – or were they protestations – put forward by French officers, supposedly loyal to King Louis XVIII, that Napoleon was invincible. Many an argument had developed over the supper table at the Lion d'Or and the Hotel de Flandres, during their brief stay in Ghent, with French officers who thought that the Allies could not win.

There was a flourish of trumpets, followed by the commencement of a twenty-one gun salute. Wellington with Blucher and a vast entourage, which Clifton knew included the French Marshal Marmont, the only Marshal of France not to join Napoleon, rode slowly onto the parade ground. Lieutenant-General The Earl of Uxbridge, commanding the cavalry, moved forward to receive the reviewing party and dropped his sword by way of salute. By the look of the uniforms almost every nation in Europe was represented. Clifton noticed that the Duke preferred more sober dress. Eventually it was the Royals' turn to come under scrutiny. As he approached, Clifton saw a look of recognition in the Duke's eyes.

"Clifton. How goes it with you? I must say your regiment looks in splendid condition!" Clifton was hardly given time to reply before Wellington turned to his companion and addressed him in French. "Marshal, may I present Colonel Clifton, who commands the First Regiment of Dragoons. He and this fine regiment of his served with me in the Peninsula." Clifton noticed the keen eyes surveying him and his men. So this was the famous Marshal Blucher, a tall, broadly built, moustached man, bedecked in Hussar uniform for the occasion. It was said that he regarded his troops as his children and that they would follow him anywhere. Clifton had been told that he was over seventy years of age. Well, if he was, he did not seem to lack either in energy or enthusiasm. Later Clifton recalled Wellington's parting words: "It will be a stiff fight when it comes and we must win!"

Lieutenant Jean Lacroix, Eagle Bearer of the 105th Regiment of the Line, awoke in his billet in the town of Solre-sur-Sambre on the morning of the 14th June. He yawned, stretched, and rubbed the sleep from his eyes. The strong, bright sunlight shone directly into his eyes and the glare made it difficult to see beyond his immediate position. The regiment, which formed part of the First Corps d'Armée, commanded by Lieutenant-General Count d'Erlon, had arrived in the town while it was still dark and had been warned that they would be crossing the river early the next day. Not too long to wait now.

He looked across the room to where the Tricolour, on its blue pole and surmounted by the Eagle, rested against the wall. The draped colour, when unfurled, displayed the regiment's battle honours and that momentous moment when he had received The Eagle from Napoleon's hands was burnt into his memory. As Premier Porte-Aigle he had sworn to defend it to the death. His two protectors, as he referred to them, otherwise Sergeants Giraud and Mesnil, more renowned for their brawn than their brains, sat with their legs stretched out in front of them and their backs to the wall, with their halberds alongside. Both men were fast asleep.

Lacroix reflected. The return of the Emperor, to whom he was devoted, had led to the reappearance of the army in all its former glory, with every confidence in its leaders. The veterans, of which Lacroix considered himself to be one, enthusiastically looked forward to the distinction of erasing the stain on the country's honour. France was surrounded by its enemies – Prussia, Russia, Austria, and Great Britain. Now the Prussians and the British were close to hand, and once they were defeated their other allies must think again. Once more the cry of "*Vive l'Empereur*" would ring round Europe.

Lacroix had no doubts. The raising, clothing, drilling, and organising of the Army had taken place in a very short period of time. There were always more recruits – in the main, old soldiers – than available weapons and equipment. Vast numbers of workmen were employed in the manufacture of arms and ammunition, the repair of fortresses and the erection of entrenched works. It was impossible to travel anywhere without meeting continuous processions of guns and wagons bearing the material of war.

Lacroix shouted across the room, "Wake up, you two!"

Giraud and Mesnil woke with a start, convinced for a moment that the enemy was attacking. Both men quickly got to their feet and prepared to rush outside. Then they saw that Lacroix was still resting on the bed. Mesnil noticed him first and nudged Giraud to draw his attention. Mesnil smiled sheepishly.

"I could have sworn I heard someone call. Must have been a false alarm."

"Now you are awake," said Lacroix, "get yourselves outside and find out what there is to eat."

Later a bugle sounded to assemble the regiment to hear Napoleon's Order of the Day. It was read by the colonel. Its final message, which brought hope to every heart and a tear to many an eye, including Lacroix's, stated, "To every Frenchman who has a heart the moment is now arrived to conquer or die!"

Stiles was brought to his senses on the regiment being ordered to turn out at a little after four in the morning of the 16th June. Three days biscuit was issued and after looking to their arms and equipment the Royals moved off. Stiles, in Number Seven Troop, although nothing as such had been said, felt that contact with the enemy was imminent. He had been with the troop ever since his promotion to the rank of corporal, which was just over three months ago. He had every confidence in Lieutenant Gunning, who commanded his troop, Captain Clark, who commanded the squadron, and the men, who with the exception of a few 'Johnny Newcomes', were Peninsula veterans. Until recently there had been doubt as to who was to command the army. Rumours had been rife. Some said that it would be the Prince of Orange, more commonly referred to either as the 'Young Frog' or 'Slender Billy', who would have the honour. He and his fellows went mad with joy when a General Order announced that the Duke was in charge. What glorious news! Nosey has got command! Won't we give them a drubbing now! They had celebrated far into the night in a general state of intoxication. Men had puffed furiously at their pipes; drunk powerful Holland gin; danced, sung, and nostalgically recalled Peninsula deeds.

They had been marching for some hours and the road ahead was thronged with troops, guns and wagons. There was such congestion that from time to time the column came to a halt. Whenever an opportunity occurred the cavalry cut across country to hasten their progress, which so far could only be regarded as slow. Now they approached a large town and Stiles eased himself in his saddle. For some time they had ridden to the sound of the guns and the noise of the cannonade had grown in intensity. Judging by the volume of smoke above the trees, Stiles supposed that the battle must be on the hill beyond the town, which he heard Gunning say was Nivelle. On entering, they found that most of the populace was in the streets, generally milling around and reacting with a mixture of excitement and fear as explosion followed explosion. Clattering peals of musketry were plainly audible and the effect on the groups of civilians was to send them running around like sheep. Those who were not on the streets hung out of the windows or stood in doorways. Stiles soon became aware of a different attitude shown by some, who stared with open hostility at the passing troops, by now jaded and dusty. 'They can't wait to see us killed,' he thought. They met the first of the wounded Belgian and Dutch soldiers, sometimes attended by six, eight, ten or more men, apparently untouched, who were expressing the opinion that all was lost.

Further down the column, Lieutenant Charles Bridges watched the growing number of wounded with increasing apprehension. Ever since Maguilla, when that fool Strenowitz had planned that ambush, he had lived in dread of being either wounded or killed. He looked at the injured as they passed, some with blood pouring from them. He saw a man with a head wound. Another reeled with uncertain steps, his face as pale as a sheet and bearing a terrified look. A soldier passed supported between two comrades. Blood streamed down his face and his knees buckled at every step. The blood created a growing stain on the grey overcoat, rolled and carried on the man's left shoulder. Not for the first time Bridges cursed his stupidity. Why, when he returned from France in 1814, had he not sold his commission? If only he'd known that after what at first sight had seemed to be the possibility of a lasting peace, England and France would so soon be at each others' throats. Perhaps the battle might be over before they reached it, or they might be ordered to withdraw. He would give anything to be able to walk round his father's constituency in Berkshire. Anything would be preferable to this.

Clark led his squadron up the hill beyond Nivelle and along a fine road bordered by elm trees. He expected that they would soon enter the field of battle as the cannon's roar sounded ever closer. Suddenly the firing slackened and became all the time more intermittent. Clark was uncertain as to their precise location until the new adjutant, John Shipley, rode up and told him that they were at a place called Quatre Bras. It was apparent that a fierce battle had been fought, as the tired horses began to stumble over the bodies of the dead. Clark, who would have freely admitted to being tired himself, thought in a somewhat detached way that their mounts must indeed be fatigued. He knew from past experience that horses preferred to step over, rather than on, corpses. There were voices all about him. Commands were being given. Men enquired after comrades, most of whom must be lying lifeless on the ground. Not all were still. Some cried for help or raised themselves as best they could, with imploring gestures. Bugles sounded and echoed as the noise of the fighting had subsided. The peace was only occasionally shattered by the growl of a cannon or the rattle of muskets.

The evening was warm and the light was rapidly failing. The dark shapes of men moved in the increasing darkness against the background of a wood to his right, and Clark wondered what the outcome of the day had been. He was certain of one thing – the battle had been fought without the assistance of cavalry and he regretted that they were too late. Now they were approaching a cluster of buildings where four roads met. This must be Quatre Bras. Orders were given to bivouac in an adjoining wheat field, beyond the crossroads, where the stalks of the crops rose five to six feet in the air. Clark gave the order to dismount and had barely got his feet to the ground when the adjutant appeared.

"Colonel Clifton's compliments. Will you please have the horses linked in column, with their saddles and bridles in place, in the event we may be needed as a matter of urgency." That accomplished, the men sank to the ground alongside their equally weary steeds.

Lacroix cursed under his breath. It would not do to show his feelings openly. They'd had a delayed start that day, the 16th June, having spent the night at Marchienne-au-Pont, which was only seventeen miles from the start line which they had crossed yesterday morning. It seemed to him that things were already starting to go wrong, but he supposed that delays were inevitable considering the number of troops on the advance. The Army had become too strung out and most of the morning had been spent in regrouping. Now that they were marching once again, each step taken raised his spirits, and the men about him seemed to be as enthusiastic as before. There were spontaneous shouts of "*Vive l'Empereur!*" and "*Vive la France!*", to which Lacroix added his own voice. Apart from beating the hated English, the ultimate prize lay before them – the capture and plunder of Brussels. Had not the brigade commander, General Bourgeois, promised them rich pickings?

The day wore on. Lacroix was aware that the 2nd Corps was to the front and the two corps totalled a formidable forty thousand men. The numbers inevitably meant slow progress. He felt an impatience that it would all be over before they got there. He was hot and sweaty and the dust thrown up by the thousands of marching feet hung in the air.

Lacroix could feel the grit on his tongue and on glancing at his companions he saw rivulets of perspiration cutting through the dust, caked on their faces. It gave them a strange macabre appearance and no doubt he looked the same to them.

A colonel galloped past towards the head of the column, with the result that they were ordered off in a different direction. The word was passed down that they were now to take on the Prussians and were now bound for St Amand.

Mesnil called across to Giraud. "As long as we are to fight I suppose it doesn't matter who it is."

"I would prefer it to be the British!" Giraud retorted. "My brother was killed at Salamanca."

From time to time further messengers enquired after their progress. St Amand was reached but they took no part in the battle and were soon on their way back in the direction from which they had come. This time it was said that their destination was Frasnes. From what Lacroix overheard, Marshal Ney was in desperate need of them, at some place called Quatre Bras. The feeling of frustration once more came over him. All this marching and countermarching, and as yet they had not fired a shot in anger. Hopefully this would soon be corrected. That night, still some way short of Quatre Bras and to the rear of Frasnes, the corps bivouacked. The battle was over, so his colonel, Lebreuf, was informed. The British had held out.

Stiles woke to the sound of muskets popping. It was dark, he felt tired, and at first wondered where he was. He put a tentative hand out from under his blanket and felt the cold damp earth and stalks of straw. It was strange. He had dreamt of Margaret. They were making love on the edge of the lake in Nyn Park and they had lain on the bank, locked in each other's arms, as though reluctant to let go. Reality focused his mind. Was it only last September, nine months ago, when he had walked across the fields about Northaw just after the harvest?

The firing increased, but apart from himself only John Williams, a fellow corporal in the troop, appeared to be awake. The rest slept on regardless.

"What's happening, Francis?" asked Williams.

"Sounds as though something's up," Stiles said. "Whatever it is it can't be much, otherwise they'd have all of us mounted. By the look of this lot," he said, pointing towards the sleeping men, "it will take more than a few musket shots to rouse them."

They both looked towards their front but could see nothing. The darkness was impenetrable.

"Must be about an hour to dawn," Williams said. "Hardly worthwhile trying to get back to sleep."

"I don't know about that," Stiles replied. "Remember the old saying – never miss an opportunity to eat, sleep, or relieve yourself."

Williams ignored the comment. He was in too sombre a mood. "Wonder what's going to happen today? I've had this feeling ever since we set out yesterday that if there's a battle, I'm not going to survive. The thought has been so much on my mind that I've lain awake all night."

"You can't go by feelings!" said Stiles. "Feelings don't mean a thing!"

"Why do I feel this way then?"

Stiles could tell by Williams' tone of voice that he had not succeeded in reassuring him. He was relieved when hoof beats drew near and what Stiles took for a patrol passed nearby. He could just about make out the blur of white faces. "Must have been that lot," he said and with that he lay down and was immediately asleep. Williams lay, eyes wide open, staring into the dark.

Clifton turned the men out before dawn. The regiment stood to and was dismissed to take breakfast when the French showed no signs of activity. Some time later Clifton sent for Dorville, Wyndham and Clark, his three squadron leaders.

"Sir William Ponsonby tells me that the Russians took a beating yesterday at Ligny and have retired to Wavre. On the Duke's orders the Army is to withdraw to conform. I don't know what the infantry will make of it. By all accounts they put up a stiff fight against the French, and but for the Prussians we would be in a good position. Still, we cannot remain here with our flank exposed. The cavalry is to cover the withdrawal and will therefore be the last to leave. Alexander, the task for your squadron is to transport the wounded back to safety. Obviously those with serious wounds will be left behind. They would not profit by the journey and could not possibly bear the rigours of travelling on horseback. You are to join us later near the wood of Mont St Jean, where, other things being equal, we will bivouac for the night. I cannot be more precise at the moment. Go down to the inn at Quatre Bras to receive your instructions. Charles and Phillip, be so good as to inform your officers what is to happen. I will talk to you again when I have more detail."

Stiles stood among the trampled wheat. The wood to his right, from which he'd heard sounds of battle last evening, stretched away into the distance, following the line of the road. Some way off he could see a village, beyond which the road ascended, and there, quite plainly, was the bivouac of the French Army. Some half-hearted skirmishing was going on and the faint sound of firing was carried back on the light breeze. It was hot. The heavy and oppressive air pressed down, making breathing difficult. He transferred his gaze back towards his own lines, where the infantry lay about cleaning their arms or tending cooking pots which were poised over numerous fires, from which wreaths of smoke rose gently on the still air. He had already eaten and for the time being felt satisfied. At least the rations had caught up with them. He hadn't relished the thought of fighting on an empty stomach. Stiles had seen Captain Clark ride off earlier but now saw him returning and calling his officers to him. He said to no one in particular, "We'll soon find out what it's all about."

Stiles and the other members of the squadron led their horses across the narrow bridge at Genappe and up the main street, closely lined by houses on either side. The clatter of the hooves echoed back loudly in the confined space. In most cases men lay draped over saddles, although some were able to sit astride. From time to time Stiles had solicitously enquired after his charge's condition, but on receiving only a grunted reply for his trouble he decided that enough was enough. He would enquire no more. The wounded man was a Highlander with a nasty looking leg wound, who now and again groaned softly. Stiles, left to his own thoughts, smiled as he recalled the sight of the man's bare arse, exposed for all to see, when his kilt had been lifted as he was being hoisted head first over the saddle. The procession, preceded by a few carriages wound its way slowly along.

When they had been given the news of their duty, Stiles had seen a look of relief on Williams' face. He had almost smiled. When they had left their overnight camping ground, they had gone back down the road to Quatre Bras, and near to the farm had passed a large number of dead Highlanders and French cuirassiers thickly strewn about. One Scotsman had been sprawled on his back with his right leg drawn up. He had a deep wound in his belly and a look of utter hatred on his face. His musket, with bayonet attached, lay at his side, and he was surrounded by dead Frenchmen. He had taken a few with him, which at least proved the 'Tin Bellies' weren't invincible. The smell of death hung heavily on the air, and the blood, which had at one time seeped from wounds, had lost its brightness and had blackened. Flies covered the corpses and intermittently rose in clouds over them before settling again.

Eventually they had arrived at the inn, where the wounded waited, and as Sergeant Nott had said it would now be "Shank's Pony" for the squadron. Stiles, as he walked and led his horse, wondered how the remaining two squadrons were faring. Earlier he had caught a glimpse of Jim Burnside. With any luck he might see him later and find out. A halt was called and the wounded were casually examined by one of the assistant surgeons. Stiles became aware that his man had stopped groaning. As he bent to adjust his horse's girth he caught the man's eye, which blinked as he met his gaze. Well, at least he was still alive.

"Do you want anything? Some water perhaps?" There was no answer. The eyes were now closed. Stiles hoped that they wouldn't have to go much further. Still, it was easier marching than on that awful retreat in the Peninsula when, day after day, they'd been up to their knees in mud, starving and chilled to the bone. Here there was dust and a hot stickiness to contend with. He looked at the sky. Thick black clouds were now heavily piled one on top of the other. In the distance a cannon fired, immediately followed by a flash of lightning and a deafening crack of thunder. Then the heavens opened.

Slowly through the thick mud churned up by countless horses' hooves and many thousands of feet, Clark's squadron, having handed over the wounded, picked its way towards the bivouac on Mont St Jean. The rain still fell in torrents, and the tired and hungry men at last came in sight of the regimental lines. Dusk had come early, for June, and the landscape was momentarily lit by flashes of lightning accompanied by loud crashes of thunder. Stiles, during these brief illuminations, could see that they were on a plain, which sloped upwards towards the front before the ground disappeared from sight and then came back into view some distance away. The hidden ground was the valley through which they had passed that morning with the wounded. It was too dark to see them, but somewhere out there were the French. Normally he would expect to see their camp fires, but not on a night such as this. They would be fortunate to find any dry kindling. He had only to look round their own encampment to see a few miserable attempts, which had resulted in more smoke than flame. Not that there was anything to cook and there was little point in trying to dry out his sodden clothes in these conditions. Stiles was so wet that he was past caring. On being given the order, he and the others dismounted. Stiles attempted to tether his horse but the ground was too soft to hold the picketing post. Keeping hold of the reins, he took the corn bag from behind the saddle and fed his mount. He had some biscuit left, which he quickly munched and washed down with water. In the distance were some farm buildings, but any hope of finding shelter was remote. Others would already be there. Anyway he couldn't just wander off. There was nothing else for it. They would have to lie on the ground and roll themselves in their cloaks and blankets and keep a firm grip on their horses by passing their arms through the reins.

Clark gave his horse to his servant. He left Gunning in charge and went in search of Radclyffe who commanded the Royals' Left Squadron. If ever there was a man capable of looking after himself and his men, Charles Edward Radclyffe was that man. Charles Edward must be named after the "Young Pretender", mused Clark, but pretender he certainly was not. Charles had risen from the ranks and had been promoted from sergeant to adjutant back in 1797. He now held the rank of brevet major, and was as strong as an ox and a born leader.

Clark walked across the ground with his boots sinking into the stiff mud at every step. The rain still beat down and was kept lying on the surface by the standing crops, which mostly were flattened, either by the weather or the many feet and hooves which had trodden over them. He came across groups of huddled men, some of whom had lit fires but with little to show for their efforts. Many held horses, not daring to let them go for fear that the thunder and lightning would cause them to run off. It was well known that loose horses would make their way back to their last camp, which would put them among the French. At last he found Charles Radclyffe with his officers, seated round a smouldering fire. A pot hung on a tripod and its contents were being stirred by Radclyffe's servant.

"Hello, Charles," said Clark.

"Why – it is Alexander," replied Radclyffe. "You look as though you could do with a drink! Will brandy do you? I'm afraid it's all we have got. Sit yourself down!" He indicated a space on a log which was serving as a bench. "We've got some beef stew cooking. Can't say when it will be ready but it will take some stewing, in which case we will be here all night. You are quite welcome to some if you wish to stay."

Clark expressed his gratitude and sat down.

"Keeling," said Radclyffe to his servant, "stop stirring that and give the captain a glass of brandy and a cigar."

Clark took the proffered glass and lit the cigar. Having taken a deep drink of the spirit, which gave him instant warmth, he said, "How did you come by the food?"

"I could see that we would be among the last to arrive," replied Radclyffe, "so I sent Keeling and another man on ahead. On their way they found an overturned cart and on rummaging around discovered a piece of beef wrapped in a cloth, and some brandy bottles. He realised that the infantry would be here well before us and the chances of finding any dry kindling would be remote, so the pair of them decided to demolish the cart for its wood. Isn't that so, Keeling?"

Keeling nodded his head in assent, at the same time responding with a loud, "Yes, sir!"

"That is not all," Radclyffe continued. "I heard him complaining to his accomplice that if it hadn't been for some light-fingered bugger who had stolen the canvas cover, we would have had shelter as well. Anyway, that's enough of that. What sort of day have you experienced?"

"Not altogether successful," said Clark. "Some of the wounded died on the way. In my opinion they would have been better left where they were but had been prepared to put a brave face on things and make light of their wounds. In all, I suppose we lost about ten on the journey back, and when I left them, others didn't look too good. I hear you have had an eventful time!"

Radclyffe drew on his cigar, replenished Clark's glass and then his own. "The others can see to themselves," he said. "I don't know that we have had a hard day but it's been trying. We didn't leave Quatre Bras until about two o'clock this afternoon. The infantry had long since retired and it would seem that their absence had escaped the enemy's attention. There was only the cavalry left, along with some batteries of horse artillery, to mask the Duke's intentions. We could see the French cavalry massing in the distance, but we had known for some time that we were not in danger of being attacked, as we could see the smoke of their cooking fires. As you know, they never fight before they have eaten."

Radclyffe held out his glass towards his servant, who poured a liberal measure and served Clark similarly.

"Anyway, where was I? Oh yes, we withdrew by alternate squadrons along the Brussels High Road, in the direction of Genappe, skirmishing as we went. You remember what a sultry morning it was! After a while, the clouds built up. Great big ugly black things, which got blacker and blacker, piled one on top of the other. A gloom was soon cast over everything except the hill where the French had lately camped, which was bathed in sunlight. Then a cannon fired – I suppose it was one of theirs and it was just as though that was the signal the elements had been waiting for. Lightning lit us, so that we must have been silhouetted against the dark background, and at the same moment a sharp crack of thunder almost deafened me. In no time at all the ground was soaked, and if it was difficult for us to make progress, think what it must have been like for our pursuers."

"We all got back to Genappe in one piece. The French occasionally drew near, with large groups of horsemen shouting "Vive l'Empereur!", but they did not seem to have their hearts set on attacking us. There was such a congestion crossing that narrow bridge over the Thy. By then, the ground was very churned up and the water was fairly tearing its way through the arches of the bridge, so there was no hope of fording the river. We just had to make the best progress we could. It was left to the 7th Hussars to provide the rearguard. We trotted up that cramped main street, and the water poured down off the roofs onto us. We took up our position above the town with the Greys and Inniskillings on one side of the chaussée and the Household Brigade and the Kings Dragoon Guards on the other. We could see that the 7th were having some trouble with the French Lancers in the narrow confines between the houses, and they got some rough treatment. Lord Somerset sent in the 2nd Life Guards to even things up and we retired to where we are now – beyond the crest of the ridge. We didn't suffer any casualties, but Phillip Dorville lost one man. That's it really, but I must tell you there was an exchange of artillery fire. The rocket battery took part in our reply and their first shot demolished a French gun. After that rockets went everywhere, except to where they were aimed. At one stage we saw one coming towards us but luckily it veered away. Looks as though we are in for a fight tomorrow. It is to be hoped that the Prussians turn up on time."

There was a lull in the conversation. Clark, though warmed through by the brandy, was soaked to the skin and said so. He also lamented the non arrival of their baggage. Radclyffe pointed to one of his lieutenants, Charles Forster. "If it will provide you with any consolation, Alexander, Charles purchased, at great cost, a double oilskin against such an eventuality as this".

"Is that correct, Charles?" he asked. "What is your conclusion?"

"I am as wet as the rest of you," replied Forster.

Radclyffe continued. "The weather could be a lucky omen for us. If you remember, it has rained heavily on the eve of some of the Duke's greatest victories. Is that meat cooked, Keeling? If we don't eat soon, it will be daybreak!"

Keeling prodded the lump of meat. "With this fire, sir, I think it is the best I can do! Shall I serve it?"

They ate, after which Clark returned to his men. The rain continued to fall.

Stiles dozed fitfully, never dropping off to sleep for long. John Williams was nearby but had scarcely spoken a word, and apparently he was still convinced that this was his last night on earth. Some of the old Peninsula hands, for the benefit of the 'Johnny Newcomes', said their present plight was nothing compared with Spain and Portugal. Whether the new recruits believed what they were told was another matter but they seemed suitably impressed and were not complaining. Probably they did not want to show themselves up. If anything, thought Stiles, the exchanges had taken their minds off the morrow. If he and the others could survive years in the Peninsula, there was hope for them all. He wished that the rain would stop. He had been thoroughly wet for hours and his outer clothes were caked in mud. He was certain of one thing – he had known, ever since they had arrived at their encampment, that they would retreat no further. Tomorrow they would have to fight for their lives.

Waterloo – Sunday, 18th June 1815

"Wake up, you lazy buggers! Come on, rouse yourselves, my beauties!"

Stiles opened his eyes slowly. His first thought was that the rain had stopped and it was daylight. Near to his nose were the muddy toecaps of a pair of boots, and as his eyes travelled upwards he saw Sergeant Nott grinning down at him.

"You can't stay there all day, Corporal. Not unless you want the French to catch you in bed." Stiles did as he was ordered, and having risen to his feet, stood and stretched. His mouth was dry, the result of too much gin during the night. It had been welcome at the time but he regretted it now. One of the troop, unable to sleep, had gone foraging and returned with an anker of gin.

He looked at his comrades. What a sight they were – unshaven, and filthy dirty from the mud. Their usually white belts were dyed red, as the rain had transferred the colour from their tunics. He ran his right hand over his chin, which bore three days stubble and felt like a rasp. It would have to stay like it. Everywhere he looked there were groups of men stretched round smouldering fires, crouched in hollows, or lying under such meagre cover as they had found the night before. The still forms, which at first gave the impression that the battle had already been fought, gradually came to life. He looked over to where the horses were being held. Afraid of losing their mounts they had decided in the early hours to take turns as horse handlers. He saw Betsy, his mare, pulling restlessly at her bridle. Stiles walked across the intervening space, and the mare gave a whinny of recognition as he approached. Stiles took her reins, gave her an appreciative pat on her flank, and offered her some corn.

"I'll try and smarten you up a bit," he said and took the curry-comb from his valise.

Stiles, hearing the sound of laughter, turned and saw John Williams sharing a joke with the men. He appeared to have lost his fit of depression and was gently chiding them to get the fire going. Some oatmeal, rum, and a large amount of biscuit had been discovered nearby. This hadn't been the end of their good fortune. Later a few stray cattle were rounded up and the troop had received its share of beef. Everyone's mood was now lighter. Stiles decided not to comment on Williams' changed humour. It would not do to ask. Either he'd had a complete change of heart, or was it an act of bravado. He restricted himself to "It's a better day, John."

"Aye, Francis, it is," was the reply and then Williams turned to the man who was supervising the cooking.

"How's that stirabout doing?"

Slater gave the mixture of oatmeal and water a stir, dipped his finger into the concoction, and tasted it. "Won't be long now, Corporal, but the stew will be a while yet."

From the camp, which was behind the second line of infantry, Clark rode slowly towards the ridge. It was heavy going for Jock, who was up to his fetlocks in mud. Clark, still wet to the skin, wanted to take a look at the lie of the land on the other side. He reflected that if they were to be called upon to fight now, they would go coolly into action. Before leaving his squadron he had given orders to Gunning that the men should look to their arms and equipment and that the armourer, Sergeant Ingham, should be instructed to sharpen the sabres on both sides. "It will be useful," he had said, "to have a double edge if we come up against the French cuirassiers in their body armour." First he rode over to Ingham to have his sword prepared and he had not been surprised to find it had gone rusty in its scabbard. Now he approached the crest. The ground, though still very wet, was already benefiting from the warm sunshine and was beginning to dry out. Somewhere a lone piper was playing, and as he came over the summit he saw the ground sloped down towards a hedge-lined lane, which ran parallel to his front, some one hundred yards away. The lane bisected the broad chaussée, which led southwards to Charleroi, and behind him northwards to Brussels. British troops were spread out to the left and right, and now he saw, as well as heard, a lone piper of the 79th. There was the sound of firing as the infantry cleaned and fired their weapons, but generally an air of serenity prevailed as the Army waited. Beyond the lane the ground fell away still further into a valley, before rising again.

"Would you like a closer look at them?"

Clark looked down and saw an officer of the 28th holding a telescope towards him. Clark accepted with thanks and raised the glass to his eye. He followed the chaussée as it ran off to the south, and there to the left of the road were the French still bivouacked.

"How far off do you think they are?" asked the infantryman.

"I'd say about fifteen hundred yards," Clark replied. He closed the telescope with a snap and returned it to its owner. "There doesn't seem to be any urgency about them. Rather similar to yesterday morning, when one would have expected them to be about their business earlier in the day. Good luck to you! Now I must return to my men." Clark wheeled his horse and rode back the way he had come.

Lacroix and his companions had spent a miserable and uncomfortable night, but Lacroix had at least managed to get some protection from the weather by sheltering under the overhang of a farm building. He knew that somewhere in front of him were the English and their allies. Why was it always the English who stood in their way? The trouble with them was they never knew when they were beaten. Well, they would soon be disposed of. The Emperor would chase them off the field; then they would destroy the Prussians and pick off the other nations who threatened France. Then perhaps they could eventually go home and enjoy the peace. Lacroix looked forward to carrying the Eagle into the battle, which should settle matters once and for all.

When day at last dawned, the French cooked and ate. There was no haste. Lacroix could see for himself that the heavy and miry ground would not only impede the infantry but would also prevent easy manoeuvring of the cavalry and artillery. At least the sun was shining.

"You're a countryman," he said to Giraud. "How long do you think it will be before the ground hardens?"

"It must be a matter of hours," Giraud replied. "Depends how much sun there is. With all this rye about, marching is not going to be easy. I can't see anything happening before noon!"

The trumpets and bugles sounded assembly. Drums beat all round. Having fallen in, been dressed and inspected, Lacroix, flanked by

Mesnil, Giraud, and the Colour Party, marched with the 105th to their position. They had scarcely completed their formation when there was a flourish of trumpets, which announced the Emperor's review of the Army. Bands played and Napoleon, attended by many staff, passed in front of the long, drawn up lines. Lacroix was certain that the Emperor had never been so enthusiastically received and he felt immense pride as the loud cries of "*Vive l'Empereur!*" rose up on all sides. He felt they were telling Napoleon that they were at one with him; they would do whatever was asked of them and were certain that victory would be theirs. Lacroix, who considered himself a realist, appreciated that this was a means of building confidence, and, as this spectacle could be viewed and heard from the British lines, the awe-inspiring display of noise and power could have an alarming effect. He shouted with the others till he became hoarse. His eyes followed the Emperor's progress, marked by the raising and waving of shakos, busbies and helmets, as the troops, now raised to fever pitch, cheered wildly. The collective sound as it swept over Lacroix was reminiscent of waves breaking on a shore. There were thousands of pennants and brilliant uniforms. Lacroix, who had to shout to make himself heard above the din, yelled at Mesnil and Giraud, "We're going to win and we'll make them pay. *Vive l'Empereur!*"

Stiles was as ready as he would ever be. Earlier when he'd sharpened his sword, he'd watched the sparks fly from the blade as it was held against the turning grindstone. He had two good edges now. It had seemed a long morning but he had filled in some of the time by trying to clean himself. His present condition was well short of his usual standard, but it was the best he could do in the circumstances. He and Betsy had eaten well, and an issue of rum had helped his sense of well-being. The sun's position indicated that it was about an hour to noon and still the French didn't come. He and the others, from their position on the reverse slope, had caught faint sounds of cheering and somewhere bands were playing. It was probably the French working themselves up. Now he and the rest were mounted and waiting for the next order.

The Centre squadron, with Clark at its head, moved forward. Stiles, as Standard Coverer, rode closely behind Clark and was followed by numbers Seven and Eight Troops. Clark was pleased that he had reconnoitred the ground earlier. He estimated that once they got to the ridge it was about a hundred yards down to the lane, and at a push they could jump the hedge. It would be just like steeplechasing. He had every confidence in his men. Even though there was a sprinkling of raw recruits, the majority had seen action before, and there was, of course, Stiles who was literally watching his back. Involuntarily, he moved his right hand to the hilt of his sword and slightly moved the weapon in its scabbard. No trouble there; the sword moved effortlessly. He wondered what Harriet would think if she could see him now. He was approaching the place, indicated to him by Clifton, where his squadron was to wait. He gave the order to halt. They were in a hollow, still some way from the crest. Apart from the other two squadrons of the regiment, to his left were the Inniskillings and beyond them the Greys – waiting, like themselves, for orders.

Back in Number Eight Troop, John Gibbs, who had joined the regiment six months earlier, was waiting for his first taste of action. His main fear was that he would let himself and the others down. He hoped that it wouldn't come to that. At the moment there was a strange silence, broken only by the sounds of horses snorting and the jingling of harness as they tossed their heads. He felt strangely excited and his mouth had gone dry. In the files either side of him were men who were veterans of the Peninsula. They told him to stick close and they would watch out for him. The troop sergeant-major had put it more bluntly: "Keep your eyes open or you'll get a French bayonet up your arse!"

Elsewhere, in Number Four Troop, John Dixon, who had been eighteen years in the regiment, appreciated more than most what was before them. In spite of his length of service he was still only a private. He had reached the rank of corporal on three occasions, only to be reduced to the ranks for breaches of discipline. If he should die today, he could face his Maker with a clear conscience. Well, almost. The regiment was his life and his family, and he trusted Major Dorville to see him through. The sun shone warmly. Not a bad day to die, but he hoped he would see off a few of those French buggers first. It didn't seem to make any difference how many engagements he'd been in – the waiting was always the worst part. It was all right once you got started.

A cannon fired, followed by a barrage. The shots didn't seem to be coming their way. Clark pulled out his watch and opened the case. It was thirty minutes past eleven o'clock.

"The 105th will advance!"

With the drummers beating the step, the regiment, followed by the 28th, advanced in column, two hundred files wide and twenty-seven deep, towards the top of the downward slope. Lacroix was towards the head of the column and had placed the butt of the blue pole in the carrying socket. He looked up with pride at the Tricolour which, freed from its case, displayed the battle honours. At the peak of the staff, the golden Eagle glittered in the sunlight. It must have been an hour or more since the first cannon had sounded. That had been followed by a stiff bombardment to their left, and word had passed that the object of the guns' attentions was an outpost held by the British. They were now passing through the gun batteries, many of which were twelve-pounders. The Emperor called them his "Beautiful Daughters". As they cleared the guns, Lacroix, for the first time, saw the British lines. He knew that the attack was to be made against the centre. Now he found himself shouting, along with the others, "*Vive l'Empereur!*" and "*En avant!*", until their own guns, with the path once more clear for them, fired over their heads and their voices could no longer be heard.

Lacroix shortened his step as he descended the slope. Before long they were on the valley bottom and then the climb upwards began. Greasy mud and long twists of rye made marching difficult, but Lacroix, flanked by the two bearded giants, Mesnil and Giraud, who carried halberds to protect the Eagle, made steady progress. Skirmishers were pushed out and Lacroix felt pressure from his left as the column of five thousand men veered slightly to its right. The guns had stopped firing. 'Not far now,' Lacroix thought. To their front was a deployed line of Allied troops, who fired a ragged volley, then turned and ran. Their shots had some effect as gaps had appeared in the front rank. The sergeants were shouting for the ranks to close up, while all the while the officers in front held their hats aloft on their sword points. The drums once more took up the beat: Rum-dum-dum-dum – the "*Pas de Charge*", which was the signal for renewed cries of "*Vive l'Empereur!*".

As far as Lacroix could see there was nothing between them and the crest. They were going to break the British centre and up until now they hadn't fired a shot. All the frustrations of having missed Quatre Bras and Ligny disappeared. The column halted just short of a holly hedge, and its leading ranks threaded their way through and immediately crossed a lane before continuing the climb. Lacroix hesitated for a moment as he wished to ensure the safety of the Colour; until at least sufficient numbers of the regiment had negotiated the barrier. Further volleys were fired, and at first he assumed that they were their own, but then he became aware that the head of the left flank was reeling back. For some reason they were retreating, but still pressure came from behind to move forward. There was confusion. Blows were struck against friends. Then came a cry, "Cavalry!" At first all he could see was a line of helmets along the ridge in front of them. He watched in fascination as over the brow of the hill came the English horsemen. The two front ranks of the column fired, and Lacroix saw some saddles emptied as the balls struck home. Because of the formation no one else was able to fire. Muskets were pointing everywhere and in some cases were knocked out of their bearer's hands. Quickly panic spread. The once orderly column became a rabble, with the majority seeking self-preservation.

Lacroix shouted, "It's time to get the Colour to safety!" He turned towards the rear, with Mesnil and Giraud beating a path for him and the Eagle.

The cannonade had grown in intensity and despite their relatively safe position on the reverse slope, the Royals were being hit by overshoots. Stiles watched the cannon balls and shells as they cleared the crest. The former, because of the softness of the ground, had not bounded along as they might have under normal conditions but in most cases buried themselves in the mud. As usual, it was the ones you didn't see that were the problem. Then there were the shells which landed with their fuses fizzing. You had to get out of the way quickly. Thank God the French didn't have shrapnel, otherwise they would have been in real trouble. As it was, Stiles had seen men and horses killed and wounded. He was only too pleased when the order was given to move forward, further along the hollow, which brought them four hundred yards from the crest. The relief was immediate, and not for the first time Stiles patted Betsy's neck and spoke reassuringly to her. To his left the 6th Dragoons – or, as they were known in the cavalry, the "Skins" – had also moved up with the Greys alongside. This was the Union Brigade, twelve hundred sabres in all. Stiles then saw Lord Uxbridge riding at speed towards the brigadier. It looked as though something was about to happen. It wouldn't be long now.

Ponsonby sent for the commanding officers. As he answered the summons Clifton saw Muter and Hamilton, his counterparts of the Inniskillings and the Greys, approaching the brigadier.

"Gentlemen," said Ponsonby, "I have received my orders. You are to bring your regiments into line and you will then await my signal to attack. I will ride to the ridge with my ADC. I understand that we will be opposing columns of infantry, and our attack is to be to the east of the chaussée. Muter, as the senior, watch for my signal. I will raise my hat. When you see me do that, the Royals and Inniskillings will follow me forward. Hamilton, your regiment, the Greys, will form the reserve. Any questions? No, well, good luck to us all!"

As he was leaving, Clifton heard Ponsonby call for his charger but his groom was not in evidence. He heard the brigadier shout angrily, "Get me any damned horse! Any damned horse will do!" Clifton looked behind him and saw Ponsonby mount what looked like a troop horse and ride off towards the ridge.

Suddenly Stiles was aware that the enemy's guns had stopped firing. A little later the sound of a ragged volley reached his ears, followed soon after by the sight of men coming over the ridge and running wildly in his direction. By the anxious glances they were casting over their shoulders, they might well have been pursued by the Devil. As they drew near they threw their arms, packs, and anything else which might impede them, to the ground. Stiles saw that they belonged to a Belgian-Dutch brigade. As they passed the Royals they were greeted with boos and hisses, but it seemed that nothing would stop them and they disappeared hell for leather into the distance.

The two deep line of the Royals continued to watch to the front, the members of each squadron looking towards its leader waiting for the order to go forward. Sabres had been drawn and were carried at the slope. Stiles could not see the French but could hear them approaching. He didn't know what was happening on the other side of the ridge but could plainly hear their drums, beating the "*Pas de Charge*" – rum-dum-dum-dum; rum-dum-dum-dum, now getting increasingly louder and accompanied by unified shouts of "*Vive l'Empereur!*" There it was, as he had heard it many times before, the beat of *Old Trousers*. When the time came, he must keep close behind Captain Clark. Where Clark went he must follow. Stiles fixed his eyes on the ridge where Ponsonby waited with his ADC. He saw the general dismount. He seemed to have lost his cloak. Stiles saw Ponsonby bend down to retrieve it, and scarcely had he put it round his shoulders and regained the saddle, when the ADC put his hand to his head and lifted his hat. It was the signal. Muter cried, "Forward!", which was immediately echoed by Clifton and Clark. The trumpets sounded, the men cheered, and the Royals went off at a dash.

The big black horses moved forward and thundering hooves marked their progress. Clark felt confident. He knew in detail what lay over the other side of the ridge. The Centre squadron quickly picked up into a canter, the hoof beats drumming out the urgency of their mission. This was the opportunity for which the regiment had waited since that abysmal day at Maguilla. Now was the chance to put the record straight.

As he cleared the summit Clark saw the French for the first time. They were, he estimated, eighty to ninety yards away. Some had forced their way through the hedge and crossed the lane but they seemed to be in disarray. He stole a quick glance to his right and then to his left. There were Radclyffe and Dorville with their squadrons closely behind them. At the moment all was so well ordered, with the men keeping a near perfect line, that it might well have been an exercise. Now the gap was closing; down to fifty yards. The notes of the trumpets sounding the charge rang out, and down came the sabres pointing directly at the French.

The pace increased to a gallop. Clark saw puffs of smoke as some of the massed infantry fired. He heard the buzz of musket balls as they passed close to him and a loud cheer from the ranks behind. All that was between them and the French were some British infantry, doing their best to get out of the way of the advancing horsemen, even to the point of falling prone to the ground if all else failed. As they passed through, Clark and his men were given cheers of encouragement. Now they had crossed the lane, easily clearing the hedge, and it was plain to see that the French were gripped with panic. Clark altered course slightly so that the squadron would wrap itself round the front and side of the now disorganised column. It was slaughter made all the easier by the terror which engulfed the enemy and in a few minutes it became a rout. The French were so closely packed that they could not use their weapons. They were fleeing down the slope, with Clark and his men at their heels, cutting, slashing and riding them down. The horses, not to be outdone, bit and kicked. The trooper's swords were red with dripping blood, and by the hundred the men of the 105th threw down their arms and surrendered.

Stiles, watching Clark like a hawk, saw him draw up and he reined in Betsy. So far it had been much easier than he had anticipated. They were surrounded by Frenchmen whose sole object was to throw down their weapons and cry, "Pardon". Based on his past experience, he didn't altogether trust them and he kept a wary eye on the group about him. Out of the corner of his eye he detected a movement. One of the supposed prisoners had picked up a musket and was aiming it at Clark. Stiles yelled, "Look out, sir!" Clark saw the danger but the Frenchman fired, and Clark, who had turned his head quickly, felt the ball graze the bridge of his nose. It stung sharply and the blood flowed freely down his face, as he gasped for breath following his recent exertions. It was the last move the Frenchman made. Stiles urged his horse forward and brought the edge of his sword down on the man's head, cutting him to the chin. An audible gasp went up from the prisoners and one of them, intent on avenging his comrade's death, fired at Stiles. John Williams had seen the movement and put himself between the intended victim and the assailant. Williams took the shot in the head and fell to the ground. There was a loud scream as the assassin was bayoneted by a soldier of the 28th.

Stiles looked down at his dead friend's lifeless body. There was nothing he could do for him now, but at least death had come quickly. John's premonition had unfortunately come true. All round him and mingled with the living were the dead and wounded; stretching back up the slope to the point where they had first made contact with the enemy. If he was selfish in his attitude, then so be it. He was still alive and he had no doubt that many more would die before the day was out. Men of the 28th now arrived in greater numbers and the disarmed prisoners were led away to the rear.

Clark paused to take stock. They were three hundred yards from the hedge and the French were in full retreat. He turned to Gunning.

"There is no more we can do here. We have other quarry to pursue." Then to his left and forty yards away he saw a Colour being hurried to the rear by a French officer. The Eagle surmounting the

Tricolour caught the sunlight, as though beckoning him. Clark gave the order: "Right shoulders forward. Attack the Colour!"

Lieutenant Charles Bridges decided that he'd had more than enough. So far he had managed to keep out of harm's way and had followed rather than led. For the sake of appearances he'd waved his sword about and shouted. He had even run a wounded Frenchman through. Now he turned his horse, dug his spurs into the beast's flanks, and raced off to the safety of his own lines.

For Lacroix there was only one imperative. One thing which mattered above all else was to get the Eagle to safety. He was heading back to the rear seeking sanctuary but he could not be sure where safety lay. Giraud, Mesnil, and his other protectors were with him, but amongst the disordered ranks of the fleeing troops it was impossible to maintain a straight course or for that matter, organised protection. For the first time fear gripped him and soon he was running aimlessly, hemmed in among a mass which was exerting so much pressure that he could not have let go of the Eagle had he so desired. Briefly he looked up at the Tricolour, which was standing away from its pole, and then at the English Cavalry coming up fast and cutting a channel towards him. At first it looked as if a corporal was making straight for him, but in the space of a few moments his place was taken by one who could only be their leader. A huge man with a blood-streaked face, astride a big black horse, came at him sword in hand.

Clark found the path to the Colour barred by the sheer mass of the retreating French. He continued to cut and thrust his way through, and by the shouts of encouragement from behind he knew that he still had support. Only a few more yards to go now. There was the Eagle in the middle of the throng. His wounded nose stung but the bleeding had stopped. His gaze quickly took in those opposing him. Some defiant. Others resigned to their fate. The Eagle bearer was clearly aware of his intention, and a look of fear showed on his face.

Stiles following closely behind his leader, saw the Eagle and its bearer, but also could not help but see the guards on either side, who somehow had managed to keep in contact with their officer. The three were surrounded by a large body of men, but whether they had any real intention of offering resistance was a matter for conjecture. Those two guards, with their halberds, would be a different matter. They were ugly looking brutes. Both were giants, with big moustaches, and one, Stiles saw, as he drew nearer, had a flattened nose. It was as though someone had taken a hammer to it. He noticed these details in a detached way, all the time urging Betsy forward and sticking as near to Clark as circumstances permitted. His sword arm was aching as he cut through the French infantry, and the success of his progress was marked by the screams of pain from his would-be opponents. There were many bodies on the ground, some undoubtedly dead, some wounded, and others feigning death. The thought flashed through his mind – it wouldn't do to get thrown. They were almost upon the Eagle bearer. Stiles, alongside his captain, was literally pushed to one side, as Clark urged Jock forward, preventing Stiles, who to that moment had been convinced that the Eagle was his, from riding straight at its bearer. Instead he took the man with the flattened nose with a cut across the neck. Lieutenant Gunning skewered the other guard. Clark thrust at the officer and ran him through the side. Above the clamour which surrounded them, Stiles heard the piercing scream. The Frenchman staggered, clutched at his wound, but was unable to fall because of the press around him. The Colour, on its bright blue pole, slowly came towards Clark, who tried to catch it as it passed.

Clark shouted at Stiles. "Secure the Colour! Secure the Colour!"

At that moment the very top of the pole with its Eagle, fell across Betsy's neck. Stiles, having let the reins fall, caught it, passed his hands down the shaft, and handed the trophy to Clark. His immediate reaction was – he'd got it! *He'd* picked it up but *they*, as a body, had done it.

Clark almost snatched the Colour from Stiles and immediately tried to tear the Tricolour from its mounting, but it was well secured.

"Pray, sir, do not break it!" he heard Stiles say. Damn his impudence, he thought, as he renewed his efforts but ultimately he had to admit defeat.

"Very well, Corporal," said Clark, "take it to the rear with care. It is mine!"

Stiles took the Eagle and rode off.

He rode up the bank. The battle had moved on and he went with mixed feelings. In one respect he was proud and more than pleased to be riding to the rear with the trophy, but the success of the squadron, so far, led him to believe that greater glory awaited and he wanted to be part of it.

He heard a voice calling from behind, "Wait for me!" Half turning, he saw Stephen Anderson, a private from Number Eight Troop.

Stiles paused, "Where are you going?" he asked.

"I'm off to the dressing station. I've been nicked in the ribs. I was going earlier but Captain Clark called for assistance. I heard what he said as you left. He may think the Eagle is his but he wouldn't have got to its bearer on his own. If anything, it's yours. You got your hand on it first."

A similar thought had been going through Stiles' mind but it wasn't up to Anderson to say so. He decided to overlook the insubordination in the circumstances and looked at the site of Anderson's wound. The blood was flowing freely from the gash on his side and there was an ever-growing stain on his jacket.

"Come on," he said. "You'll be better off getting yourself patched up!"

They rode together to the summit, having passed many dead – some piled one on top of each other. There were the wounded– some sitting, others lying. The extent of the wounds varied. They saw soldiers from both sides, clutching their stomachs and trying to hold in their innards, which bulged through gaping wounds. Others were less severely wounded but glad to have respite from the fighting which had left them demoralised. Anderson went off to seek the regimental surgeon. Stiles stopped and looked back. On the opposing ridge the cavalry were among the French guns. It was easy to pick out the Greys, but at that distance the remainder were a jumble. He could not detect whether the others were the Royals or Inniskillings. Whoever they were they had gained the ascendancy. The French would not be so cocksure now. Then he heard trumpets sounding the recall, but they were either not heard or the troopers were so carried away that they chose not to obey.

Before riding on, Stiles took a closer look at the flag. He had no knowledge of French but on one side read, "L'EMPEREUR NAPOLEON". There were some other words beneath that including, "105th regiment". On the reverse side were what seemed to be place names – "Jena" (he'd heard of that), "Eylau", "Eckmund", "Essling", and "Wagram". These must be the battle honours. Above the flag the tasselled ropes hung below the Eagle, which on its plinth had inscribed the numerals "105". Now for the first time he felt the strain, but was aware of a sense of achievement. Stiles had no idea what time it was but it didn't seem all that long ago since the charge, and here he was on the way back, while others were still involved. His heart, which all the while had been racing, was now slowing down and he became aware that he was hot and thirsty. He removed the stopper from his canteen and took a long drink of water.

"Where are you taking it, Corporal?" The words, spoken from behind and in a thick Scottish accent, caused him to swing round. A few feet away was a giant of a man, a sergeant, sitting astride one of the largest grey horses Stiles had ever seen. He too carried an Eagle but held it as though it were a toy, whereas Stiles was beginning to find his charge not only cumbersome but heavy.

Stiles replied, "I've been ordered to take it to the rear and to ensure that it finds a place of safety, but I have to admit I'm not certain where I am going,"

"Well, laddie," replied the sergeant, "I can only suggest that as we have the same objective we ride along together until we find someone in authority. My name's Ewart. Ewart of the Greys." Stiles introduced himself.

They had not gone far when a staff officer detached himself from a group on a hill and rode up to them.

"The Duke requests you take the Eagles to Brussels. Hand them over to the military commandant for safe keeping and be sure to give details of their capture, the names of your regiments, and your own names of course. The Brussels chaussée is over there," he said, pointing to his left. The officer rode off.

"That settles it," said Stiles and they turned towards the road, past cheering British troops and French prisoners, many of whom openly wept on seeing the Eagles.

Charles Bridges had left the field at speed and lost no time in gaining the Brussels Road. He soon found his progress impeded by carts and wagons bringing up ammunition, and no doubt the same vehicles would later be used to convey the wounded to the rear. If he was challenged, he would say that he was taking an urgent message to the military commandant in Brussels. Bridges realised that he would have to come up with a more convincing story, if and when his superiors asked him to explain his absence from the fighting. He had already half decided he would say his saddle had turned, causing him to leave the field. Anyway, among all that confusion he would not be missed for some time. In spite of the traffic he was able to make reasonable progress and had the advantage that when he came to points of congestion, he could temporarily leave the road. At first he had considered hiding in the woods but the trees were widely spaced and offered little protection. The gaps between the trees were wide enough to drive a battery of guns through and he had heard the colonel tell Clark that if the worst came to the worst, the Army's line of retreat lay through the woods. As he rode, deep in his own thoughts, he was unaware that he had been seen by a fellow officer.

George Stead, the regimental surgeon, had chosen the position of his casualty station carefully. The barn, adjacent to a farmhouse, lay a quarter of a mile from the ridge and just off the main road to Brussels. He and his two assistants, Prosser and Alderson, had completed their preparations. Three tables, still wet and shining, had been scrubbed by the orderlies, and the instruments were neatly laid out. Saws, knives and probes (yet to be used) gleamed. Straps, gags, ligatures, bandages, and a generous supply of rum waited for the first of the seriously wounded patients. The water in the buckets was as yet clean, but from the sound of the battle now raging beyond the crest, it would not be long before all three tables were occupied and their grisly work began. The light inside the building was poor and they would need to light the lamps.

Stead had been with the Royals for ten years and knew most of the men. There were a few malingerers among them but he knew who they were – unlike in his early days, when as a young and inexperienced surgeon, he'd had the wool pulled over his eyes. Stead had been four years into his service before he had amputated a shattered limb. He could picture the man now as he had been lifted onto the table, his lower left leg almost torn off and hanging by shattered bone and a few shreds of flesh. In some ways it had been more like being a butcher than a surgeon. Luckily he'd had a good senior, James Sullivan, who, seeing the look of terror on the man's face, had spoken reassuringly to him, had some brandy poured down his throat before a piece of folded leather was pushed into his mouth, lest he should bite his tongue off. The attendants had pinioned the man's hands, shoulders and undamaged leg. Stead had been urged to work quickly by Sullivan and in a flash had amputated the limb. It was a pity the patient had died of mortification a few days later. What was it that Colonel Wyndham had said to him when they sailed to the

Peninsula? Yes, he remembered – "Well, my boy, you will be in for some real doctoring now."

It hadn't always been major surgery, although, to a greater degree, wounds had provided his main work. There had, from time to time, been cases of the pox, which always increased in number when the regiment spent more than a few days in any location. Neither were those outbreaks confined to the other ranks. When Sullivan left, he became surgeon, and two years ago he had been joined by his assistants. He never ceased to wonder how the wounded, for the most part, bore their pain with stoicism. He was not indifferent to their suffering but did not have the means at his disposal to make it easier. Suddenly he was aware of his sombre thoughts and decided that he would be better off thinking about the days he had spent in Bath. As an unmarried man he had been the subject of attention, too much so at times, of the mothers who looked for husbands for their daughters. Stead had found himself very much in demand at a variety of social gatherings, and in all modesty his good looks were an advantage. Well, enough of that also.

"Tom! Robert!" he called to his assistants. "We might as well take the air while we have the opportunity. Let us go outside." They went into the sunlight. Stead lit a cigar. The main road was busy with traffic, mostly going towards the front, although the occasional traveller, some on horse, others on foot, made their way to the rear. His attention was particularly attracted by one horseman, who was making fast and erratic progress towards Brussels. He knew him.

"Damn my eyes, Prosser, ain't that Bridges over there going at a famous pace?"

Prosser looked, but whoever it might have been was now hidden from view. "Can't be certain," he replied.

Stead consulted his timepiece. It was thirty minutes after two o'clock. He looked up. Some men were making their way towards him. Some walked with difficulty, others were assisted, and a few were being carried. Stead looked at the empty pit, dug for corpses and amputated limbs.

"Time to get on with some real doctoring, gentlemen!" They re-entered the barn.

Up till now all had gone well. He'd captured the Eagle, and Stiles had departed with it. 'Hope he takes good care of it,' thought Clark as he turned his attention back to his squadron. He could see the troopers of the Royals, Greys and Inniskillings well up the slope among the French cannon, cutting and sabreing the gunners. It was a pity they didn't have the means of towing away or spiking the guns. The cavalry must have dashed up the slope to get there so quickly. It was time to get them back. Wright, his trumpeter, was nearby with some other men. He led the group forward across the valley bottom, which was stiff with mud and then upwards. Clark then faintly heard the recall sounding to his rear, but the men ahead ignored the command.

"Wright, sound *Recall*!" he ordered. The trumpet call echoed but it took several repeats before the men responded and began the return journey.

Clark noticed that what had started as a leisurely response had assumed a greater degree of urgency. Horses were being urged on almost to no avail, as the animals, blown by their exertions, failed to answer their rider's urgings. The reason for the haste became apparent when French Lancers and Chasseurs appeared over the hill before him and who, judging by their shouts, were bent on revenge. There was no time to get an organised formation in place. The Greys, from the moment they had taken part in the charge, had left the Union Brigade without a reserve. It was up to each man to get back as best he could.

Clark shouted at those nearest to him, "Get back! Get back!" They needed no urging. Now he was being passed by the returning soldiers, but could see, only too well, that the French, with their fresh horses, were arriving at speed. Some of the Chasseurs were firing their carbines, but Clark was not too concerned. It would take a good shot, under these conditions, to find his mark. He decided that he would wait for the last possible moment before joining the dash for home. Then he saw Sir William Ponsonby being pursued by a group of Lancers. He did not seem to have much chance and was being rapidly overtaken. There was nothing that Clark or anyone else could do to help the brigadier.

Clark decided it was time to go. He turned Jock and headed towards the British lines. The mud, still thick in the valley, slowed his progress. Many horses gasped for breath and their riders looked anxiously over their shoulders. Some, it seemed, were resigned to their fate and had turned towards the French waiting with swords in hand. Clark had now reached the spot where the initial action had taken place. Jock picked his way through a mass of French dead and wounded, and Clark ignored the plaintive cries for water. He felt his horse stagger and then it fell slowly to the ground. Jock was done for. Clark picked himself up. He had felt his scabbard jerk and on examination saw a hole where a ball had passed through it. Judging by the wound in Jock's side, the round which had so narrowly missed him had dealt his horse a mortal blow. He was still four hundred yards from safety and wondering how he was to get back, when support for the stragglers came from the Light Dragoons, backed up by Picton's Infantry.

'Well,' thought Clark, 'my hour has not yet come.' He managed to catch hold of one of the loose horses, swung up into the saddle, took one last look at Jock, and rode back to the crest.

Bridges having escaped from the fighting, felt his sense of elation diminishing with every step that took him nearer to Brussels. What was he going to do? How was he going to explain himself? These were the questions running through his mind. The plain answer was that he did not know. It was reasonably safe here on the road but once he reached the city, it would be another matter. In the course of his journey so far, he had been asked on numerous occasions by officers going in the opposite direction how the battle was going. He had adopted a standard reply. "It is going in our favour, but you will need to excuse me. I am carrying an important dispatch." Then, to emphasise the point, he would put his hand to his sabertache. He might be done for if he met someone in authority who might demand to see the message. Worst still, he might be cross-questioned by a member of the Provost Marshall's staff. He did not want to be apprehended as a deserter. He couldn't be too far from the Namur Gate. What sort of guard would there be? What questions would they ask?

Bridges, on the verge of panic, saw an inn. Perhaps it would be better if he got off the road for a while. The wood, which had run continuously from behind the battlefront, still adjoined the road and would provide him with a hiding place from which he could watch unseen. Perhaps he would wait an hour or two, until he sorted things out in his mind. Yes, he decided, that is what he would do. He turned his horse off the chaussée towards the inn.

Stiles found Ewart to be a rather dour companion – a man of few words. After their initial exchanges, for the most part, they had ridden in silence, and on being stopped to be congratulated, which happened quite often, Ewart had grunted what sounded like, "We're in a hurry!" and left Stiles to do the talking. From the conversations Stiles had with well-wishers, it appeared that rumour was rife. Some were convinced that the battle was already lost, but he was able to reassure them on that point. They had now reached the stage that when Stiles stopped to answer questions, Ewart rode on. Stiles was also eager to deliver his Eagle so that he could return to the regiment. He longed to be back with his fellows. He was perhaps more concerned as to what might have happened since he had left them.

Bridges watched the road, now bathed in sunlight. It had been warm out there and he was pleased to be in the cool of the wood. The inn had been a great temptation but he had not dallied. It might have proved dangerous. He had remained on his horse while an ostler went inside for a bottle of wine. It was a trifle sour but the more he had drunk, the better it had tasted. Now there was only a quarter of the bottle left. His thoughts turned to food and for the first time he realised that he was hungry. Perhaps the wine had given him courage and improved his appetite.

Something was happening. Two men on the road were attracting attention. He could only see their heads because of the surrounding crowd. One of them, on a grey horse, was riding on. He appeared to be carrying a flag. Now the other followed. He too was carrying a flag and by his uniform he was a Royal dragoon. Bridges thought this might be the opportunity he had been seeking. He quickly remounted and rode back through the trees, so that by the time he reached the road he would be a hundred yards or so behind the dragoon, who was hurrying to catch up with his companion. As he came onto the chaussée, Bridges put his horse into a canter. As he got nearer, while still not recognising the soldier, he saw that he wore a corporal's stripes. He also saw that he carried a French Eagle.

"Corporal! Corporal! Stop, I say!" Was the man deaf? Stiles heard someone shouting and turned round. Coming towards him, at a fair pace, was an officer. 'Damn my eyes,' he thought, 'it's Lieutenant Bridges. What's he doing here? No doubt I'm about to find out.'

"Corporal," said Bridges, "did you not hear me call out to you?" Stiles thought that was hardly a realistic question bearing in mind the noise and bustle on the road, not to mention the sounds of battle which had reached a new intensity. He said nothing but waited for Bridges to speak. Bridges had had time to think. He would tell Stiles, who obviously recognised him soon after turning, that he had been ordered to take the Eagle into Brussels. That would be his way out. What a stroke of good fortune.

Stiles listened to Bridges, all the while aware that once again Ewart had left him behind. He didn't like Bridges and certainly didn't trust him. Stiles remembered, only too well, how the lieutenant had scuttled away like a frightened rabbit, near Maguilla.

"The details are a trifle sketchy," he heard Bridges say. "The colonel," Bridges hoped that that Stiles had not got his orders from Clifton, "the colonel has especially requested that I deliver the Eagle, but neither he nor I are aware of the details surrounding its capture. What took place?"

"Well, sir, it was like this. I was one of a party led by Captain Clark, who captured it. I was the first to get my hands on it and the captain said I was to take it to the rear. Then me and a sergeant of the Greys," – Stiles pointed in the general direction of Ewart's receding figure – "who also got one, were ordered by one of his Lordship's staff officers to take the Eagles into Brussels. We have to find the military commandant, sir, and be sure to give full details of our regiments, ourselves, and the manner of their capture."

Bridges proceeded to draw further details from Stiles and as he did so continued to develop his plan, but thought it wiser to wait a moment or two before replying.

"Corporal Stiles, you have performed a very brave deed. I would not wish to deprive you of your hour of glory but I am acting under the colonel's orders and I am sure you will wish to rejoin your comrades as soon as possible. The regiment has need of you. I will take the Eagle into Brussels and ensure that your name, together with that of Captain Clark, is put to its capture. Give it to me now like a good fellow!"

Stiles was far from convinced and was reluctant to comply. He'd got so far with it. Bridges sensed his hesitation. "You *do* appreciate that you could wait some hours before you see the military commandant. Don't you think that *I* will have a greater chance of being seen more speedily?" With that, Stiles handed the Eagle over to Bridges.

Almost as an afterthought, Stiles asked, "How's the battle going, sir?"

"Going well and getting better all the time from our viewpoint," Bridges replied, almost beside himself with the feeling of relief that this chance meeting had brought about. He would not be going back to that blood bath if he had any say in the matter. Without so much as a farewell, he dug in his heels and rode off clutching his passport to safety. As his horse picked up speed he determined one thing – he would only give one name as the captor of the Eagle and that would be the name of Stiles. He would be damned if he would mention Clark. That would teach Clark and the others to look down on him.

Gradually the remnants of the Royals returned to the ridge. Clark, looking about him, saw that many of the men had wounds and there were a large number of riderless horses. He was relieved to see that Phillip Dorville was unscathed and rode towards him. The day had started well enough but he found it difficult to shake of the depression which had overtaken him as he thought of the human cost. He had sent Gunning, who was badly wounded, off to Stead. By now the surgeon would have his hands full. Clifton was also heading in their direction, but there was no sign of either Radclyffe, or Windsor, or for that matter Bridges. His eyes searched the slope but he could not see any of them among the dismounted who were walking back.

Clifton greeted them warmly. "Well, Phillip and Alexander, at least you two have survived. Charles Radclyffe has been severely wounded and I have been informed that Windsor and about twenty men were brought down by a volley at the very beginning."

Dorville interrupted. "It seems to me that we were so successful with our first attack that the men got carried away."

Clifton looked at his subordinates. "The report will have to come later. At the moment I estimate our strength is the equivalent of two weak squadrons. Colonel Muter has taken over as brigadier and wants me to remain in close contact. You know, of course, that Sir William Ponsonby is dead, as also is Hamilton of the Greys. It is time for the remainder of you to take a rest. Phillip, take what is left of the regiment to that wood over there." He pointed in its general direction. "I am sure that there will be more for us to do!"

Clark felt the ball smash through his ankle and his horse collapsed under him like a sack of flour. He managed to roll clear, tried to stand but could not support himself on his right leg. He was assisted into a sitting position and he looked at his right ankle. The round must have passed clean, through. Blood marked both the entry and exit points of the wound, which hurt like hell. He felt faint.

Dorville, who had seen aim go down, hurried over. "You had best see the surgeon. Stead is about a quarter of a mile back. I'll get someone to go with you and find you a replacement horse." Somehow, with assistance, Clark got himself up into the saddle and, more importantly to his mind, stayed there. The short ride to the regimental hospital, which meant crossing to the chaussée and following its line in the direction of Waterloo, seemed endless.

On arrival, Clark saw that Stead and his assistants were working at full stretch. Outside the building was a pit, which contained an assortment of amputated limbs, and along one side of the barn lay many corpses awaiting burial. He could not help wondering whether his injured leg would be added to the grisly heap. At the barn door he dismounted with difficulty and the man deputed as escort supported him so that his injured limb was kept clear of the ground. Stead was busy probing a thigh wound. As he tried to locate the ball which had caused the injury, the soldier, stretched out on the table with his arms and legs pinioned, writhed in agony as Stead continued searching but did not utter a sound. Clark turned away and a little later heard, "That's got it!" as the search ended successfully. Stead, wearing a much-bloodied apron, plunged his hands into a bucket of water. He called for a red hot iron to cauterise the wound and left it to an orderly to apply the dressing.

Stead turned, saw Clark, noticed the wound on his face and that he was being supported on one leg. "You had better get up onto the table and let me have a look at you. Just a minute, though," as Clark moved forward. "Grimshaw, wash that table down and fetch some fresh water," The orderly did as he was ordered, and Clark soon found himself laying on the hard surface, Stead peered at Clark's ankle wound and then at the graze on his nose. "We will have to cut this boot off, Alexander. I can tell you that the round has passed straight through but I need to examine the wound." The boot was removed. Stead bent his head. "Bring that lantern nearer, I can't see a thing! U'hm, you have been lucky. No splintered bone. Another inch higher and I would have to amputate. We will just clean you up and apply a dressing. Then you will be off to hospital in Brussels. You will need to stay off that leg for some time."

"Will I regain the full use of my leg?" Clark asked, not for the first time feeling anxious.

"No reason why you shouldn't," Stead replied. "By the amount of work we've had to do you must have had a busy day. When did this happen?"

"I take it you mean my ankle," said Clark, wincing as Stead busied himself. "It happened, as far as I recollect, about seven o'clock. We had been up on the ridge, but this time on the westward side, for the better part of three hours, strung out in a long thin line. Gradually what had been two squadrons was reduced to one. Colonel Muter had been wounded and Clifton had taken over as brigadier. The French had been firing cannon at us, but the problem was their skirmishers. It must have been one of them that did for me and my horse. Up till then I seemed to have had a charmed life, apart from this," he said, pointing to his nose. "It was the second time I'd had my mount shot from under me. Earlier I'd lost Jock. I can tell you, it's been the most trying experience and made anything we saw in the Peninsula look like child's play. You should have seen the charge we made early on in the battle. We cut through them like a hot knife through butter. I am certain that if we had delayed for two or three minutes longer, the battle would have been lost. The French were almost to the crest."

Stead straightened up. "Well, that's done. Now, you must go off to Brussels. I will find out what transport is available. I'll tell you one thing – Bridges found no difficulty in moving to the rear earlier today."

"You have seen him?" asked Clark. "I thought he must be among the casualties. He has always been suspect, ever since we attempted to rescue the wounded from Maguilla."

"I certainly saw him," Stead replied. "As far as I could tell from here, there was nothing wrong with him. He was going at a famous pace towards the rear!"

Stiles felt uneasy. His return journey had given him time to think, and the more he thought the more suspicious he became. Why had Lieutenant Bridges been sent after him? Had he been right to hand over the Eagle? He really hadn't had much choice in the matter, if for the only reason that Bridges was his superior officer. Once or twice Stiles thought about retracing his steps but he would never find Bridges now and anyway what would he say to him. The cannon's roar grew louder as he passed through the village of Waterloo. In fact the gunfire had not stopped all afternoon. Someone was getting a pounding, that was for sure. By now it was early evening. A large number of wounded, some singly, others in groups made their way to St Joseph's church, which was being used as a hospital. Stiles noticed the corpses stacked outside the building. To Stiles' mind the whole scene did not augur well. With mounting apprehension he hurried on his way.

He eventually found his comrades, and his worst fears were confirmed. He'd had a difficult time finding them as they had moved from the position they'd held that morning and were now to the west of the main Brussels road. The ground was covered with the dead and dying of both sides but he gave most of his attention to the red clad figures among them. Mutilated horses wandered or turned in circles while others lay still or raised their heads as if seeking assistance. Betsy whinnied as she came up to the poor beasts. Stiles' first impression was that there were not many mounted men of the Royals left. Probably not more than eighty or ninety in all. A squadron's strength at most. They were drawn up in a single line on the crest, behind a regiment of Hanoverians.

Stiles went looking for Captain Clark but could not see him. Major Dorville was there but the colonel and many of the officers were absent. He spied Sergeant Nott and rode over to him. There was a temporary lull in the fighting.

"You're back then, Corporal!"

"I'm looking for Captain Clark," said Stiles.

"He's left the field," Nott replied. "He was wounded again and had his horse shot from under him. You took the Eagle back to Brussels?"

"Well, almost," said Stiles. "I was on the outskirts of the city when Mr Bridges caught up with me and said he would take it on."

"What was Mr Bridges doing there?" asked Nott. Stiles was unable to reply as at that moment cannon fire was renewed, with ferocity by both sides. Nott shouted, "Take your place in line. It looks as though the French are coming again."

Stiles urged Betsy into a gap. Not much could be seen to the front as the smoke from the guns hung heavily on the still air. A hail of roundshot and shells came towards them, knocking down the infantry like ninepins. A shell fell to earth a few feet in front of him, buried itself in the soft earth and exploded with a volcano-like eruption. Mud, stones, and iron were hurled into the air. Stiles fought hard to control his mount which, momentarily, reared and plunged. The bombardment continued and took its toll on the cavalry, then, as suddenly as it started, the firing stopped. Through the clearing smoke Stiles could see the top of the ridge and the tops of bearskin caps appearing above the summit. In the brief silence which followed, the French drums beat the "*Pas de Charge*" and the accompanying shouts of "*Vive l'Empereur*" broke like waves hitting the shore. In the Allied ranks orders were given. Stiles quickly checked his carbine, ran his fingers under his chin strap, and moistened his dry lips. It looked as though the imperial guard was being sent against them. In some ways it was as it had been before the charge, earlier in the day, except that as the heavy cavalry was so depleted, salvation would have to come from elsewhere. They must have skirmishers out, thought Stiles, as musket balls whistled past. His immediate neighbour fell from his saddle, clutching at his throat, in a vain effort to stem the flow of blood.

The French came on and on. Stiles saw that they were approaching the guns. Why didn't the artillery fire? As if in answer to his question the guns roared. In the brief moments before the black smoke obscured the view, Stiles witnessed the slaughter caused by canister, grape and shrapnel, the last of which burst above the massed French troops and carved great holes in their tightly-packed ranks. Then the scene was blotted out. He heard the screams and cries of the wounded and the dying and the sound of controlled volleys of musket fire, fired only as the British could – with discipline and courage. Still the cannon roared. He looked to either side and saw that the desperately thin line of cavalry was weakened still further. Soon there might be none of them left. There was a great cheer. The smoke cleared and the French were gone. The Army was advancing. He hardly trusted his eyes and looked at Nott. The sergeant's smoke-blackened features broke into a huge grin. He was shouting something and Stiles realised that Nott was yelling, "Boney's beaten! We've won! We've beaten the buggers!" As if by way of confirmation, the sun's dying rays momentarily lit up the field.

The horses were picketed, and Stiles, having watered and fed Betsy and given her a good rub down, walked back towards the fire. There was no shortage of food, fuel, or drink. The fleeing French had left plenty of those commodities behind. Although he had not eaten all day the fever of excitement still gripped him, and for the moment at least he had no appetite. They had advanced as far as the opposing heights, formerly occupied by the French, and in so doing passed through the debris of battle. It had begun to get dark as they marched, and in the gloom, as it had been impossible to tell friend from foe, they had been halted and told to bivouac. The Prussians had taken over the pursuit.

Stiles looked back across the battlefield. The moon had risen and shadowy figures moved about, lighting their way by lanterns which shone dimly in the distance. They haven't wasted much time, he thought. They were probably scavengers going among the dead and making short work of those who still lived and those who tried to stop them. They would search for pickings all night and the morning light would reveal many a naked corpse. There would also be wives searching for their loved ones. "Francis," he heard someone call his name. He looked over to the fire where Jim Burnside was sitting among a group of men. A pot was suspended over the flames and the aroma of cooking meat filled the air. Now he did feel hungry and saliva filled his mouth.

"It's good to see you are unharmed," said Burnside. "I looked for you earlier and became concerned until I heard that you had gone off with the Eagle. Come and sit down a while and have some grog!"

Stiles sat. "There aren't many of us left," he said. "You must have suffered greatly. What happened after the charge?"

"We didn't do too well to start with," replied Burnside. "I think our squadron was more exposed to the Frenchies' column, as they got off a volley which killed Captain Windsor and brought down about twenty men. I saw Captain Phipps' horse shot at the same time. Anyway, after the charge we all got mixed up – Royals, Greys and Inniskillings – and we went on up to the French guns. We did some more damage, and the group I was with wanted to go on further but my horse was blown, so I turned and came back. Just as well I did! I had about cleared the thick mud in the valley bottom when I heard shouting and saw the French Lancers coming over the hill. I can tell you, a chill went down my spine. Despite urging him on, my horse could barely trot, but I was one of the lucky ones. As I reached our former position I looked back and saw many of our brave fellows run through. It was not a pretty sight. Some managed to survive, but there were many riderless horses which made their way home with blood on their saddles. I heard later that Sir William Ponsonby had been killed and we lost many men."

"Was that the worst part of it?" asked Stiles. "I was shocked to see how few of you were left when I rejoined and had difficulty finding the regiment."

"I'm not sure if that *was* the worst part," replied Burnside. "In fact what followed later surpassed even that. There have been many times today when I thought that Jim Burnside had had his last woman."

"We were withdrawn to a wood and allowed to dismount. By then we were down to about the strength of two squadrons. It was about four o'clock when the order came for the brigade to remount. This time we crossed the Brussels High Road and they brought us into single line behind a square of infantry. I think they were either Hanoverians or Brunswickers, and I heard Sergeant Brooke say that they were raw and needed stiffening. We were ordered to hold our position in case they should run. The French put in attack after attack, with their cavalry, on the infantry squares which somehow held their formation. The French survivors of these attacks came towards us, but by then they had lost their momentum and were really seeking a way back to their own side, as though not risking passing too close to the squares which had inflicted heavy damage. They didn't cause us much harm."

"It was their guns and skirmishers in between the charges that hurt us. It was later that our brigade and that of Lord Somerset had to be put in against the French cavalry. Half of us went down. Then we were ordered to charge some cuirassiers whom we met halfway. Both sides seemed so tired that the shock of the impact was not great and few were killed. We stood about thirty yards from each other and fired our carbines until some time later we disengaged. It was about this time that Tinsley received a mortal wound. I managed to get him back, but he was dying as I looked at him. He said that I was to give you this – his journal." Burnside handed over a waterproof covered package, tied by a piece of tape. "The rest you know," Burnside continued. "I must say that when I heard that you had gone to the rear, I thought that at least one of us was safe. I didn't expect to see you back here."

Stiles carefully put the journal in his pocket. "Well, Jim," he said, "we've both survived, although I'm sure that after today things will never be the same. I don't know about you but I've had a bellyful of fighting. There's been enough to last me a lifetime!" He lapsed into silence. The thought crossed his mind that he would have to write home, so that his family and Margaret would know that he was safe, but that would have to wait for another day. He had regained his appetite and hoped that the food would not be too long. Burnside nudged him in the ribs with his elbow and passed him a brandy bottle. Stiles wiped the neck with his hand and raised the bottle to his lips in a silent toast to his fallen comrades.

Appendix

Casualties

The Union Brigade had sustained a high casualty rate. According to Clark the Royals went into action, at Waterloo, about three hundred and twenty strong. Other sources put the figure somewhat higher but eighty-five were killed, seventy wounded, and one was missing. Horse casualties were one hundred and sixty-five killed and thirty-five wounded. The much reduced regiment, with the remainder of the Army, advanced into France, and early in January 1816 returned to England.

There is no doubt that the charge of the Union and Household Brigades saved the day. Wellington, who was never satisfied with the handling of cavalry – a conviction that was more than justified by the undisciplined foray among the French guns with tragic results – was provoked into issuing orders specifying formation and maintaining an adequate reserve.

The Eagles

The Eagle of the 105th Regiment de Ligne taken by the Royals, with that of the 45th captured by the Greys, were sent by Wellington along with his despatch to the Prince Regent, the day after Waterloo. Major Percy, his only unwounded ADC, was given the task of transporting them. All the way from Dover to London, the two Eagles, protruding from the windows, on each side of his coach, were cheered on their way.

Five days after the battle, Clifton, as acting brigadier in his report to Colonel Hervey, now commanding the cavalry, wrote:

I have particularly to mention my entire satisfaction with
the conduct of Brevet Lieutenant-Colonel Dorville, as
well of Brigade Major Radclyffe and Captain Clark, *the
latter's conduct contributing to a great degree to the
capture of the Eagle*. The above mentioned officers I
beg to recommend to His Grace for promotion.
(Supplementary Despatches vol. X P. 568)

The Dispute

It was not long before a dispute began in the regiment as to who
had captured the Eagle. Was it Clark or Stiles?

Stiles was given the initial credit, and by the end of June 1815 he
had been promoted to Sergeant. In April 1816 he was commissioned
as an Ensign in the 6th West Indian Regiment. He went onto half pay
in December 1817 and died on the 9th January 1828. It is not clear
that he ever served with his new regiment, as evidence seems to point
to that regiment having been disbanded.

Apart from his service with the Royal Dragoons (the regimental
musters give details of his recruitment in London and his progress), he
remains a man of mystery. As far as can be ascertained, there is no
retained record of Stiles, apart from the Army Lists, once he became
an officer, either at the Public Records Office or at the headquarters
of the Jamaican Defence Force.

Captain Alexander Kennedy Clark spent two months in Brussels
recuperating from his wounds. One week after the battle he wrote to
his sister Jane Maxwell telling her of his recovery and his capture of
the Eagle:

I had the honour to stab the standard bearer of the 45th
Battalion of Infantry and take the Eagle which is now in
London. It is a very handsome blue silk flag with a
large gilt Eagle on top of the pole with its "*wings
spread*".

This statement is factually incorrect. Although Clark only had the
Colour in his hands for a short time, the Colour was a Tricolour
inscribed with the Battle Honours of the 105th, and the Eagle's wings
are not spread.

In 1839, Clark, in writing from Leeds, states:

> I did not see the Eagle and Colour (for there were two
> Colours but only one with an Eagle) until we had been
> probably five or six minutes engaged... What became of
> the other Colour I do not know but it is rather singular
> that I last autumn saw a dark blue silk flag with the
> words *105ème Regiment d'Infanterie de Ligne* in gold
> letters upon it in the hall of Abbotsford along with other
> military curiosities. How it got there I could not learn,
> the present Sir Walter Scott telling me he had no
> knowledge of how it got into his late father's possession,
> or where it came from. Could this have been the very
> flag that was along with the Eagle, or was it a camp
> colour? The flag of the Eagle was red, white and blue;
> this was all blue.
> (Waterloo Letters No. 37)

Returning to 1815 and Clark became increasingly anxious as his
act of valour appeared to have been overlooked. On the 9th of July he
wrote to Dorville, who had been promoted to brevet colonel, and it is
clear that he is seeking promotion:

> It is a terrible blow for me to be absent at this moment.
> If I was able to be on the spot, it is possible I might
> succeed in procuring brevet rank but as it is, I have no
> person sufficiently interested in my progress in the army
> to exert themselves on my behalf.

He then put the thought to Dorville that if only Clifton would act
(Clifton had already done so in his despatch to Colonel Hervey) and
bring his conduct to the notice of the officer commanding the Brigade
and get him to recommend him to the Duke, then all might be well.
He continues:

> I give you my solemn word of honour that I do not
> believe the standard bearer was touched by anyone until
> I reined up my horse and ran my sword through his right
> side above the kidneys, when he fell more than half

down and I could touch part of the silk cord but could not hold it... If you can do me a good turn I shall be grateful. But you will also do me a favour if you will candidly give me your opinion on this business. If you think I have no claim, please tell me and I shall be obliged to you for your candour.

Dorville took the matter up with Clifton, who ordered Radclyffe to find out what really happened and to report to him. In due course Radclyffe forwarded the following to Clifton:

I certify that Captain Clark gave me a statement, of which this is a true copy, respecting the capture of the Eagle of the 105th French regiment of Infantry, some days before he found it necessary to request that I should take the evidence of Anderson and Wilson.

Clark's statement:

When my Squadron, the centre one of the Royal Dragoons, had advanced about two or three hundred yards beyond the second hedge on the British left and the heads of the columns of the French Infantry had been broken by our charge, I perceived a little to my left an enemy's Eagle with which the bearer was making away with the intention of carrying it off to the rear. I immediately rode to the place calling out to secure the colour and at the instant I reached the spot ran my sword into the officer's right side who carried the Eagle. He staggered and fell forward. But I do not think at this time reached the ground on account of the pressure of his companions. I called out a second time, "Secure the Colour! It belongs to me!" This was addressed to some of the men close behind me at the time. The officer was in the act of falling and as he fell with the Eagle a little towards the left, I was not able to catch the standard so as to hold it. Corporal Stiles and some other men rushed to my assistance and the Eagle was secured, it falling across his horse's neck, as he came up on my left, before it reached the ground. I immediately ordered the Corporal to carry it to the rear and I remained, although wounded, in charge of my squadron.

A. K. CLARK

Capt., 1st Dragoons.

Captain Clark being desirous to have the statements of Stephen Anderson and John Wilson of the 1st Royal Regiment of Dragoons, on the subject of the capture of an Eagle of the enemy taken on the 18th June, and having applied for the two men in question to join the Regiment, which was not granted on account of their having no appointments, has requested me, as senior officer, to take their depositions. I have done so and the following is the substance of what they have stated to me relating to it.

Anderson was to the left of Captain Clark when he stabbed the officer. He and the officer fell and the Eagle fell across the heads of his and Captain Clark's horses and against that of Corporal Stiles. Captain Clark called out twice together "Secure the Colour." Corporal Stiles seized it and carried off the Eagle to the rear. He was wounded soon after and rode part of the way from the field with the Corporal.

Wilson was about to quit the field when he heard Captain Clark call out to secure the colour and turned about to assist in taking it. He was a horse's length to the right of Captain Clark when he stabbed the officer who carried it. The Colour and Eagle fell against the neck of Corporal Stiles' horse who snatched it up and galloped off to the rear. A man of the Greys, I believe a Sergeant, took another and he saw them both afterwards on the road to Brussels.

C. E. RADCLYFFE

Royal Dragoons, Lieutenant Colonel

Note: Neither Armstrong or Wilson are shown as having been wounded at Waterloo. They were not absent from duty at the end of June when the Muster was taken.

In due time, but judging by the following letter, not until July 1816, Clifton sent for Stiles, who after his interview with the Colonel wrote to Gunning:

Ipswich Barracks

31st July 1816

Sir,

This day Colonel Clifton did send for me about the taking of the Eagle and the Colour. He asked me if I had any person who saw me take the Eagle; I told him you see me. I believe, as the officer of the French was making away with it. I belonged to your troop, at the time and you gave me orders to charge him, which I did and took it from him. When I stated it to him this day, he wants to know the particulars about it and me to write to you for you to state to him how it was. I would thank you to write to the Colonel, as you were the nearest officer to me that day. Sir, by doing so you would much oblige.

Your most obedient humble servant,

Francis Stiles

Sergeant[1] in Royal Dragoons (28)

There is no record of a reply from Gunning to Clifton.

Clark's Continuing Representations

Over a period which ended in 1838, twenty-three years after the battle, Clark was to submit his statement, or as he preferred to call it, his Memorial, on ten occasions to higher authority. The first person to receive it was the Duke of Wellington. Initially Clark was requesting brevet promotion, and when this failed he later pursued promotion by purchase. All requests were turned down largely on the grounds of precedent but he received an offer of a Majority (with the 7th Dragoon guards) in 1825. In 1831, having been promoted to

---

[1] Strictly speaking he was an Ensign and had been so since April.

Lieutenant-Colonel the previous year, he brought the Memorial into play again, when he unsuccessfully applied for the Order of the Bath. It would seem that, in Clark's estimation, he never received the recognition which he felt was due to him. At one stage he went so far as to suggest that, had Picton and Ponsonby not been killed, they could have attested in his favour. What they might have seen in the confusion of the battle is another matter. The only other Royals' officer nearby was Gunning, who does not appear to have been asked for corroboration other than by Stiles.

Clark became a Companion of the Royal Military Order of the Guelph (a Knight of Hanover) in September 1831. When his aunt, Mary Kennedy, died in 1835, he inherited her estate and assumed the name of Kennedy under the terms of her will. In 1839 he applied for and was granted an augmented Coat of Arms, which among other things added the Eagle of the 105th, and in 1854 he was promoted to Major-General, followed by further promotion to Lieutenant-General six years later. Two years earlier he had been appointed Colonel of the 6th Dragoon Guards. Two further honours awaited him. In 1860 he became Colonel of the Royal Scots Greys. His son John, by now a full colonel, had been "sounded out" regarding his father's appointment and told him, "Do not allude to the Royals". Finally in November 1862 came his KCB. He died on 30th of January 1864, at 69, Oxford Terrace, Hyde Park and is buried in the family vault in the churchyard of St Michael's, Dumfries.

Conclusion

It seems reasonable to reach the conclusion that neither Clark or Stiles could have captured the Eagle without the assistance of other members of the Centre squadron. Clark is convinced he did, but in his letter to his sister, written only seven days after the battle, he wrongly describes the Colour and the Eagle. Would Stiles, knowing how severe the military system could be, have risked possible physical punishment and dismissal? Why did Clifton, in his despatch, refer to Clark's conduct *contributing to a great degree to the capture of the Eagle*? It must have been Wellington who recommended granting a commission to Stiles, the same reward granted to Ewart of the Greys. The Duke was not empowered to appoint ensigns but had to bring such matters to the attention of the commander-in-chief, for approval by the Prince Regent. Was it a question that Wellington, having secured Stile's promotion, was not prepared to entertain the matter further?

If the circumstances surrounding the capture of the Eagle were uncertain in the immediate days, months and years after the battle, the distance in time of a hundred and eighty years has not brought a solution nearer.

For a short thirteen months between 1949/50 when I served with the Royal Dragoons, the matter of who captured the Eagle at Waterloo was still in dispute. Although not a day-to-day topic, the officers maintained that the Eagle had been taken by an officer. The sergeants, equally firmly, said it was captured by a corporal.

What happened to:

♦ LIEUTENANT CHARLES BRIDGES

It is a matter of fact that he left his post at Maguilla and, the Field at Waterloo and that Stiles handed the Eagle over to him.

Clifton called a special meeting of officers at Major Dorville's house to enquire into Bridges' conduct at Waterloo. Bridges was asked why he had left the regiment before or during the charge made about noon. He first said that his saddle had turned. Then that his horse had run away with him and landed him in the Prussian camp. He was given the options either of resigning from the regiment, or being put under arrest to be tried by court martial. He chose the former but did not leave the Royals until December 1816.

♦ LIEUTENANT-COLONEL A. B. CLIFTON. (BEN THE RULER)

He commanded the regiment until 1829 when he went onto half pay. He became colonel of the regiment in 1842 and held that position until his death in 1869.

♦ LIEUTENANT GEORGE GUNNING

He served with the Royals until 1822 when he went on to half pay.

♦ PRIVATE JAMES (JIM) BURNSIDE

Promoted to corporal in 1816.

♦ BREVET LIEUTENANT-COLONEL PHILIP DORVILLE

Went on to half pay in 1827.

♦ BREVET LIEUTENANT-COLONEL CHARLES EDWARD RADCLYFFE

Went on to half pay in 1821 and died in February 1827, at which time he was brigade major to the cavalry in Great Britain. He had been badly wounded in the knee at Waterloo and the bullet had never been extracted.

♦ THE ROYAL DRAGOONS

They would not see action again until the Crimean War, the intervening years seeing them employed as "policemen and revenue men". They served with distinction throughout the Boer, First and Second World Wars. They were in the latter conflict one of the last cavalry regiments to be mechanised, and remained for the greater part of their remaining years an armoured car regiment.

On the 31st March 1969 the Royal Dragoons and the Royal Horse guards merged to become the "Blues and Royals".

- 105TH REGIMENT DE LIGNE

The regiment was disbanded at Perigeux on the 29th September 1815.